WHAT SHE FORGOT

a gripping psychological thriller

S.W. VAUGHN

More by This Author

TERMINAL CONSENT – a standalone crime thriller

How do you stop a killer whose victims are volunteering to die?

P.I. Jude Wyland series

DEADLY MEASURES – a prequel novella

THE BLACK DIRECTIVE

House Phoenix series)

BREAKING ANGEL | Book 1

DEVIL RISING | Book 2

TEMPTING JENNER | Book 3

SHADOWS FALLING | Book 4

WICKED ORIGINS | Stories & Novellas

"But each day brings its petty dust
Our soon-chok'd souls to fill,
And we forget because we must,
And not because we will."
--Matthew Arnold

PROLOGUE

the darkest evening

I didn't mean to kill her. Not like that. She just wouldn't stop screaming, no matter how much I begged her to. She wouldn't stop.

Killing her was messy. But it's done now, and I can't take it back.

This new one, she doesn't scream. She's eager, maybe a little too eager. She promises she's never going to tell anyone what we do, what she saw me doing. She says I excite her.

She says a lot of things. I'm not sure I believe any of them.

I tell her that she's special, that she's my only love. It keeps her under control. I need to control her, even though we're out here so far away from anyone and anything. She has to keep my secrets. I don't want to kill another one. All she has to do is stay, and be mine when I want her, and things will work out.

But I'm starting to think she's crazy. Maybe crazier than me.

Now I don't know what to do anymore. She's still mine — so young, so beautiful, so eager to please. She swears she'll never leave, that she'll always be here waiting for me. And I want to believe her. I really do.

I just can't be sure. After all, can I really trust a crazy person? It doesn't seem like a good plan, with everything she knows about me. I may have to kill her too.

I'm thinking maybe that'll be okay. Maybe killing won't be so hard this time.

And I can always get another one to replace her.

1

Madeline

I was the one who got away.

His name was Stewart Brooks. They called him the Singing Woods Killer, and for five long, horrifying months, he made the quiet suburban town of Dayfield, New York, his hunting ground. His reign of terror cast a shadow that hangs over this place, even today, as one by one he claimed four mothers' daughters.

I should've been the fifth.

Like his other victims, I was sixteen when he dragged me into the woods. They said he kept me for a week, but I don't remember any of that. I don't remember the abuse, the pain, the starvation they told me I'd suffered. I remember nothing. They filled in those stories for me, the doctors and the shrinks and the police with their cold, invasive examinations and their droning, exhaustive interviews. I never read any of the news articles, not even the ones they wrote about me. I couldn't stand to risk seeing photos of his dumping grounds, of glimpsing those endless trees again.

There's only one thing I know must have happened. For that, I carried the painful, heart-wrenching proof, and I still bear those scars. But even there, my memory is a black hole, a complete and terrible blank spot where nothing lives.

I remember the terror of being taken. I remember *knowing* I was going to die. I can still feel that awful hollow sensation, the idea that I would cease to exist, become nothing. And my memories would die with me. I would never remember my friends or my family or that camping trip with Carson and Tricia the summer after freshman year, or my tenth birthday when Mom got me a guitar and I obsessed over it fiercely for two weeks and then put it in my closet and never touched it again, or how much I love pistachio ice cream and walking barefoot on warm sand.

That feeling — the terrible, shuddering black nothing of death — always comes back to me when it's too quiet, and I have to watch television, turn on music, make up awful stories in my head. Anything to distract myself before the feeling can consume me.

I remember running through the woods. Running from death.

I remember that I killed death itself.

I can still see my escape, if I close my eyes. The dark, thick silence of the woods, the trees looming out of the blackness from nowhere to slow me, scratch at me, as if they were on *his* side. His harsh breathing and heavy footsteps catching me, his weight falling on me. The broken branch I jammed into his throat to get him off, because all I could feel was death, the awful rotting empty spot deep in my stomach that I never wanted to experience again. I pretended all that blood was a warm shower, washing away the shivery ache of death.

Twenty years ago on the evening of June 4, somewhere deep in the Singing Woods, I killed Stewart Brooks.

He's dead, long gone, reduced to dust and bones in a numbered pauper's grave at the Woodlawn Cemetery. My psychiatrist keeps telling me it's okay that he's dead. It's okay that I killed him. I can forgive myself for murder. Because now, he can never hurt anyone again.

But this morning, I saw him again. Watching me. Taunting me.

I'm crazy. Everyone knows it. *I* know it, but that doesn't matter.

He's come back for me, and the vast, yawning empty is still waiting to claim me after all these years.

The hunt is on.

2

Monday, June 2, 7:30 A.M.

The morning starts out like any other Monday, with Renata dragging and groaning her way through school preparations and finally hauling herself into the car five minutes late. It's my week for the morning carpool, and like any other teenager, my daughter is mortified at being driven around by her mother.

"Ugh," she says as she flops into the passenger seat and hauls her backpack in behind her, as if it's full of bricks instead of books. School is such a chore for the young. "How long until I can get my license, again?"

I watch until she puts her seatbelt on, and then put the car in reverse and start backing out of the driveway. "Six months," I say, as if I haven't told her that a hundred times since she passed her permit test last week.

She heaves a dramatic sigh. "Why do I have to wait so long?"

"Because the state of New York hates teenagers." I'm hoping to prod a smile from her. It almost works, but she actively fights the tug at her lips. Sixteen-year-olds aren't supposed to laugh at lame mom jokes.

God, how is she sixteen already? Sometimes I feel like all I did was blink, and my sweet little girl who used to love cupcakes with too much frosting, everything Harry Potter, and of all things, monster trucks, had traded places with this beautiful, distracted woman-child who has a phone permanently grafted to her hand, who whispers and giggles with her friends over real-life boys instead of fictional ones, who keeps secrets from me when we used to share everything.

This year is going to be hard. I'm already overprotective, I know that — and sixteen is the banner year. The danger year, at least in my trauma-warped, disordered mind. I can see myself smothering her with my own fears, the ghosts of my past, all those dead girls and me. If I'm not careful, I could drive a wedge between us that will never go away.

Renata keeps her gloomy, half-asleep silence until we pull up in front of the first stop, a pale green Colonial at the end of a cul-de-sac. This is the Klines' place, and Jenny Kline is my daughter's 'bestest friend in the whole wide world.' They've been practically inseparable since kindergarten. Jenny and Rennie. When I stop the car, Jenny comes bounding out the door, beaming as always despite the early hour, and vaults into the back seat. "Morning, Mrs. Osborn," she says, and before I can say good morning back, she and Renata are chattering away like a couple of magpies in that nearly incomprehensible language every generation of teens seems to develop as a defense mechanism against lurking parental ears.

We have two more passengers to pick up. Tonya Washington, three blocks from Jenny, is the shyest of the group and tends to spend the whole trip staring out the window, chewing on a thumbnail. The last stop is for Drew Ritter, who was Renata's first official boyfriend. But since they were both six years old at the time, there's been no lingering awkwardness from the 'breakup.' These days Drew wears more jewelry and makeup than my daughter. I'm no longer sure what that means for modern kids, but no one seems to mind, so I don't either.

It's not far from Drew's house to the high school, and when we arrive, the drop-off line is relatively short. I pull up behind the distinctive canary-yellow Humvee that happens to belong to my obnoxiously perfect neighbors, the Clarks, and turn to Renata while we wait. "What's going on after school today, honey?"

A stricken look flashes across her face, and I realize I've committed the cardinal sin of calling her 'honey' in front of her friends. "Soccer practice," she mumbles, sinking down in her seat with a huff. "Seriously, Mom, I already told you that last night. Jenny's mom is picking us up. I'll be home around five."

"All right. That's fine, then," I say. I can't apologize for the slip now, because that would be even more embarrassing. "Do you still have a game Friday night? Your father said he should be home in time to make it. He's only working a half-day on Friday."

"Really? That'd be cool, if you can both come," she says. "Yeah, it's at six."

I nod and smile, glad she's still at least somewhat interested in having her parents involved in her life. My husband, Richard, owns a very successful landscaping business and often works long hours, but he makes a constant effort to stay involved in our daughter's life so she won't feel his absence. He's a wonderful father, a wonderful husband. My rock, even after what we went through in the early years, when my condition was not as controlled as it is now. Unlike my mother, he stuck by me through the hard times, and now we're better than ever.

We married young — I was only twenty at the time, although Richard was twenty-eight — and everyone said it would never work out. But here we are, and I couldn't be happier with our family, our life. Sullen teenager and all.

This too shall pass, I tell myself. Again.

Finally, the two perfect Clark boys get out of the Humvee and it drives away, and I pull forward into the drop-off section. Renata pops her door at the exact same time Jenny opens the back passenger door, but the back driver's side door stays closed. Even at the high school, the kids aren't allowed to exit a vehicle on the traffic side. "Bye, Mom," Renata calls reflexively over her shoulder, just before she shuts the door and moves away from the car, as if she's hoping no one saw her getting out of it.

When they're all out and the last door closes, I grip the wheel and hold back a sigh. I can't believe how hard it is to let her grow up. Everybody tells you that's your job, to raise your children well enough so they don't need you, but no one mentions how much it hurts to actually succeed, to no longer be needed.

Parenting might be the only job where success can make you miserable.

The crossing guard waves me on, and I pull away slowly and complete the gentle arch of the circular drive in front of the high school, signaling to turn onto the main road. I have an appointment at nine, but that's still over an hour away. Not enough time to go home and do anything, too much time to sit in the lot at the office park and wait. So I decide to run a few errands in the meantime.

Dayfield isn't big enough for our own Wal-Mart or Target, or any kind of mega-center, but we do have a twenty-four-hour supermarket, and it's only a few miles from the office park. Price Cutter dominates the mini-plaza at the north end of town, taking up three-quarters of the frontage while a nail salon, a liquor store, and a former pet supply place that's been available for lease for two years huddle in its shadow.

This early in the day, there are plenty of decent parking spaces available. I pull into one next to a cart return near the front end of the lot, where I'm facing the strip of scrub pine and birch trees that separate the plaza parking lot from the homes on the other side. It's something I don't think about often, how many trees there are around here. This town is surrounded by forest on all sides, and randomly sprinkled with patches and swathes of trees throughout.

In fact, the eastern border of the Singing Woods is right behind this very plaza.

Goosebumps race across my skin, and I close my eyes and breathe slowly. I clear my mind the way Dr. Bradshaw taught me. White light in, dark thoughts out. The danger is over. Stewart Brooks is dead.

Finally, I feel steady enough to get on with my day. I get out of the car, push the key fob button to lock it, and head for the store. As I'm passing the cart return, a flash of movement catches my attention and I glance toward the trees edging the parking lot. I'm thinking it was probably a squirrel, a bird, someone's cat out for a morning stroll.

There's a man standing in front of the trees, like he just stepped out from them.

Shocked panic drills into me and freezes my blood before I'm fully conscious of what I see. He's perfectly still. Dirty black jeans, stained camouflage hunting vest over a dark thermal shirt, big boots, a shapeless cap jammed over dark, stringy hair. Smooth-shaven. Eyes like storm clouds, glaring thunderbolts at me.

His face. *His* face. Exactly as he looked twenty years ago. It's impossible, I know that, but there's no mistaking him. I've never been able to erase the face of death from my mind.

Someone is screaming. I barely realize it's me, don't understand that I'm falling until a sudden, explosive pain smacks my knees when they hit the pavement, and a gray blur rushes toward my face. The only sound in the whole world is an intense ringing in my ears, like a bomb went off right next to me.

All at once, there's someone trying to pull me up.

I jerk back hard and lunge to my feet, flailing my arms like mad. The back of my hand whacks something cold and hard, making a hollow metallic *boing*, and I cry out and stumble blindly a few steps. Oh God, he's back, he's going to take me again. This is not happening. It *can't* happen.

"Madeline!" The voice is definitely female — *not him* — laced with concern and fear. "What's wrong? Paul, I think you should call 911."

My jumbled senses clarify in an instant, and I force myself to breathe and turn toward the voice. "No, wait. I'm sorry," I say, panting as I focus on the two older people standing by the cart return, watching me like I'm a wild bear who's just torn loose from a steel jaw-trap. I know them. Paul and Diane Blanchard. Their granddaughter, Eve, is on Renata's soccer team, and we've attended enough games together to be on a first-name basis, though we never exchange more than small talk.

Diane gives me a worried frown. "You nearly passed out, and ... are you all right, dear? You look terrible."

I am not all right. But instead of answering the question, I ask one of my own. "Did you see a man over there by the trees?" I wave in the general direction of where he came out, horrified but not surprised to see no sign of the man who couldn't possibly have been Stewart Brooks. "Dark clothes, dark hair, hunting cap?"

Diane shakes her head and glances at her husband, who clears his throat awkwardly. "No, we didn't see anyone," he says. "Are you sure I can't call someone for you?"

I'm cold all over, and for a moment I don't know if I'll be able to answer him. Finally I say, "Thank you, but I think I just need to sit down for a minute." I'm already making my way back to the car, fumbling for my keys. "I skipped breakfast this morning," I mumble as I press the unlock button and see the headlights flash.

There's no way I can tell these people I barely know that I just saw a dead man.

Diane starts to say something else, but I get in the car and close the door on her words. I feel pretty bad about that. She was only trying to help, and I must've hit either her or Paul, whichever one of them had grabbed me when I collapsed. The back of my hand is throbbing where I whacked it into the cart return, and there's a nasty red mark that's already starting to bruise along the edges. At least one of my knees is skinned, too. I can feel blood trickling down my shin.

I sit in the car with the doors locked, all thoughts of grocery shopping gone. Somehow, I must've been hallucinating. The man who'd abducted me and killed all those girls was long dead.

But it *was* him. I know that face. It's the only thing I remember. His face as he chased me, as he died.

As I killed him.

Not for the first time, I think I should've left Dayfield when I had the chance. I never should've come back home. I could be somewhere else right now, living with a fresh start. But I'd moved back in with the ghosts.

Still, I wouldn't trade my family for anything. My husband, my daughter.

They're worth it.

The slam of a car door somewhere in the parking lot pulls me away from my frantic, half-formed thoughts, and I grab for my phone to check the time. I'm not sure how long I've been sitting here. Five minutes, maybe ten. If I can pull myself together, maybe I can still run into the store for a few things.

I'm stunned to find that it's almost nine. I've been in the car for over forty minutes.

I start the engine and jab the power button for the driver's side window, suddenly too aware of the heat and the stale air I've been breathing all this time. My appointment is going to be very hard today, because I'll have to tell Dr. Bradshaw what I saw. Or thought I saw. I can already see her disappointment. According to her, I'd been making real progress.

Now that progress is gone, and I'm not sure I can face the idea of losing my mind again.

3

the woods are lovely

She's here.

It's been so long, and here she is. I can't believe it. I'm sickened, furious. *Bitch.*

Why is she here? There's nothing for her in this town. I've made sure of that. Nothing to claim, nothing to hold.

I can feel the old rage coming back, and it's all I can do not to kill her right now. How *dare* she? Walking around like she's normal, like she belongs. Like she isn't an absolute lunatic. She should be locked away somewhere, ranting and raving her poisoned mind to padded walls and security cameras.

I knew I should've killed her before. I could've gotten to her again, easily. But I didn't, because I actually felt some sympathy for her, for our time together. What a fool I've been. She was the loose end I should have tied off years ago, before it came to *this.* But I never thought she'd have the gall to be here, after all that happened.

I loved her once, but my life is different now. I'm not that man anymore. But she refuses to believe that.

I can't let her confront me. She'll ruin everything.

Again.

Damn that woman. I had everything under control. The past was in the past, my mistakes buried down deep, where no one would ever look. I was free. And now, just the sight of her makes me shake, makes my hands itch to take a life again.

Her life.

I have to do something about her. But I can't be rash, can't be impatient like I was the last time. I'll wait. I'll plan. And I will destroy her.

Before she can destroy me.

4

Monday, June 2, 9:20 a.m.

Dr. Gillian Bradshaw is a monolith of a woman. Tall and solidly built, almost Amazonian, with thick brown shoulder-length hair and the darkest eyes I've ever seen, so brown they're almost black. Though she tends to wear pant suits with long, flowing jackets, I've often imagined her in a winged helmet and breastplate armor, the kind with hammered breasts that used to grace the covers of '80s pulp fantasy books. I think she could pull off that kind of look.

Her presence makes me feel safe, and has done so ever since I started seeing her fifteen years ago. Following my ordeal and my eventual release from the hospital, she was the third psychiatrist I was sent to. On the heels of less-than-productive sessions with the previous two, both tiny, twiggy women who were identically awful with their fake smiles and false sympathy and nonsensical questions, I'd latched onto this gentle giant, this superwoman with calm mannerisms and nerves of steel.

But today, nothing feels safe.

I'm seated on the couch. Huddled, really, pressed into the corner with my hands squeezed together and my gaze restlessly roaming the room. Dr. Bradshaw's office has barely changed over the years, an observation that usually comforts me.

Not this time, though.

She's angled toward me in her chair, her posture loose and easy. No notebook or half-glasses to frown over at me, no recording device. Her concern shows in her eyes and the lines around her mouth.

"Well. I'd ask if you missed your meds, but you never do," Dr. Bradshaw finally says as she folds her hands on a knee. "How certain are you that you really saw this man?"

"I ... I don't know." I want to scream that I'm positive, that he was just as real as the two of us are right now, but I can't. I know that's not possible. I have to believe it wasn't real, because to let myself actually think that the man I killed has come back to life is an invitation to madness. "Paul and Diane didn't see him," I say.

Dr. Bradshaw's eyes soften in sympathy. "You do realize what's coming up in two days, don't you?" she says with some reluctance, as if she hates to remind me.

I glance at the large calendar on the wall, because for a moment I don't realize what's coming. Her calendars are always birth month flowers, and this month it's white roses for June. Today is Monday, the second, and in two days it'll be June 4.

Exactly twenty years to the day since I killed Stewart Brooks.

My breath leaves me in a rush, and a sense of relief settles over me like a blanket. That must be why I'm seeing him. It even makes sense that I haven't been consciously aware of the impending anniversary, because why would I want to remember? I've certainly never wanted to celebrate the occasion.

Dr. Bradshaw smiles as she sees me relax. "You're going to be okay, Madeline," she says. "In fact, this may be related to your condition. I've heard of cases where sufferers mistake perfect strangers for people they know, sort of the reverse of seeing imposters."

I nod as my throat goes dry. It had been years since I'd experienced the symptoms of my disease, once we'd settled on meds that worked, and I'd hoped I never would again.

I've been diagnosed with Capgras Syndrome. It's a rare disorder, a delusion of misidentification where the inflicted person believes that a person or people they know have been replaced by lookalikes, doubles, imposters. Capgras sufferers usually have these episodes with close family members, but it can happen with any acquaintance, or even themselves.

Most people developed this syndrome as a complication of psychosis. But it can also be brought on by traumatic brain injury, which I suffered in the woods the day I killed Stewart.

"I know it won't be easy for the next few days, but you'll get through it," Dr. Bradshaw was saying. "Still, if you'd like me to prescribe a mild sedative—"

"No. Thank you," I say quickly. I'd struggled with nightmares and insomnia for years after my abduction, compounded by the awful tragedy that struck only a week later. Sedatives had been my only relief. But they'd left me foggy and disconnected for weeks at a time, and weaning myself off them had been a separate kind of nightmare. I don't want to go through that again.

"All right, then," she says. "Let me know if you change your mind, though. You know you can call me anytime." She settles back in her chair, and her demeanor shifts. We're in session mode now. "Shall we pick up where we left off last time?"

I manage a small nod as familiar heat pricks my eyes, the way it does every time I think of him. The wounds are still as fresh as the day it happened. I've talked to Dr. Bradshaw about my father before, but never as in-depth as we have been for the last few sessions.

It's hard, because I don't think I can discuss him without having to bring my mother into the conversation, too. And she's still alive to torment me.

Dr. Bradshaw is waiting for me to start, but I'm not sure I can. When I think about my father, it's my mother's face I see. Red and blotchy, mascara oozing down her cheeks like tar, lipstick the color of dried blood smeared around her screaming mouth. *It's all your fault, you little bitch! You might as well have shot him yourself!*

I take a deep breath. White light in, dark thoughts out. "I just wish he'd left a note," I finally say in a small voice, a child's voice. "I wish I knew *why*."

"Why do you think?"

Because of me. It's my fault! For the second time in ten minutes, I want to scream. "I have no idea," I say, ignoring the echo of my mother's voice in my head. "That's the real problem, isn't it? No one knows the answer."

My father, Wendell Grant, was a good man. Not a perfect man or a pillar of the community. Not a saint. But he was a good father, a good husband as far as I knew, with a family he loved and a career he enjoyed, teaching tenth grade history at Dayfield High School. He rarely raised his voice, never hit me or my mother. He drank occasionally but wasn't an alcoholic, smoked the odd cigar but wasn't addicted to nicotine or any other drug.

He was neither remarkable nor forgettable. He just ... was.

And then he wasn't.

Exactly one week after I escaped the Singing Woods Killer, my father took his own life. He held a revolver under his chin and fired a bullet into his brain. There were no warning signs at any point. When I came back from the woods, he'd been nothing but overjoyed that I was alive and safe, and that the man who'd hurt me could never hurt anyone else again.

To lose my father like that, on top of everything else that happened, just wasn't fair.

And to have my mother blame me for his death was devastating. She'd eventually tried to take back what she said, but I couldn't forget. Between that and the horrible things I'd said to her because of the Capgras, things have never been easy with the two of us since.

That's an understatement. We barely speak, unless we have to.

It also didn't help that she'd had me committed to a mental institution for two years, until I was a legal adult and could check myself out without her permission. That was where I'd had to bear the burden of what happened in the woods — and the long, terrible aftermath — alone.

"I can give you a clinical reason, but there's nothing comforting in symptoms or diagnostics," Dr. Bradshaw says. "And you're right that there's no way to know why. What you *can* deal with are your feelings."

I shake my head. My feelings about my father's suicide are the last thing I want to confront. But out loud I say, in that small child's voice, "I'll try."

A sympathetic expression eases across Dr. Bradshaw's face. She rarely pushes me to express myself when it's obvious that I don't want to. Instead, she looks at her watch and gives me a smile. "Maybe you can think about it for next time," she said. "Our session is nearly over. Meanwhile, I'm going to call in a prescription for a higher dose of pimozide, just to help control your symptoms until you've gotten past the new stressors." She doesn't say *the anniversary*, and I appreciate that. "You can pick up the scrip this afternoon."

"Thank you," I say, tugging at an invisible wrinkle in my pants, my scraped knee aching all over again. I really need to clean that up soon. I'm still unsettled by what I saw, or imagined I'd seen, but at least I'm not frantic like before.

"You're going to be okay, Madeline," Dr. Bradshaw says. "Oh, and one more thing. I know you won't like this idea, but I strongly recommend that you attend the survivor's group meeting tomorrow night at the church. You haven't been to a meeting in over a year, and that's fine. You're doing great without it. But I really believe, with what's coming up, you're going to need a little additional support."

My stomach twists at the thought of the survivor's group. I'd gone regularly for a long time, and the meetings had been mostly helpful, but eventually I'd had to stop going. Because of Dallas Walsh.

His daughter, Angeline, was the first victim of the Singing Woods Killer. Since that dark time, his wife has left him, taking their remaining daughter and moving far away from Dayfield, and Dallas has become a complete alcoholic, so far gone he's practically a parody of a town drunk. Only there's nothing funny or endearing about it.

He's a mean drunk, an angry drunk. And he absolutely despises me.

Because I lived, and his daughter didn't.

"Madeline?" Dr. Bradshaw says gently.

I blink to dislodge my thought train. "Yes, maybe ... I'll probably go," I say. She's right that I could use some extra support, and the group leader, Delphine Pearce, is always wonderful and sweet and never allows anyone to badmouth their fellow attendees. I actually have missed her calming presence. Besides, it's been so long that Dallas may have stopped attending by now.

"I will go," I say with more resolve.

"I'm glad to hear it," Dr. Bradshaw says with a smile. "Don't forget to pick up your prescription this afternoon."

I tell her I won't, and we say our goodbyes as I leave the office eager to shake off the stress of this morning and *do* something. Already, memories of the past are crowding into my head, trying to get my attention, and I need to distract myself. I'm glad that I have no recollection of what happened to me in the woods, grateful for the black hole in my mind where a full week of my life remains shrouded forever in darkness.

I don't want to remember anything.

5

Madeline—the past

Ugh, my hair wouldn't do a thing this morning. But I was going to be late, so I threw it in a ponytail and swiped hopelessly at my bangs with a comb, and then rushed downstairs with my backpack already on. Carson would be here in a few minutes, and we had a lot to talk about on the way to school. Like my party this weekend.

Sweet sixteen. Finally.

Mom was at the table in the kitchen, reading the paper. I buzzed past her toward the cabinets, on a mission for breakfast-to-go and some kind of snack to bring for lunch in case I ended up starving to death. Today was pizza day, and the school pizza was super hit-or-miss. Sometimes it was really good, like it could've come straight from Angelo's on Poplar Street where everybody hung out on Fridays.

But other times, it tasted like wax and wet cardboard.

I found a box of cherry Pop Tarts, grabbed a shiny foil package and slipped it into my backpack. Breakfast, check. As I rooted and slammed through more cabinets, the paper rustled behind me and Mom cleared her throat. "Good morning to you too, slowpoke," she said, teasing me. "What happened, did you drown in the shower?"

"My hair is a freak show, that's what happened." I flipped a grin over my shoulder and opened the next cabinet, staring at the contents. "Hey, Mom, do we have any more of those cheese cracker sandwich things?"

She didn't answer. In fact, she didn't answer very loudly. Her silence was deafening.

"Mom?" I turned around slowly and found her staring at the paper, horrified, her eyes wide and her skin scary pale. "Mom, what's wrong?"

"Oh, my God," she said in a high, funny voice. Her hands started to shake hard enough to rattle the newspaper. "Oh, my *God.*"

Heavy footsteps sounded from the direction of the living room, and my dad rushed into the kitchen with an alarmed expression. "What happened?" he said. "Judith?"

"Wendell, my God," she whispered, and handed him the folded paper. Then she looked at me with tears in her eyes. "I'm so sorry, honey ..."

"*What?*" I said, suddenly feeling frantic and clammy. "I still don't know what's wrong!"

Dad made a choked sound and froze with the newspaper in front of his face.

"It's Angeline," my mom finally said, standing from the table and walking toward me slowly, one arm extended as if she wanted to touch me but wasn't sure she should. "The girl in your class."

I blinked. "Angeline Walsh?" I said dumbly, not understanding. I knew her, but I didn't *know* her. Just enough to say hi in the halls and stuff, plus she was in my bio class and once we did a mini-lab together because we had a substitute who wanted to 'mix things up' and help us 'make new friends.' We didn't really hang out, though.

I knew she'd gone missing almost a week ago. Everybody in school knew, and most of them thought she'd run away from home, even though her parents were totally freaked out.

"Yes, honey. That's her." Mom was right in front of me now. Her tears were dripping, flowing, carrying her makeup down her face. "She's ... gone."

"Gone?" I echoed. I still didn't get it, because I already *knew* she was gone. I looked from Mom's haunted, distraught face to Dad, who still hadn't moved an inch. Like he was playing some awful game of

Statues all by himself, and there would be no one to ever tag and unfreeze him. "What do you mean, gone?"

Mom took my hand in both of hers and squeezed, the way she did when she had to tell me that my grandfather passed away a few years ago. Actually, her face had looked like this too, drawn and scrunched and blotchy red. My heart started to pound really hard in my chest, and all at once, I didn't want her to explain anymore.

"She's dead, Maddie," my mom said. "She's been ..."

"Murdered." The strangled word burst from my father's throat, and the newspaper fell on the table with a flat slapping sound that seemed as loud as thunder. Even from here, and upside down, I could read the headline on the open page.

Brutalized Body of Missing Sixteen-Year-Old Found in Singing Woods

"Wendell!" my mom snapped, shrill and startled. "Don't *say* that!"

I barely heard her. I couldn't breathe.

Angeline Walsh was dead. A girl I'd waved at, talked to, worked on a stupid science lab with, testing germs and toxins on plastic water bottles. That girl, someone I had known, if only a little, was now a 'brutalized body' that had been dumped in the woods like garbage.

This was so much different than my grandpa passing away in his sleep. So much scarier. This was Death with a capital D.

Tears blurred my vision. Everything went dark and kind of smothered, and it took me a minute to realize it was my mother, hugging me. I hugged her back, more shocked and horrified than sad, and tried to tell her that I was fine.

The words wouldn't come out.

Mom was shaking and sobbing, way more of a wreck than me. And in that moment while we were hugging, as a few of her tears dripped on my shirt, I had a startling thought that I realized was very ... adult.

She wasn't crying for Angeline. She was crying for *me*, imagining how she would feel if *I'd* been the one murdered and found in the Singing Woods. She was more afraid than sad.

"I'm okay, Mom," I finally said. "I'm okay."

She drew back with a sniffle and swiped at her eyes. "Are you sure, sweetheart?" she said, glancing back at Dad. "You can stay home from school today, if you want to."

"No, it's fine. Really," I said as I tried to remember what a reassuring smile felt like. My face wanted to twitch and contort in horror, but it was all just plain shock. People didn't get murdered in Dayfield, *especially* kids my age.

Kids who'd been in my biology class.

God, this is so stupid. Angeline's voice spoke in my head, and my stomach did this weird, twisty thing. I could see her standing beside me at the glossy black lab table, a look of bored disgust on her face as her fingers played restlessly with one of the glass slides for the microscope. *I mean, seriously, who cares about iron and zinc in water, right? Those are minerals, anyway. They don't kill you. This sub sucks, we were supposed to dissect frogs this week.*

The loud chime of the front doorbell popped the memory I'd been stuck in, and I scrambled toward the living room, anxious to escape my mom's misplaced misery and my dad's eerie, deer-in-the-headlights stance. They were scaring me more than the news about Angeline. "That's Carson," I called back to them, running for the entrance. "I got it."

I pulled the door open, and there was Carson Mills, my best friend. Her shoulder-length blonde hair was perfect, as always, but her big blue eyes were wet and her nose was a little red. "Oh my God, Mads, did you hear about Angeline?" she gushed immediately, walking right past me and heading for the kitchen. She was over here all the time, and my parents pretty much treated her like a second daughter. "It's so awful, isn't it?"

"Uh, yeah, we just heard," I said, too late to warn her not to go in there. I sighed and followed her, knowing what a huge fuss my mom and dad were about to make.

Carson vanished through the kitchen doorway, a flash of bright blonde in a skimpy pale blue outfit. "Hey, Mr. G. Good morning, m-o-m," I heard her say. Since fourth grade, she'd called my mother 'em-oh-em' spelled out, for 'my other mother'. Mom thought it was adorable.

"Wow, is that today's paper?" Carson said as I rushed into the kitchen. "Poor Angeline. I can't believe it!"

I breathed a sigh of relief when I assessed the situation. My parents were almost back to normal, standing together by the table with my dad's arm around my mom, rubbing her waist the way he always did when she was upset. They both managed smiles.

"Hi, Carson," Mom said. "I'm so sorry about your friend, sweetie."

Carson gave a little shrug and opened the fridge, helping herself to two bottles of flavored water. She tossed one to me, and I barely caught it. "Thanks. We didn't really know her, but it's still so terrible," she said as she shut the fridge door. "Anyway, me and Mads have to run. We're *so* gonna be late."

Dad frowned. There was still an awful, vacant look in his eyes, like something vital had been knocked right out of his head by those words in the newspaper. "Do you girls want to ride in with me?" he said. "I'm leaving in five."

"No, we like the walk. Fresh air, sunshine, all that good stuff," I said quickly, grabbing Carson's hand and pulling her toward the back door before she could answer for us. "Love you guys. See you later!"

"Love you too, honey," my mom called back just before door clicked shut between us, and I let out the breath I'd been holding. That was close.

Carson giggled as we crossed the back yard, headed for Mrs. Vanderwall's driveway that opened onto Geary Street. It was faster getting to school this way than going around the front of my house, which would make us have to walk an extra block and a half, and my backyard neighbor didn't mind if we cut through her place as long as we didn't step on her flower beds. "Come on, Mads, what's wrong with you?" my best friend said, giving me a playful shove. "Why don't you want to ride to school with your dad?"

I rolled my eyes. "Are you kidding me? He's not just my dad, he's a *teacher*," I groaned. "I'd be totally humiliated."

"But your dad's pretty cool," she said, still grinning. "And also, he's kind of hot."

"Ew!" I elbowed her and stuck my tongue out. "That's disgusting."

"Whatever. He is, though." Her smile fell away as we turned onto Geary, and she fussed with her hair. Which, I noticed, didn't mess up her style one bit. "Seriously, though, can you believe it about Angeline?" she said, her voice dropping to a dramatic whisper. "I heard they found her all cut up, like some wacko science experiment. It's freaky."

God, this is so stupid.

Those are minerals, anyway. They don't kill you.

We were supposed to dissect frogs this week.

I shuddered as the dead voice of Angeline Walsh twisted through my mind, and suddenly I wanted to throw up. "Can we not talk about that, please?" I said, surprised at the heat behind my tone.

Carson drew back with comical shock, and then she hugged my shoulders. "I'm sorry, Mads. I'm being a total ghoul," she said. "You're right. Let's talk about something awesome, like your party this weekend!"

"Yeah. I can't wait." I was still shaking off the shadows, my enthusiasm just a little bit fake. "Mom said we get the whole community center to ourselves, the pool and everything."

Carson flashed a sly smile. "I bet you still didn't invite Dark and Stormy, did you?"

A blush heated my face, and I pressed my lips together. She meant Ian Moody, a totally gorgeous senior I'd been crushing on since seventh grade, at least. But last week was the first time I'd actually interacted with Ian for longer than five minutes. It wasn't really a date, since we just bumped into each other at Sally McKenzie's party and started talking. We'd ended up hanging out for hours, though.

He was everything I dreamed he would be. Sweet, funny, smart, and oh-my-God drool-worthy. I still couldn't believe he'd talked to me.

"Uh, no," I finally said out loud, trying to sound casual. "I mean, he's a senior. I'm sure he has better things to do than hang out with a bunch of sophomores at a lame birthday party."

Carson grinned. "No, he doesn't."

"How do you know?"

"Girl, you're lucky you've got a friend like me." She draped an arm around my shoulders. "I invited him yesterday, and he said he'd love to go."

"Oh my God! You didn't!" I squealed, my face going even redder. But I was delighted. Butterflies in my stomach and everything.

We shifted further into familiar, happier conversation territory, and the lingering shock of hearing about the girl who died began to fade. I gradually forgot Mom's desperate sobs and the scary blank look in

Dad's eyes. I even forgot Angeline's voice. The tide of the day swept me up, depositing me on the mundane shores of Average Teenage Life ... and I forgot everything.

As if the violent murder of a classmate was nothing more than a loose eyelash that I'd blinked away in the bathroom and washed down the sink, never to be remembered again.

6

Monday, June 2, 12:15 p.m.

After my session with Dr. Bradshaw, I'd gone home to wash up and change, and to grab the materials I needed for my class this afternoon. Now I'm at the Ticonderoga, one of Dayfield's three casual dining restaurants, for lunch with Jan Shearman. I don't have many adult friends, but Jan and I go way back. I actually met her in high school — she was a student teacher, just five years older than me, who started at Dayfield High in my sophomore year. *That* year, the one that ended so badly for so many families in this town.

Including mine, though my bad ending had been extended through the rest of my life.

I'd connected with Jan from the start, with her tall stature and Alpine looks, bobbed red hair and pale skin with light freckles, a confident smile. She'd also been one of the few people from my old life who still wanted a relationship with me when I returned from my little two-year 'vacation' at the Brightside Retreat for Teens and Young Adults. These days, she's a full-fledged gym teacher and coaches my daughter's soccer team.

The good thing about gym teachers is that they get all the lunch periods free, and the high school is only a few blocks from here. So Jan often gets the chance to skip school and hang out with me.

Jan orders her usual, a cold shrimp and black bean salad, and I get the cottage cheese plate with crunchy tortilla strips on the side. We talk about normal things, the soccer team and whose lawn my husband is working on and the flat tire I had last week and Jan's uneventful date over the weekend with Brad Calverton, the ninth grade English teacher. By the time our entrees arrive, I still haven't brought up this morning and seeing Stewart Brooks. If I tell her, she'll be worried about me.

But if I don't tell her, and she hears about it through the grapevine — I'm sure there's some kind of overblown rumor about me making the rounds right now, started by the Blanchards after the scene at the Price Cutter — she'll be hurt that I didn't confide in her.

I'm toying with my cottage cheese, pushing my fork around idly, when Jan puts her iced tea down on the table and cocks her head at me. "Okay, Maddie, what is it?" she says, with nothing but friendliness and warmth in her voice. "I know there's something wrong."

My eyes fill up, and I have to blink at the ceiling for a few minutes. Of course she can tell that I'm not right.

"Something happened this morning," I say without looking up from my plate. "I saw something ... someone ... impossible." I take a deep breath and raise my head. "I saw *him*."

Jan looks confused for just a few seconds before realization sets in and sympathy floods her face. But there's something else there too, an expressive quirk that's familiar to me. A certain whiteness around the eyes, a narrowing gaze, a cautious set to the jaw. I'd seen it so many times on the faces of nurses and orderlies at Brightside. It's an unspoken question, a mental gauge attempting to measure something very specific: how crazy is this person I'm dealing with right now?

I hate seeing that look from Jan.

"I know it wasn't actually him," I say quickly, relieved when her jaw relaxes and her eyes refocus. "That's impossible. But he just looked so real, and honestly, it scared the hell out of me."

"Of course it did," she says a little too forcefully. "I mean, after all you've been through, it had to be terrifying."

At least she's trying to believe me. I think.

I grab my lemonade and take a long sip. "I saw Dr. Bradshaw right after," I tell her. "She says it could be part of my condition, so she's upping my meds just in case." God, how I want to believe that's the reason. I've made peace with my disorder, come to an understanding that I can't always trust myself. My eyes work just fine, but sometimes my brain lies to me about what I'm seeing. Still, I've never flat-out hallucinated people before. "She also reminded me of the date, and how it's two days from ... the twenty-year anniversary."

"Oh, sweetie." Jan reaches across the table and takes my hand. "What an awful time for you. Is there anything I can do to help?"

I shake my head and smile. "Not that I can think of, but I'll let you know if I do," I say. "Mostly, I just don't want to think about it."

"I don't blame you," she says, and looks at her watch. For some reason I get the sense that she's uncomfortable talking about what happened all those years ago. But it's not really that strange. No one wants to reminisce about the Singing Woods Killer, about the four girls he killed.

Or about the one he didn't.

"I'm sorry, Maddie, but I've got to get back to work," Jan says as she digs through her purse, coming out with two twenties that she lays on the table. "Lunch is on me today. Don't argue, it's my turn."

Her smile is almost brittle, and I start to wonder what she's so worked up about. *I'm* the one who hallucinated a brutal killer outside the supermarket. But I push that unkind thought aside and return the expression. "Thanks, Jan. Tell Renata I said hi, when you see her for soccer practice today." Even as I speak, I wince slightly, remembering this morning's Festival of Embarrassment in the car. "I mean, as long as her friends aren't around to hear that her mother exists," I add, trying to keep my tone light.

Jan laughs. "Kids," she says, shaking her head. "Don't worry, she really does love you. She's just going through a phase."

"Tell me about it."

I manage to sound normal, despite a hot, unexpected stab of anger. Jan doesn't have children. She has no idea what it's like for a parent trying to navigate the teenage years. And maybe I'm a little jealous too, because Renata loves soccer and her coach, and my daughter might actually spend more time with this woman than me.

In fact, this woman might not even *be* Jan. My friend would never say something so patronizing.

She could be an imposter.

"Are you okay, Maddie?" Jan says, half on her feet. "You look really pale."

I shake myself and blink a few times. Where did all *that* come from? I'm not jealous of Jan. I'm proud that Renata has such a great role model, and I'm certainly not angry with her for not having children of her own. She's a teacher, for God's sake, and she's wonderful with the kids. Of course she knows how teenagers are.

"I'm fine," I tell her, returning to myself again. "I just had a spell for a minute, that's all. My blood sugar must be low or something."

She circles the table and gives me a hug. "Well, I worry about you," she says. "If you need anything, you just give me a call, okay? Any time, day or night."

"I will. Thank you."

Jan heads out, and I stay at the table for a few moments longer, trying to collect myself. I absolutely don't like the thoughts I was just having, especially the part about whether that was really Jan. Those were the kind of thoughts I had early on after my ordeal, the kind that led to accusations, hurt feelings, fear, and full-on panic attacks.

Could I really be relapsing somehow? Had I forgotten to take my pill this morning? No, I remember waking up at 5:30, shuffling into the bathroom to pee, and then shaking out a little blue pill to swallow after I washed my hands, just like always. I remember, because I thought the tablet looked different somehow. A slightly darker blue than it should have been. But it was early, and one of the light bulbs over the mirror had been flickering.

I hope I'm not just getting worse.

The first time it happened, the first time I had symptoms of Capgras, was with my father. It's something I don't like to think about because it's one of the last memories I have of him. The hurt and bewilderment on his face, the sick terror. I hate that I caused him to look that way, to feel so betrayed, even if I couldn't control what I was doing.

They'd kept me in the hospital for three days after I was found in the woods, due to the head injury. I'd just come home and was lying on the couch with a movie playing on TV that I wasn't watching. My mother was upstairs, compulsively cleaning my bedroom and probably crying, which she'd done almost constantly since I was found, and my father had gone into the kitchen to get me a glass of water.

After a few minutes, a man came out of the kitchen who looked just like my father, but he wasn't. I knew he wasn't. He was an impostor, wearing my father's face and clothes, walking like him, talking like him. This was someone *pretending* to be my father, holding a water glass out to me.

I stared at him. "Who are you?"

The man who looked like my father laughed hesitantly, and his brows drew together. "What do you mean, honey?"

"I'm Madeline," I said. I didn't like this man calling me 'honey'. "My dad went to get me a glass of water. Did he ask you to give it to me?"

"Maddie ..." His face went slack. "Sweetie, it's me," he said as he set the glass on the coffee table and started to sit on the couch next to me. "What's wrong —"

I panicked and scrambled away, pushing myself into the furthest corner of the couch. "*Who are you?*" I screamed. "I want my daddy! Go away! Mom, *help!*"

The man stood like a shot and backed away slowly, his expression shattered. "Madeline," he whispered with tears in his eyes. "I don't understand."

Feet thundered down the stairs, and then my mom was there, her arms around me. I buried my head in her shoulder and started sobbing. "What happened?" she said in a small, confused voice. "Maddie? Wendell, what ...?"

"That's not my dad!" I sobbed, squeezing my eyes shut so I didn't have to see the man who looked exactly like my father, but wasn't. "I don't know who he is. He tried to give me water. Where's Daddy?"

"Oh, God." Mom's voice was thick, horrified. "Oh, baby, what did he do to you? What did that filthy animal do to my beautiful daughter?"

I'd thought she was talking about the man in the living room, the man who was impersonating my dad. It wasn't until years later, after I'd done the same thing to her multiple times but the medication was finally starting to help, that I realized she'd meant the killer. Not my father.

A waitress comes to my table to ask if I want a refill on the lemonade, snapping me back to the present. I decline politely and hand her the two twenties that Jan left, telling her to keep the change. Our total lunch bill can't be more than thirty, and is probably much less, but I don't mind leaving a healthy tip.

I stop in the restroom to freshen up and then head outside, where my black Sonata sits in one of the curbside parking slots. The town of Dayfield is one of those places people describe as 'quaint', with lots of brick buildings and wooden shutters, landscaped tree-lined sidewalks, and ample on-street parking without the modern monstrosity of parking meters to interrupt the charming atmosphere. Right next door to the Ticonderoga is the Rainforest Café, where Richard and I had our first date.

And across the street is the Dayfield Community Center with its public pool, tennis and basketball courts, game fields, and picnic areas. The large building on the grounds holds the town library, several workshop rooms, an auditorium, and a few small administrative offices. It plays host to all sorts of community events, from weddings and family reunions to fashion shows and rock concerts. My husband and I were actually married there. That's where my class is being held, in about fifteen minutes.

I'm concentrating on fishing my keys from my purse as I walk toward the car when a surprised voice calls out, "Maddie?"

I'm so startled that I nearly drop the keys. I whirl toward the sound, my heart in my throat, and then relax instantly when I see my husband standing on the sidewalk. He's just come out of the café with a coffee in each hand. I can't believe I didn't see his truck, which is parked about ten spaces from my car. He drives a big, distinctively purple Tundra, but his tow trailer isn't hitched to it right now. He must've left it at his job site for the coffee run.

"Hey, honey," I say with nearly forced cheer as I walk toward him. It's not that I'm unhappy to see him. I just don't want him to ask what's wrong, and then spend the rest of the day worrying about me when I can't tell him. And as I get closer, I spot another good reason to hold off the mention of what happened this morning, sitting in the passenger side of the Tundra and glaring at me through the windshield: Ian Moody.

Ian and I have a long, complicated history, and things didn't end well between us ... though I still don't know why, because he ended them completely out of the blue, without giving me a real reason. I'd been surprised as hell when Richard came to me just before our wedding and told me he'd taken on a business partner, and it turned out to be Ian. But my husband didn't know that Ian was my ex. He'd offered to cancel the partnership if it made me uncomfortable, but I told him I didn't mind. I wasn't the one who had to work with the man Carson used to call Dark and Stormy — with good reason, as it turned out.

But it was too painful to think about Carson now.

"What are you doing here?" Richard says, grinning like he's just won the lottery as he gives me an awkward one-armed hug while trying to balance the coffee cups. It melts my heart that he's still so happy to see me, every time we've been apart. Even if it's just a few hours. "Wait, let me guess. There was a big sale at Danvers, and we *really* need six more avocado savers."

I giggled and kissed him, briefly wondering if seeing us together made Ian jealous. But I doubted that. He'd made his feelings crystal clear years ago, if not his reasons for them. "No, I think three is still plenty," I say with a smirk. Richard's still teasing me about the three-pack of avocado savers I'd bought at the department store about seven months back. It was an impulse buy, because I'd been looking up new recipes earlier in the day and saw that avocadoes seemed to be suddenly popular, and healthy, so I'd been thinking about trying them. Then I found these 'avocado savers' on clearance for a dollar, marked down from fifteen. It felt like serendipity at the time.

When Richard saw them sitting on the kitchen counter, he'd laughed so hard that he couldn't speak for a few minutes. Finally, he'd blurted, "Why do we need to save the avocadoes? They're perfectly safe in this house — none of us has ever eaten one in our lives. It's cruel to cage them in those. Let 'em roam around, like ... free-range avocadoes."

I'd ended up laughing just as hard. And the avocado savers ended up in the back of the utensil drawer, gathering dust and spawning fits of laughter every time one of us caught sight of the still-unopened package. Free-range avocados, indeed.

"Anyway," I say, "I just had lunch with Jan, and I've got a class this afternoon." I flash a smile at him. "That's my excuse. What's yours?"

He holds up the coffees and shrugs. "Playing hooky for a few minutes," he says. "Though I don't know why we decided on coffee. It's hot as hell out here, and we've still got four or five hours of outside work today."

"Well, you might be crazy," I say.

"I am crazy. About you." He leans down to kiss me again, and then winks. "I'd better get going before Ian cooks to death in there," he says. "See you tonight, babe. Love you."

"Love you," I call as he walks back toward the truck. I feel bad not telling him about my incident this morning and hope he doesn't hear it from someone else first, but I'll explain everything tonight when he gets home. He'll understand. He's the most patient man I've ever met — unlike his business partner.

As I turn away and head for my car, I can feel Ian's green-eyed glare burning into me.

7

Monday, June 2, 1:00 p.m.

The pottery class I teach on Mondays and Thursdays at the community center was actually Richard's idea, but I was thrilled with it. He'd managed to arrange just what I needed, right when I needed it.

Before he'd gone into business for himself, Richard worked for the town's department of public works, doing roadwork and landscaping. The community center grounds were a large part of his route, and he became friends with Selma Ferguson, the center's director. Once he started Osborn Outdoor Services, Selma rearranged the budget to give his company the maintenance contract for the center, because she liked the way he took care of things. With such a large, regular client right out of the gate, the business really took off.

Then, years later, I'd gone through a bad patch when Renata started middle school and got involved in after-school activities. I was alone most of the day, depressed, and afraid of my condition worsening. Richard remembered that I'd made pottery while I was at Brightside and kept up the hobby for a few years after, though my wheel had been sitting covered in the garage and gathering dust for quite a while at that point. So he'd talked to Selma about starting up a pottery class at the community center.

She'd been delighted to offer something new to the community; I'd been surprised and happy to have something fun and meaningful to fill my time. And now, here I was.

I find that I enjoy teaching, helping others find their own shapes to tease out of the clay, the way I used the activity to quietly reshape my broken self after what I'd endured at Brightside. My students are mostly beginners, adults looking for a new hobby, but I have a few who've taken my class several times and show real artistic promise. It's a delight to discover them and encourage them, even if they never progress beyond making beautiful pieces for themselves, family and friends.

I've just brought the last of my materials from my car into the classroom and stepped out, planning to head down the hall to the small staff lounge for a cup of coffee before class begins, when I see a familiar and unwelcome figure emerge from the lounge. Trevor Downes teaches a class that helps seniors learn to use the Internet for everyday things, which I suppose is useful and maybe even noble, but he's also a total creep. He leers at everything with breasts, gets drunk and grabby in public, and he has an unhealthy obsession with serial killers. Including and especially the Singing Woods Killer. More than once, he's cornered me to ask uncomfortable, inappropriate questions about my ordeal. He wants the lurid details.

Even if I could remember anything, I wouldn't tell him.

I sigh and walk toward the lounge, even though he's noticed me and hasn't moved from the doorway. I'm not going to let a bug like Trevor make me afraid or push me away from my hard-won, more-or-less settled life. I'm an adult, and I can handle one creepy little man with a disgusting hobby.

"Trevor," I say as I reach the lounge. "Could you please move, so I can get in there?"

"Hello, Madeline." He takes a step in exactly the direction I don't want him to — backwards into the lounge. He's not going to leave. "How are you doing today?"

I want to ignore him, but it's hard for me to be rude. Even when I have a good reason for it. "I'm fine, thank you," I say without looking at him, headed for the Keurig on the back counter beneath the window.

"Are you sure?" He's coming closer, and my skin crawls at the hint of avaristic glee in his voice. "It's just that I heard you had a bad morning," he says. "I'm only asking because I'm worried about you."

"Well, *don't* worry about me," I say as I grab a mug from beneath the counter and sock it into place under the coffee machine. I pluck a pod from the rack beside the Keurig without reading the label and drop it into the holder, quickly closing the cover. "You don't even know me, Trevor."

"Oh, come on. I heard you were hallucinating, and that you freaked out in a parking lot and slugged Paul Blanchard." He's right next to me, propping an elbow on the counter, staring as I push the button to start the machine. "Was it him? The killer?" he says. "You can tell me about it. I promise I won't laugh."

My teeth grind together, and I silently urge the stupid coffee machine to brew faster. I can't believe the Blanchards are letting people think that I hit Paul on purpose. "I don't want to talk about it," I say, and then realize that might sound like a confession to him. I don't want him to keep digging around for details. "Look, it's none of your business. And I have to get to class now. Excuse me."

I take the mug from beneath the spout while the Keurig hisses and gurgles out the last few dregs of coffee, hating myself for that 'excuse me.' I'm still being polite, and I shouldn't. It only encourages him.

As I walk out of the room, Trevor calls behind me, "There's a big anniversary coming up for you in a few days, isn't there? Twenty years since you killed a man." After a smug pause, he says, "What did that feel like, Madeline? Did you feel guilty? Numb? Or maybe you enjoyed it."

I don't know what will happen if I let go of the rage building inside me, so I keep walking. *Do not engage*, I tell myself over and over as I make my way down the hall and back inside the classroom, where a few early arrival students are seated at their wheels. I greet them by name, trying to sound upbeat and normal, when inside I'm cracking like a pot that's been left too long in the kiln.

There's nowhere to hide in this room, so I sit behind my desk with my eyes closed, sipping nuclear-hot coffee that I didn't manage to add cream and sugar to, working on my calming technique. White light in, dark thoughts out. White light in, dark thoughts out. Again and again, until the world behind my eyelids is bright enough to give me a headache.

I breathe and set the coffee aside, standing to greet the class. No one seems to be worried or giving me strange looks, so maybe I've succeeded. Or maybe they're all just too polite, like me.

We've just wrapped up a section on pinch pots, and today I'm going to start them on the coil method. There are fifteen students, and I have each of them take a brick of earthenware clay from the front table to bring to their wheels. When they're seated, I go through the steps, taking the plastic from one of the clay bricks to demonstrate how to form a base, how to roll the clay into coils, where to weld the first coil to the base.

Soon they're off and running, and I move around the room offering tips and compliments. I've nearly managed to forget about Trevor and his hurtful questions, and the hour-long class flies. Before I know it, it's time to start wrapping things up, securing the works in progress, and giving my brief talk about what to expect the next time.

As I'm going through a short description of the possibilities using the coil method and encouraging my students to think about where they'd like their pieces to go for the next class, a man comes into the room and takes a seat near the back. At first I think nothing of it. This class has open enrollment, and I often get students who come in mid-session and pick up wherever the class has left off.

But soon I notice that the new arrival is staring at me intently rather than looking around the room like most prospective students. And he seems familiar, somehow.

A brief stab of panic makes my words falter, but it's not him. The man doesn't look anything like Stewart Brooks. He's stocky, average height, with thinning strawberry-blond hair, dressed in a rumpled button-down shirt with no tie and badly cut slacks. I can't make out the color of his eyes from here, although I can feel the weight of his stare. Where have I seen him before?

I wrap up my spiel quickly and dismiss the class, hoping the mystery man will leave with them. But he doesn't. He waits until the room empties, and then strolls toward me as I dash to the other side of the desk, hands in his pockets. I can see his eyes now, and they're a deep, striking, almost unnerving shade of blue.

That's when I recognize him, and my stomach starts to churn. His name floats up from the depths of my subconscious to hover at the forefront of my mind, flashing red like a warning beacon.

Frank Kilgore.

"Good afternoon, Miss Grant. Sorry ... it's Mrs. Osborn now, right?" he says, showing absolutely no response to the glare I've fixed him with. His hands are still in his pockets, and he's smiling like he has every right to be here.

He doesn't.

"I just want to ask you a few questions," he says as he stops on the other side of the desk with his cocky grin. "It won't take long."

"Get away from me." My voice emerges stronger than I thought it would, but my hands are shaking. First the ghost at the supermarket, then Trevor, now *this*. "You don't get to ask me anything."

"Actually I do. It's a little thing called freedom of the press." I can't help flinching when he takes his hands from his pocket, and he laughs, vulture that he is. He's holding a microcassette recorder in one hand, and he pushes the red button that starts the little tape inside the device recording. "Interviewing Mrs. Madeline Osborn at the Dayfield Community Center," he says into it, and then points the damned thing at me. "Mrs. Osborn, how do you feel about the upcoming twentieth anniversary of the murder of Stewart Brooks?"

I clamp back a shout that would've been peppered with a lot of choice words. He's trying to bait me, to goad me into a screaming rage so he can print more terrible things about me in that rag he works for. Not that he won't print them anyway. But I'm not going to give him the satisfaction of a legitimate quote.

"No comment," I say tightly. "Leave my classroom, Mr. Kilgore."

Instead of leaving, he leans forward. "This is your chance to be heard," he says. "I don't just write for the Tribune any more. I've got a news blog that's read by people across the country, and my readers think you're insane. Here's your opportunity to prove them wrong."

I narrow my eyes at him. "I wonder what could have possibly made them think that," I say, knowing he'll twist my words out of context. Not caring. "This is the last time I'm telling you. Leave me alone."

He straightens and arches an eyebrow, and a horribly smug expression spreads on his face. "How's your daughter doing, Mrs. Osborn?" he said. "I understand she turned sixteen recently, the same age as you were when you killed Stewart Brooks. Her name is Renata, isn't it?"

Rage explodes red behind my eyes. "Get out of here!" I scream, storming around the desk toward him. He starts backing away, hands raised, a smirk stamped on his face. "I swear to God, if you go *near* my daughter, I'll —"

"Kill me?" he says with a laugh. "Go ahead and say it, Madeline. I'll have it on tape, and then everyone will know how crazy you really are."

It's an effort to hold myself back, to keep from lunging at him and slapping that smile off his face. "If I so much as *think* you've been near my daughter, I'll call the police," I say. "And I'll tell them what you did all those years ago. I have proof."

His mocking grin is a little less certain. "No you don't," he says. "If you did, you would've gone to them already. And besides, I didn't do anything."

He's too late trying to defend himself. Now I'm the one smiling, a brittle expression that feels like cut glass on my face. "Stay away from me, and my family," I say. "I'm not kidding. I will turn you in."

"What's going on in here ... Madeline, are you all right?"

I jump a little at the sound of a woman's voice from the back of the room, and then relax when I see who it is. "I'm fine, Selma," I say without taking my gaze from the scumbag reporter. "This man was just leaving. Weren't you?"

Frank Kilgore leers and stops his recorder, stuffing the device back in his pocket. "Yes, I think I have plenty of material," he says. "Thank you for your time, Mrs. Osborn."

I bite back an equally sarcastic reply to his sarcastic thanks as he pivots and strolls from the room, under a suspicious glare from Selma

Ferguson. Once he's gone, concern fills the director's face as she starts toward me. "I heard yelling," the older woman says, glancing over her shoulder as if Frank might come back and start in again. "Are you sure you're okay, dear? You just look so exhausted."

Relief and frustration war within me, forcing me to the verge of tears. I blink them back and brave a smile. If I start crying now, I'm going to have a very messy breakdown right in front of Selma, and I don't want to put that burden on her.

"It's been a long day," I finally say, turning away to swipe at my eyes. I'm sure Selma notices, but she doesn't draw attention to it, and I'm grateful. "That man ..."

"Whoever he is, I've got half a mind to report him to the police," Selma says. "He was clearly harassing you."

The righteous indignation in her tone prods a real smile from me. "His name is Frank Kilgore. He's a reporter," I say, unable to keep the strain from my voice. "We have a history. A bad one. He's written about me in the past, made me sound like some kind of ... psycho."

"Oh, you poor dear!" she gushes, giving my shoulder a comforting pat. "I do hate reporters. They're such vile people, always trying to glamorize human suffering." She shakes her head disapprovingly and purses her lips. "I'll tell Mike that he's not to allow that man in the building, so he can't harass you again."

"Would you?" Some of the tension runs out of me. Mike Roberts is the receptionist for the community center. He's a big man who can look very intimidating, if you don't know what a sweetheart he really is. "That would be wonderful. Thank you so much, Selma." It's good to know that not everyone thinks I'm crazy.

She smiles. "It's no trouble at all," she says. "Now, why don't you head home and get some rest? I'll grab one of the volunteers to sort your room out and lock up for you."

"You're an angel," I say. The adrenaline that carried me through my confrontation with Frank is ebbing quickly now, and I'm not sure I can stay on my feet much longer. I might actually indulge in a quick nap before Renata gets home at five.

After saying goodbye to Selma, I grab my purse from the desk and head to the parking lot. My hands start shaking again as I open my car door, and I try to will myself calm enough to drive. It's not far, I tell myself. Ten blocks, and I'll be home.

Then I can worry about how to explain all this to my husband tonight, without scaring him half to death.

8

Madeline—the past

Another girl from our class went missing yesterday. Her name is Tricia Spinks, and she definitely didn't run away. The police were at our school all day today, looking through Tricia's locker, interviewing her teachers, talking to her friends.

Carson and I knew her because she was in the art club with us, so we had to talk to the police too. I was surprised when the one who interviewed me turned out to be a woman. Detective Brenda Westhall. I must've watched too many cop shows. Most of the police on TV were men, so I just assumed a 'detective' would be some rugged guy who drank too much coffee and went to bars at night, and had a lousy love life.

But I liked Detective Westhall, and I felt bad that she had this job. It must've been awful having to interview so many people about Tricia, which probably included her parents too. Everyone was a lot more scared this time. We all knew what happened to Angeline Walsh last month, and even though the police hadn't said it yet, we knew that Angeline's killer had taken Tricia.

Carson and I walked home together right after school, not saying much. We were going to my house, and we'd planned to do our lame math homework and then reward ourselves with the new Tom Hanks and Meg Ryan movie, which I'd gotten on DVD for my birthday and hadn't watched yet. But now the idea of watching a romantic comedy while Tricia was missing, and probably being tortured or something even worse, didn't feel right.

"So, did you talk to Ian today?" Carson said out of the blue, trying to change the subject that was on everyone's minds.

I shrugged. "For a few minutes at lunch," I said. "He's sad about it, like everybody else."

"I didn't mean talking to him about Tricia." Carson's face pinched for a second, and she looked almost angry. But then she went back to normal. "It's gonna be your one-month anniversary soon," she said. "You have to hint about these things to guys, or they won't remember. Trust me on this one."

I covered an unexpected giggle with a hand. "That sounds kind of lame, doesn't it? A one-month anniversary," I said. Ian and I were officially dating now. He'd asked me out at my birthday party while we were sitting by the pool, and somehow I managed to say yes without blurting something incredibly stupid, like 'you're the best birthday present ever.' That would've sent him running for the hills pretty fast.

Carson looked affronted. She'd always been a sappy romantic, but none of her boyfriends had ever been romantic enough for her. She said they were all too immature to treat a girl right. "Listen, the one-month is very important," she said. "If he forgets that, he'll forget the six-month, and then the year. Before you know it, you'll be looking at an entire life with no flowers, no jewelry, no romantic dinners."

"Come on. It's not like I'm planning to marry him or something," I said as a heated blush filled my cheeks. "We just started dating."

"You never know when you're going to meet your soulmate," Carson said gravely. But her lips twitched, and then she burst out laughing. "Okay, fine. Just don't come crying to me when all you get for your anniversary is a blank look."

I started to laugh with her, but the sound died in my throat when I noticed a man with orangey-blond hair walking down the sidewalk toward us, moving fast. He looked determined and, I thought, a little bit crazy. There was something heavy and black on a strap hanging around his neck, and it bounced against his chest with every step.

I clutched Carson's arm and tried to steer her off the sidewalk.

"Mads, what are you doing?" she said, giggling until she followed my gaze to the approaching man. "What's wrong? Do you know that guy or something?"

"No, and I don't want to," I whispered sharply. "He scares me."

Her brows went up. "How can he scare you, if you don't even know him?"

"I don't know." I was shaking, but my feet had kept moving the whole time with minds of their own, still in the rhythm of walking. Carrying me toward this man with the black thing around his neck.

Then he was in front of us, smiling, blocking the entire sidewalk somehow. The thing around his neck was a camera, the big bulky kind with the huge lens and the tower flash. It was probably very expensive.

As an overall image, he looked normal. Handsome, even. Possibly on the verge of cute, because handsome was something you said about a man, and this guy wasn't very old. Early twenties, maybe. He wore a crisp blue button-down shirt and black pants, with new-looking sneakers on his feet. Nikes with their unmistakable swoosh logo. I shouldn't have been afraid of him.

But I was. His smile was empty, his eyes flat, despite being the most brilliant blue I'd ever seen. The blank lens of his camera was positioned to suck out my soul.

"Hello, ladies," the man said, drawing a giggle from Carson. I wanted to elbow her quiet, but I couldn't move an inch. His flat stare pinned me in place. "You two go to Dayfield High, don't you?"

"Oh my God, you're Frank Kilgore!" Carson squealed. "I've read every single one of your articles for the New Tribune, and your guest columns in the Herald."

My heart sank. This guy was a reporter, which meant it was going to be almost impossible to tear Carson away from him. At the beginning of the school year, she'd decided she was going to be a journalist. She'd pestered her parents into subscribing to every paper known to man, talked me into joining the school newspaper with her, and started having crushes on various reporters for weeks at a time before she moved on to the next one. I couldn't keep track of them all, but he must've been one of them.

Frank Kilgore grinned, revealing perfect white teeth, but there was nothing friendly in that smile. It was practiced, calculated, designed to lull people into a false sense of security. “Wow, a true fan,” he said to Carson. “Hey, listen. You two must’ve known Tricia Spinks, right? Would you mind me asking a few questions, maybe taking a picture?” He held up his camera.

“Absolutely not,” I said, surprising myself with a firm voice as I grabbed Carson and shoved her around the reporter. “We’re minors. We can’t talk to you.”

“That’s a rule for the police, sweetheart. Not reporters,” he said, recovering quickly from his shock as he started to follow us. “You don’t need permission to talk to me. Come on, it’s just a few questions.”

“No! Get away from us, or I’ll call 911!” I shouted over my shoulder, still propelling a stunned Carson along. She’d never seen me act this way. In fact, I think I never *had* acted this way. But I couldn’t help it. Something about Frank Kilgore chilled me to the core.

There was a snap and a high-pitched whine from behind us, just as Carson snuck a glance back. He’d taken a picture.

“I can make up any quote I want, you know,” he half-yelled after us. “I can even suggest you had something to do with Tricia and Angeline, and everyone would believe it. Come on, just one question.”

I didn’t dignify that with a response.

“I know your names,” Frank shouted. “Carson Mills. Madeline Grant.”

“Oh my God,” Carson whispered, turning pale. “Maybe we should —”

“No. He won’t do anything,” I said firmly, even though my legs had turned to jelly and my throat felt like sandpaper. “Come on, we need to get out of here.”

A few blocks later, I slowed down and made sure he wasn’t following us anymore before I let out a breath. “Ugh. What a jerk.”

“Ugh is right,” Carson said, wrinkling her pretty nose. “I’m crossing *him* off my crush list. It’s too bad, because he really is much cuter in person. I mean, those eyes.” She kissed the tips of her fingers and then opened her hand to the sky, like she was appreciating a pizza or something.

That made me smile a little. "Well, at least we got away," I said. "Good riddance to bad rubbish."

Carson blinked at me. "Huh?"

"It's just this weird thing my parents always says," I told her. "You know, like all the other weird stuff they say."

She laughed, and we were okay again.

Frank Kilgore didn't cross my mind again until later that night while I was lying in bed, tossing and turning because I couldn't stop thinking of Tricia and all the horrific possibilities, of what she might be going through right now. And that was when I remembered something the reporter said that I hadn't really noticed at the time, but now made me break out in goose bumps and lie there with my teeth chattering, unable to close my eyes.

He'd said, 'You two must've *known* Tricia Spinks.'

As if he already knew she was dead.

9

Monday, June 2, 3:45 p.m.

Once I leave the community center, I pick up my stronger prescription at the pharmacy and head home. A quick nap, a loaded dishwasher and a dinner's worth of marinating chicken breasts later, I'm at the flowerbeds in our fenced back yard with a glass of iced tea, trying to remember which ones are actual flowers and which are weeds.

Gardening is not exactly my strong suit. Richard always tells me he'll take care of it, but I know he doesn't want to spend an extra hour or two working in our yard when he's already spent most of the day on other people's. I don't mind, really. And our flowerbeds might not win any awards, but they're colorful and fragrant, and they attract hummingbirds.

Our back yard is fairly large, surrounded by a rustic red picket fence with a matching white-trimmed shed in the back corner. Past the back fence is a gently sloping stretch of weed-choked scrubland that leads into a patch of woods. It's not the Singing Woods — that vast stretch of untamed forest with impossibly tall trees, riddled with natural traps and pitfalls. Our little forest is domesticated, mostly short pines and birch trees with plenty of space between, and you can see flashes of the houses on Pritchard Street through them. There's even a well-worn path straight through where some of the school-aged kids cut down from Pritchard to Seneca, our street, a shortcut to the nearby town park.

But even that little spit of trees can give me the shivers sometimes, especially at night. I try to avoid the back yard when it's dark.

On my knees in the dirt, I spot a dense clump of thick green blades that I think is called crabgrass, or maybe quackgrass, growing beneath a hydrangea bush. I crawl toward it, my gloved hands holding a trowel, and hack at the stubborn stuff, eventually ripping out the plant along with a big, messy clump of roots. Hopefully, I've got it all.

As I back out from under the bush, dragging my prize with me, I can't help but remember another time in another garden, far less pleasant than this.

Richard and I were living across town in a small two-bedroom rental house. We hadn't been married long, and we were saving for a down payment on a bigger, nicer place. I'd gotten it into my head that I would grow all of our vegetables myself, so we could cut back on the grocery bill and get a down payment together faster.

Looking back, I know that homegrown vegetables really wouldn't have made that much of a difference to our budget, even if it had worked out. But I was young and determined, and probably kind of stupid.

It was a blazing hot August afternoon, and I was out in the postage-stamp back yard in shorts and a knotted midriff top, my feet bare, a scarf tied on my head. My gardening clothes. I'd tried to water the powder-dry earth around the rows of stunted, yellowing plants first, before I did anything else, which meant I was now weeding on my knees in mud.

Like I said, I was probably kind of stupid.

While I had my back to the house, the screen door leading out from the kitchen creaked open, and then banged shut seconds later. I looked over my shoulder, a smile on my face, expecting Richard.

But my brain didn't see my handsome new husband. Instead it saw a stranger, an imposter, a man I didn't know, who only *looked* like Richard. Coming out of my kitchen and into my yard, holding one of my water glasses in his hand with condensation dripping down the sides.

"You look thirsty," the fake Richard said, obviously holding back a laugh. He thought he was fooling me, but he wasn't. "I thought I'd bring you a drink. What's that on your nose?"

I scrambled to my feet and took a step back, holding the rusty secondhand trowel out like a sword. "You're not my husband," I said. "You're *not.* You want to hurt me."

The stranger with Richard's voice, Richard's smile, lowered his hands as his expression smoothed out. "Madeline ... I am Richard, I promise," he said with such care, such patience. Telling me soothing lies. "I'm your husband. You're having an episode. Please, try to remember."

"Leave me alone," I said as I moved forward cautiously, still brandishing the trowel. "You're not Richard. If you try to hurt me, I'll ... I'll kill you!" I shouted triumphantly. "Just like I killed *him*. I will, I swear it!"

"Madeline," he said, still gentle as he stepped toward me. "That's your name, Madeline Osborn. And I'm Richard Osborn. Your husband. We love each other." His voice was plaintive, pleading. "Please put the shovel down."

I screamed and rushed at him, slashing the trowel wildly through the air. He threw his arms up to shield himself. I swiped the trowel toward him, catching a sharp corner on his forearm and scratching deep, drawing blood.

He cried out in pain and clamped a hand over the gash. Blood dripped through his fingers. The man who wasn't my husband looked at me sadly, as if he expected me to feel sorry for him, and then turned and walked into the house.

My house. He didn't belong in there.

I rushed after him, yanked the screen door open and stomped into the kitchen. And relief filled me when I saw my husband standing at the sink, running cold water. The real one. "Richard, where were you?" I breathed as I went to him, the rusty trowel still clutched in my hand. "There was a man. He was in the back yard, and I ... he ... oh, God, you're bleeding!" I said as I caught sight of his arm. "What happened?"

He closed his eyes, as if in pain, and then looked at me with such sorrow that my heart wanted to break. "I broke a glass," he said carefully. "Knocked it right off the table. Don't worry, I've already cleaned it all up."

For a few seconds I wondered why, if he'd been in the kitchen all this time, he hadn't come outside when I started screaming at the stranger. But I decided I must have gotten mixed up somehow. Maybe I was standing out there for longer than I thought after he went inside.

Richard smiled at me and took the trowel gently from my hand. "Let me just wash this up for you," he said. "It's pretty filthy. Just like you, Little Muddy Face." He touched my nose with a finger. "Do you want to jump in the shower?"

"Yes. I think I've had enough gardening for one day," I said, throwing my arms around his neck for a kiss. "But the man ... didn't he ..."

"That man is gone," Richard said. "It's okay. He won't hurt you."

And we'd both gone about the rest of our day, as if nothing had happened.

Now that I understand my condition, it's so easy — and yet so hard — to look back at things, that incident in particular, and see how much I'd hurt the people I love. Richard has been so patient through it all, so understanding. That time in the garden, he could have told me that I was the one who gashed his arm, that I'd thought he was a stranger and attacked him, but he didn't. He even washed the blood from the trowel before I could see it there. Because it would have hurt *me* to know that, and he doesn't want me hurt.

My mother, on the other hand, will probably never forgive me for the awful way I made her feel when I screamed at her, threw fits, told her I didn't know who she was and didn't want her near me. I guess we're even, since I'm still not sure I forgive her blaming me for my father's suicide.

It's past 4:30 already, and I need to head inside and wash up so I can start dinner. Renata will be home from soccer practice in half an hour or so, and Richard usually comes in around six. I straighten and brush the loose dirt from my jeans, then set the trowel in the plastic caddy beside me. The gardening gloves join them, and I start across the yard to stow the caddy in the shed.

I've covered half the distance when I finally realize there's someone standing at the back fence on the woods side, completely motionless. Dark hair, dark clothes, hunting cap, malevolent glare.

Him.

Again.

I want to run at him, confront him, demand to know why he's stalking me. Why he still looks twenty years old, the same age he was on that day. I want to kill him all over again.

But pure terror takes over, and I scream. The plastic caddy falls from my hand, tips over on the lawn, and I pivot and sprint toward the house. My heart beats so fast that it feels like it's vibrating, and I can barely take a breath.

I stumble through the back entrance into the laundry room, slam the door shut and lock it hard with a shaking hand. Then I lean my back against the door, gasping in big lungfuls of air. I did not hallucinate him. I did *not.* That was a real man. It was Stewart Brooks. I didn't kill him, after all.

The police. I need to call the police.

I hurry to the kitchen on trembling legs and snatch the cordless house phone from the wall charger. Dial 911, wait while it rings twice, three times. A woman answers. "Nine-one-one, what is your emergency?"

"There's an intruder in my back yard," I say loudly, as if shouting makes it sound more believable. "Please, I need help. He's dangerous. He wants to hurt me."

"Okay, ma'am, are you in a safe location right now?"

"I ... I think so." I'm quieter now as I look around wildly, wondering if the windows are unlocked, if the front door is open. "I came inside and locked the back door. I'm checking the front entrance now."

"We'll send a car right over, ma'am," the operator says, and I hear keys clicking in the background. "Can you give me the address, please?"

"Two-oh-five Seneca Street. Dayfield," I add, in case the 911 center isn't in this town. I've never actually thought about that. I reach the front door and try the knob. "Both doors are locked," I tell the operator.

"All right, ma'am." More background typing. "Osborn. Is that right?"

"Yes, that's right. Madeline Osborn." At least I can feel my heart beating now, but the fear still hums through my veins, electric and alive. *Impossible. This is impossible.* Am I losing it? Was there actually a man at my fence? Was it Stewart Brooks? I didn't see him move at all, not this time. He was just there. Did he move this morning, at the supermarket?

I can't remember. My stupid, *stupid* brain won't work right.

"Ma'am?" the operator says. "Mrs. Osborn, are you okay?"

"Sorry, yes," I breathe out heavily. I must've missed something she said. "Can you repeat that?"

"Officers are on the way. They'll be there in about five minutes," she says. "Can you safely observe your back yard, to see if the intruder is still there?"

"I ... I don't know," I say with reluctance. Suddenly I'm not sure I want to look. If he is still there, would it prove that I'm not crazy?

And if he isn't, would it prove that I am?

"That's all right, Mrs. Osborn. You stay safe until the officers get there." The operator sounds warm and friendly, as if she truly cares about the welfare of a stranger who may or may not be insane. "Please don't hesitate to call back if your situation changes."

The call ends and I stay where I am in the foyer by the front entrance, clutching the silent cordless phone in both hands like a shield, nervously watching for the police through the narrow windows beside the door.

Praying they'll believe me when they get here.

10

Monday, June 2, 4:50 p.m.

The police arrive in a sedan with no logos, but there's a light bar across the top of the vehicle, which they leave flashing blue as they exit the car and head for the house. Two men, both in shirts and ties rather than uniforms, each with a gun at the hip and another in a shoulder holster. One looks just shy of thirty with cropped blond hair and stubble on his face, the other is mid-forties, dark hair, his craggy face clean-shaven. The older one has a piercing stare that I can feel through the window.

I open the front door as they climb the porch steps, and the younger one flinches as his hand moves to his gun. But he relaxes within seconds. "Mrs. Osborn?" the older man says, and I hear a certain undercurrent to his voice, one I don't like. It suggests that he's already judged my situation and decided that I'm wrong. "You called in an intruder in your back yard, is that correct?"

I nod, for a moment unable to find my voice. "Yes, that's right," I say after a pause. "He was behind the back fence."

The older cop raises an eyebrow and nods at his partner, who turns and heads back down the porch steps to circle around the house. When he's out of sight, the older man says, "May I come in?"

"Yes. Please," I say as I step back and open the door for him. I'm shaking all over again, but I don't think it's fear now. It's the feeling I'm getting from this man that he believes I'm wasting his time. "Thank you for coming, Officer ...?"

"Detective Tom Burgess," he says, his sharp eyes roaming all over the foyer and the living room beyond. He gestures vaguely toward the back of the house, and adds, "My partner is Sergeant Boyd McKenzie. He's canvassing the back, to make sure it's safe. Are you able to see your back yard from inside the house?"

"Yes, from the laundry room," I say. "It's right this way."

I lead him through the living room, then the formal dining room and the kitchen. I've left the door to the laundry room open, so I just point through it and watch as he walks into the room, toward the window of the back door. I don't want to see what's happening outside. So I replace the phone on the wall charger, lean against the counter, and wait.

"Do you mind if I unlock your back door?" Detective Burgess says after a minute. "So my partner can come in this way."

"That's fine," I tell him. I can't see him from this angle, but I hear the deadbolt click and the door open. He doesn't say anything, though. I imagine he's just gestured for his partner to use this door.

"Detective Burgess," I say. "Can I speak to you for a moment?"

He walks into the kitchen, somehow moving in silence. It must be police training or something. He says nothing, but waves a hand for me to talk.

I can't help sighing. "You don't believe me, do you?" I say. "About the intruder."

His expression closes off, like a book being shut. "I'm aware of your ... history, Mrs. Osborn," he says. "That's why my partner and I are here, responding to your routine call, instead of a couple of uniforms. The department has standing orders that any incident involving you must be handled by a detective."

The statement horrifies me. "You're saying the police have entirely different procedures for 'handling' me?" I say. "That really doesn't seem fair. It means that if I need help, whoever comes to help me is already going to have formed an opinion before they see the evidence. Like you have."

"It's for your protection," he says. "Due to the violent nature of the crimes that you were involved in."

"Involved in? You make it sound like I had a choice!"

"Mrs. Osborn, please, calm down." The detective raises both hands, as if he's shushing a child. "We're going to investigate this matter fully."

"You still haven't answered my question," I say. "Do you believe me?"

Before he can say anything, his partner comes in through the back door, looking flustered and irritated. "There's no one out there," he says crankily, right before he notices I'm standing there. The back of his neck turns red, and he coughs into his hand. "I did find footprints in the ground behind the fence that would've been someone standing there, looking into the back yard. They seemed relatively fresh, but there's no way to tell how long they've been there. I took pictures."

Detective Burgess nods once. "Isn't there a path through those woods behind the house?" he says.

"Yeah, from Pritchard Street. The kids use it all the time."

"So those footprints could be anyone's, then."

"Excuse me," I say. "There was a *man* standing at my fence, less than half an hour ago. Not a child. I know what I saw."

They glance at each other, and the detective clears his throat. "Mrs. Osborn, can you identify the intruder?"

Panic worms through me. If I tell them it was Stewart Brooks, they definitely won't believe me. He's dead. They know it, and I know it. But his face ... it *was* his face. There's no way I could mistake anyone else for him.

Unless it really is because of my condition.

Just then, the front door slams open and Renata's voice fills the house. "Oh my God, Mom! Are you okay? There's a police car outside! Where are you?"

"In here, honey. I'm fine," I call out, and glance at Detective Burgess. "That's my daughter," I say, in case he can't infer that from the way she called me Mom. "Excuse me, please. I'll be right back."

I head out of the kitchen and through the dining room, feeling horribly guilty — because just for a few seconds, I'm glad that Renata sounds scared. I don't want her to be afraid, of course. It's just that her reaction proves she still loves me, something she won't admit to these days without pulling several teeth.

I'm ashamed of myself for thinking that, even for a moment, but there it is.

My daughter is still in her blue-and-gold soccer uniform, sweaty and smeared with dirt, her backpack hitched crookedly on one shoulder. She drops the bag and hugs me, and I have to choke back a sob. More than anything, I'm relieved that *she's* okay, that she's safe from the man who may or may not have been in the back yard, but was nowhere near her.

"Mom, what's going on?" Her voice is small and muffled, and she steps back and gives a little gasp as she peers into the kitchen. "Are those guys police? Why are they in our house?"

"Everything's okay," I tell her, gently rubbing her back. "There was ... an intruder in the back yard, that's all. He's gone now. I just wanted the police to check things out, and I think they scared him away."

Concern and confusion appear on Renata's face. "An intruder?" she says. "Do you think he was trying to rob us or something? Did you know him?"

Her last question is a twisting knife. I can't tell my daughter the truth, or what I believe is the truth. Then she really will be terrified. "I don't know what he wanted, honey," I say. "But everything is all right now. We're safe."

"Okay," she says uncertainly with another glance at the officers in the kitchen. "Can I go tell Jenny and Mrs. Kline? They're still outside in the car. They were worried, too."

I nod and smile, vaguely nauseous at the thought of the rumors that are going to spread from this. Having the police here is practically begging for gossip and speculation. "Yes, please tell them that everything is fine," I say. "You can go ahead and grab a shower when you come back in, if you want to. I just have to talk to the police for a few more minutes."

"Thanks, Mom." Renata smiles and squeezes my hand. "I'm glad you're okay."

As she races back outside, my heart nearly explodes with love for her, and I know that I'll do anything to protect her. Always.

I steel myself for an unpleasant conversation and return to the kitchen, where Detective Burgess and Sergeant McKenzie are talking, low enough that I can't make out the words. They stop when I enter the room. "I'm sorry about that," I say. "Can I offer you some coffee, or a cold drink?"

"No, thank you," Burgess says with a look at his partner. "I'd like to get back to my question. Can you identify the intruder?"

I don't want to tell this cold-eyed, disbelieving detective that I saw the man who abducted me twenty years ago, the man I killed in the woods. So I decide to describe him instead. "He has brown eyes and dark hair, stringy, shoulder length," I say. "He's about five-eight, a hundred and forty pounds. He was wearing hunting clothes —"

"Is this the same man you claimed to have seen earlier this morning at the Price Cutter?" the detective interrupts.

My chest tightens. "I didn't ... didn't report that," I say.

"No, you didn't. Paul Blanchard took it upon himself to come to the station and mention the incident, after you refused his offer to call for help. He also wanted to report you for assault, but I thought that was a little excessive on his part." Burgess almost seems sympathetic, but it's the humoring kind of sympathy, the kind of tone he might take with someone threatening to jump off a building. "I understand that you must be having a stressful day, Mrs. Osborn," he says. "But at this point, I don't think this is a matter for the police. There's no evidence of an intruder in your yard, or a lurker at the plaza, and it's highly unlikely that the same man would happen to be in both of those places in one day."

"So you're saying it's a matter for my psychiatrist," I say bitterly. "You think I'm crazy."

"I think you're a woman who's been through a lot in her life, and you have every reason to be cautious," the detective says, choosing his words with care. "We'll stop by and question your neighbors, to see if they noticed anyone fitting the description you gave around your home. Outside of that, there's very little we can do without evidence."

I nod and press my knuckles to my eyes, trying to stem tears of frustration. He's probably right. There wasn't anyone there, earlier today or this afternoon, and it's my condition making me believe there was. All of this amounts to nothing.

But it doesn't *feel* like nothing.

"Thank you for coming out," I say in an unsteady voice.

Burgess gives an apologetic frown. "If something else happens and you have proof, go ahead and get in touch with the station," he says. "Otherwise, I'll let you know if we find anything more."

"All right. I'd appreciate that."

I walk Burgess and McKenzie to the front door, noting with relief that Mrs. Kline's car isn't outside. I thought I heard Renata come back inside and head upstairs while I was talking to the police, but I wasn't sure. At least Jenny's mother didn't try to come in and find out what happened for herself. I couldn't have explained it to her without sounding crazy.

And I'm not crazy. I'm just having an episode, the worst I've had in a long time.

I will get through this.

11

dark and deep

It's her fault. All of it. I wish I'd known just how insane she was before I had her. But it's far too late for wishing. If wishes were horses, then beggars would ride.

I still hate that saying, even though I use it all the time.

She should've just left town, as soon as she knew I was here. But obviously, she's not going to. Not with the way she's acting, like *I'm* the threat. I can't go on like this. I wanted to move ahead with my life, but she's going to make so much trouble for me.

How am I going to stop her?

She's entrenched. She has a support network. I want to dig her out of her so-called life and pop her like a tick, but I can't. Not yet.

I wonder if she thinks she's left her own dirty secrets behind, buried somewhere out of reach. If she believes she's untouchable. Well, she's not. *I* know her secrets, every awful one of them.

All I have to do is figure out a way to drag them into the light. Then everyone will see that she's not the woman they think she is. *She is not a victim*. Every single thing that happened was her doing, and she did it deliberately. She's a crazy person, a dangerous lunatic. A time bomb waiting to go off.

And I'm the only one who might be able to defuse her, before it's too late.

12

Monday, June 2, 6:30 p.m.

There's no way I can concentrate enough to cook a decent dinner, so I order pizza. Mushroom and pepperoni from Angelo's, a favorite for both my husband and my daughter. I'm more of a roasted-vegetable fan, myself. Usually I just pick off the pepperoni and I'm fine, but tonight I don't think I'll taste anything, anyway. It hasn't just been a bad day. It's been overwhelming.

Dinner and Richard arrive right around the same time. He doesn't know about the police being here yet, but he knows something is wrong. There's concern written all over his face. Before I can say much of anything, Renata asks if she can take her pizza to her room, because she wants to get her homework done, and I tell her that's fine. She hugs her dad, and actually kisses me — on the cheek, but it's still unusual — before she runs upstairs with her gooey, greasy plate.

"Okay, now I'm really worried," Richard says with a funny little smile, once he hears her bedroom door close. We're in the dining room with the pizza box open on the table, and he's piling a few slices on a plate. "I thought she said that she's too old to kiss her mom."

"Yes, she did say that. She's just worried because something ... happened," I say on a shaky breath, holding up a hand before he can start firing questions at me. "Can we sit down, and I'll tell you all about it?"

"All right," he says cautiously. "Just reassure me that whatever happened isn't still happening."

I shake my head. "I think it's over now."

He still looks uneasy as I put a single piece of pizza on a plate, and then we head to the living room and settle on the couch. "All right," my husband says, as if he's bracing himself to hear about a death in the family. "Tell me."

I tell him. Everything.

By the time I'm done, he's gone through an astonishing range of emotions and eventually landed on sympathy. "Oh, babe, I'm so sorry," he says, putting an arm around my shoulders and drawing me close. I relax against him with a sigh, still determined not to cry. If I open those floodgates, I won't get them closed again anytime soon. "Have you talked to Dr. Bradshaw yet?" he asks me.

I stiffen just a little. Of course he thinks it's not real, that I didn't actually see Stewart Brooks today — not once, but twice. Any sane person would come to that conclusion. Dead people don't show up at supermarkets and in back yards. I guess I'd been hoping my husband would believe me, just for a few minutes.

But I have to stop this. It didn't happen, *couldn't* have happened.

"Yes, I had an appointment with her. It was after the first time I ... had a problem." Maybe if I don't say *I saw him* out loud, I'll stop believing it. "She says it might be stress, because of the date. The twenty-year anniversary. Which is in two days," I finish in a whisper.

He squeezes me tighter, as if he could impart some of his strength to me with a hug. I almost feel like it works. "Of course you're stressed," he says, but without the indulgent, patronizing tone I've gotten from other people today. "And the police, what did they say?"

I hate talking about it, because now I feel like a fool for calling them in the first place. "They didn't believe me," I admit. "One of them, the sergeant, said he found footprints from someone standing behind the fence. But he said they could've belonged to anyone."

"Right. Like the kids who use that path through the woods back there," Richard says, warming to the idea. He might be trying to convince me that's what happened, or himself. "I am glad you called them, though."

"You are?" I turn a puzzled frown to him. "Why?"

"Because maybe there really was someone," he says in a tone rough with concern. "And if there's even a chance that you could get hurt ... well, I never want to take that chance. You're my whole world, Maddie."

His declaration brings tears to my eyes, happy ones this time. "I love you, too," I say with a real smile.

"Now that's what I like to see. Happy wife, happy life." He bumps my chin with a finger, and then reaches for the plate of pizza he'd set on the coffee table. "Want to watch a movie or something?" he says. "Maybe after dinner, we could sneak in a little couch time ... we'll be quiet, in case Renata comes down."

He nuzzles my neck, kissing me in that hollow spot that makes me shiver. I let out a giggle. "Down, boy," I whisper.

I'm about to make a joke about traumatizing our teenager forever with the knowledge that Mom and Dad sometimes have s-e-x when the doorbell rings.

Richard's brow furrows. "Are we expecting anyone over?"

I shake my head a little, my tongue frozen in my mouth. I hate being afraid of my own doorbell. But after all that's happened today, no matter how I try to convince myself that none of it was real, my brain only has room for a single, blaring, overriding thought.

What if it's him?

"I'll get it," Richard says, a determined set to his jaw as he puts the plate back on the coffee table and stands. Panic screams through my body. I want to tell him not to answer the door, because *what if it's him?* What if he kills my husband, just for standing between him and me?

Richard peers through the side window, then glances back at me and smirks, rolling his eyes. There's still a scream on the tip of my tongue as he opens the door, right up until the moment I hear our visitor speak.

"Oh, Richard, I'm glad you're home! I was so worried about Madeline, after the police came by and spoke to us, that I just had to come over and make sure everything was okay."

That explains the eye-roll. It's Lexi Clark, our oh-so-perfect neighbor.

She bustles past my husband, clutching an elegant glass-covered cake pedestal in both hands. "It must've been so terrifying for you, Madeline," she gushes as she approaches me with her offering. I know it must be something gourmet and amazing that she'll brush off as no big deal, and she proves me right with her next words. "I thought I'd fix you a little something to cheer you up. It's opera cake." She flourishes the dish at me. "Just a coffee-soaked almond sponge cake with buttercream ganache and cocoa dusting. Alex and the boys adore this stuff."

I stand to greet her, forcing myself not to roll my own eyes. The Clarks are an all-A family — Alex and Alexis, and their twin boys Alford and Anton. I don't know how they can stand being so adorable, even when she insists that people call her Lexi so they don't get confused with all the As, tee-hee, couldn't you just die.

"Thank you, Lexi. That's really wonderful of you," I say as I steer her toward the dining room. "You didn't have to go to so much trouble."

It's no trouble at all, I think at the exact moment she echoes the thought out loud.

Right on cue.

Lexi sets the fancy dish on the dining room table, and her eyes flick over the open pizza box with faint disapproval. Mrs. Alexis Kingsford Clark would never dream of feeding her family a greasy cholesterol bomb from the local take-out place. But she morphs her judgment into an exaggerated, sympathetic face and pats me on the shoulder.

"You poor thing," she croons. "I told the police that I didn't see anyone in your yard, but honestly, I wasn't looking out windows too often. I had so much wash to get done today. You wouldn't believe how fast two teenage boys can go through clothes. And do they *smell* when they're through with them!" She laughs and waves a hand in front of her face, just one mother commiserating with another. "Anyway, from the way that detective described the man, I certainly would have remembered if I'd seen him. He sounds awful," she says with a polite shudder.

My smile feels like a three-dollar bill, and I hope she's not here for an extended visit. I hope she has a lot more smelly laundry waiting for her at home. "Well, thanks again," I say, trying not to look directly at the perfect, extravagant 'little something' on my table. "I'll bring your dish back to you soon."

"Oh, there's absolutely no hurry. Whenever you're ready, sweetie." Lexi is already heading back to the living room where Richard stands by the front door, telegraphing the same message I'm silently urging in her direction. *Please go home.*

I trail in Lexi's wake as she continues to spout platitudes and engage in mental hand-wringing on my behalf. When she reaches the door, she turns with a look of sympathy strong enough to cover at least three disasters — as if I've had a house fire, lost a pet, and been diagnosed with a terminal disease instead of just having an intruder in my yard. "You poor thing," she oozes, throwing her arms around me.

I have no choice but to return the hug. It's mercifully brief, and Lexi tones down the sad-sack expression when she steps back. Now's she's Sincere Neighbor. "You call me anytime you need me, Madeline, okay? I'm just next door," she says.

Then, with a little wave at Richard and a bright, "Toodles!" to accompany it, she's gone.

Richard closes the door after her and waits for a beat, then screws his face up. "Toodles, sweetie, I'm just next door," he says in a mock-high voice. "As if we don't know where she lives."

I'm completely surprised when I burst out laughing so hard, I have to sit on the couch before I collapse. Richard looks comically startled — I can practically see the little balloon with the exclamation point over his head — and it makes me laugh even harder.

He joins me after a few seconds, and soon we're both doubled over on the couch, holding our stomachs. It really isn't that funny. My laughter is wild, almost frantic, disguised screams barely held in check. But it keeps me from dissolving into tears.

The amusement is dying down when a thunder of footsteps descends the stairs and Renata pokes her head over the banister. "What's so funny down here?" she says.

She sounds like a schoolmarm scolding a classroom, and I hiccup and choke as fresh laughter tries to escape. "Nothing," I say, still trying to catch my breath. "It's just ... Mrs. Clark brought us a cake, and ..." I look helplessly at Richard.

"Toodles," he says with a straight face, and then we're off again.

"You guys are so weird," Renata says, smirking as she runs the rest of the way down and slips past the couch. "I'm gonna grab some more pizza."

Our daughter helps herself to a fresh slab of grease and returns to her room, confident in the knowledge that her parents are a couple of weird old people, like everyone else's parents. Richard and I settle in to watch a movie. We pick some random action B-movie on Netflix and spend most of the time making fun of the bad plot and worse acting. The occasional whispered 'toodles' from my husband sends us both into quiet gales of laughter.

At some point I realize that I've managed to believe life is good. And that Stewart Brooks is still dead.

Finally around ten, exhausted and wrung out from the events of the day, I kiss Richard goodnight and head upstairs to get ready for bed. I poke my head into Renata's room and find her sitting cross-legged on the bed, her laptop in front of her and ear buds parked in her ears. I remind her somewhat loudly to get to sleep by eleven, so she can hear me over whatever she's listening to, and she nods and rolls her eyes at me. She's back to normal.

In the master bath adjoining our bedroom, I open the medicine cabinet and take the new prescription bottle from the brown paper pharmacy bag, crumpling the bag up to toss it in the small waste bin under the sink. For some reason, the white plastic bottle feels heavier than it should.

I open the bottle, shake one of the pills out, and stare at it. That's not right. I'd seen the higher-dosage tablets before, since I was on them for almost a year at one point. But this is lozenge-shaped instead of hexagonal, pale yellow instead of white.

Frowning, I check the label carefully in case I've gotten the wrong prescription. All the information on the bottle is correct. Osborn, Madeline. Pimozide, 2.5 mg. Take one pill twice daily, morning and evening. Store tightly capped in a dark place. May cause dizziness or drowsiness, blah blah blah.

They must have changed the formulation at some point, or decided this pill shape is easier to swallow. I put the pill on my tongue, wash it down with a swig of water, and then grab my toothbrush to finish the nightly ritual.

I can't quite shake the strange feeling that the pills are wrong, though. Especially since I had the same thought about my regular pills, the blue ones that looked *too* blue this morning. Maybe I'll ask Dr. Bradshaw about it tomorrow. I can just call her at the office.

For now, sleep beckons me like a light bulb calls to a moth, and I'm helpless to heed its siren song.

13

Tuesday, June 3, 7:45 a.m.

It's the day before the anniversary, and I feel fine. Really I do.

The morning's gone smoothly, for once. Renata is up and ready on time and in the car a few minutes early, actually smiling. She talks to me about the English paper she's doing, a persuasive essay on a topic of the student's choice, and how she's chosen to argue that schools should replace textbooks with iPads. I laugh at first, thinking the same tired old parental line about kids and their obsession with electronic gadgets.

But then, she goes on to explain that school-issued iPads would give underprivileged children a way to connect with their peers and the world that they might not otherwise get, and tells me that five million school-aged kids in the United States don't have Internet access at home, which leaves them behind the educational curve. And once again, I feel guilty for my thoughts.

My daughter is becoming an intelligent, compassionate young woman, right in front of me. She astonishes me sometimes, in a good way.

I revel in the conversation, at least until we reach Jenny Kline's house and the car is filled with the rapid-fire banter that only best friends can generate. I'm content to listen and smile the rest of the way as we pick up Tonya and Drew, drive to the school, and pull into the drop-off line.

We're about ten cars back in line, and I glance casually around the school grounds, remembering when I was a student here. Trying not to think about the reason that my high school career was cut short right near the end of sophomore year and never resumed. I still had some good memories of the times before then, and some things at the school hadn't changed. There is the patch of grass between the sidewalk and the bus circle, with the flagpole planted in the center. Here is the statue of a proud lion, the school mascot, covered with the multicolored handprints of the most recent graduating class. Over there is the huge oak tree on the grass island where students lounge for lunch in warmer weather, and biology teachers teach their fresh-faced charges about photosynthesis but mostly just want to get out of the stuffy classroom for the day.

And beneath the oak tree, dappled in shadows, is a man.

I fight to hold a gasp inside as my hands clench on the steering wheel, turning my knuckles white. *Please, not again.* I want to look away, but I can't take my eyes off the half-seen figure. He's standing with one leg bent and a foot planted on the trunk of the tree, bringing something up to his lips. It looks like a flask. He lowers that arm, lifts the other, and the orange flash of a cigarette brings his face into view. Just for a few seconds, but it's long enough for me to recognize him.

Not Stewart Brooks, but Dallas Walsh. The father of the Singing Woods Killer's first victim.

The man who hates me for being alive.

I find myself almost relieved to see him drinking so early. Maybe that means he won't be at the survivor's group meeting I'd promised to go to tonight, since it obviously isn't helping him. Then I silently call myself out on the uncharitable thought and hope that whatever he's doing to get by, it brings him some form of peace.

Though I can't imagine anything would. Not after losing a child, especially in the way he did.

Renata catches my stare and follows my gaze to the shadows. Her nose wrinkles. And as if she's given a signal to the others, all three kids in the back seat crane to look at what she's seeing.

"Hey, isn't that Mr. Walsh?" Drew says.

"Yeah, it is," comes from Jenny. "Oh my God, is he drinking? It's, like, not even eight!"

"He always drinks," Tonya mutters. She's the first to look away.

Renata makes a rattling sound in the back of her throat. "That's disgusting," she says. "I'm never going to drink. It makes you mean, and that guy's a real asshole."

"Renata Lee!" I blurt before I can stop myself, and I sound so ridiculous that I have to laugh. Fortunately, the kids find it funny, even my daughter. But as glad as I am to hear her proclaim herself anti-alcohol — though it probably won't be long before her opinion on that changes — I feel compelled to stick up for Dallas. "Try to be nice to him," I say, to all of them. "His life hasn't been easy, and everyone deals with grief in their own way."

"My mother says you can't find salvation at the bottom of a bottle," Tonya mutters. Everything she says is a mutter.

"Your mother is right, but we should forgive Mr. Walsh," I say.

And I think: *Even if he won't forgive me.*

We reach the front of the drop-off line, and the back door pops open instantly as three out of four passengers tumble out, already laughing and groaning about the school day ahead. Renata stays behind for a moment, and when she thinks her friends aren't looking, she leans over and gives me a hug.

"See you later, Mom," she says. "Love you."

"I love you too," I say, my heart lifting as she slides from the car and runs to catch up with her friends. Moments like these fortify my spirit for the not-so-good times I know are still ahead. I can bank them up like treasure, take them out and admire them when we're fighting over silly things, her stubborn to my adamant.

I drive home, finally feeling able to put yesterday behind me. Richard has already left for work, and I have no plans for the day, but I honestly don't mind staying home to catch up on laundry and vacuuming, and all the other little tasks that tend to pile up in a living, breathing household. Maybe I'll take a nice long bath this afternoon and let myself relax. I'd like to be as calm as possible when I go to that meeting tonight

Because whether or not Dallas Walsh is in attendance, it's going to be stressful.

I park in the double-wide driveway and head in through the front door, risking a quick glance at the Clarks' house on the way. They have a painstakingly restored, three-story Victorian paired with a two-story carriage house, with both structures just as immaculate inside as out, and a lawn that's so green and perfect it may as well be Astroturf. Our very nice two-story Colonial with a wraparound porch and flagstone back patio looks like a cheap prefab compared to that.

But I don't envy Lexi's two thousand additional square feet to keep clean, or her astronomical property taxes.

Inside my nice, normal home, I deposit my purse on the sideboard in the foyer and head upstairs to assemble laundry. Richard's and mine are already corralled in baskets, but only because I'm in the habit of scooping his clothes off the floor on my way out of bed in the morning. I set the baskets at the top of the stairs and head down the hall.

Renata's clothes, I'm sure, are scattered all over her bedroom and piled between the toilet and the vanity in the upstairs bathroom. I don't like to invade her privacy, but I duck into her bedroom just long enough to grab the half-full basket beside her closet and bring it to the bathroom, where I add the loose clothes from the floor. It's enough for a load, at least. She'll have to gather the rest and bring it down — and she often does her own laundry, anyway.

But if I don't do a load now and then, we get mornings of Renata rushing around in full-on fuming mode, throwing a half-load in on the fast cycle and then attempting to dry just the clothes she wants to wear that day before it's time to leave for school. Those mornings end with a damp, grumpy daughter and a frustrated mother.

I half-carry, half-drag three baskets down the stairs and to the laundry room, getting the first load started before I head into the kitchen and start a new half-pot of coffee. I keep forgetting to mention to Richard that I'd like to get a Keurig, like the one at the community center, since I usually drink only one cup after Renata gets off to school and I end up wasting quite a bit of decent coffee. Our drip pot isn't designed for single-cup use.

I'm sure he'd be fine if I bought a Keurig, but I want to ask him what he thinks first anyway. If I can ever remember to when he's home.

Once the coffee's going, I wander toward the living room, stretching my arms above my head. Maybe I'll vacuum first, and then I can sit down for a while with a book and enjoy my coffee while the laundry's going. After last night's unplanned TV dinner, the living room carpet definitely needs it.

I'm just at the arched opening between the living room and the dining room when the doorbell rings.

My heart jumps a foot in my chest, and I slide back behind the dining room wall, out of sight of the front entrance. I try to tell myself it's just Lexi, back from dropping off her perfect twins at school and wanting to tell me what a poor thing I am, and how terrible she feels for me. But Lexi never comes straight home after the morning drop-off. Her next stop is inevitably the gym, where she works out six days a week.

And if it is her, I don't want to talk to her anyway.

The doorbell goes off again like a cheerful bomb. I clap a hand over my mouth, as if whoever's out there can hear me breathing. After a moment, someone starts pounding on the door, hard, insistent raps.

"Mrs. Osborn, I know you're home," a muffled voice says, and I recognize it even through the door. It's Frank Kilgore. I can't believe that slimy bastard's come to my house.

But after yesterday, I don't have the strength to confront him again. I'm just going to wait until he leaves.

Another insistent chime, more pounding. "Your car's in the driveway. I know you're here," Frank shouts. "Listen, I just want to give you some information. I found out some things you should know. Give me five minutes, and then I'm gone and I won't bother you again. I promise."

He's lying. I know he is, because he's used this particular strategy before to gain access to me.

And then he nearly ruined what was left of my life at that point.

The doorbell bongs again, three times in rapid succession. "Madeline!" he says with a frustrated snarl. "Okay, look, I'm putting my card under your door. Please call me. There's something I need to tell you."

Complete silence follows. I nearly take the bait, almost start edging toward the entryway where I can see the door, but just in time I realize he's still standing there. I haven't heard him walk away yet.

I wait. Three or four minutes later, I finally hear footsteps moving across the porch, descending the steps. I give it another full minute, and then a car engine starts outside and drives away.

Shuddering with relief, I walk across the living room to the foyer. There's a small white stock card on the floor, a few inches past the door. The business card he said he was going to leave. I pick it up gingerly by a corner and carry it to the kitchen as if it's a dead thing. There, I grab an old, stained ceramic bowl from the back of the cabinet, drop the card in, and set a match to it. When it's burned to ashes, I rinse them down the sink and replace the bowl, out of sight in the cabinet.

I want nothing to do with Frank Kilgore, ever again.

14

Madeline—the past

Carson and I were going to her house after school, and I was really worried about her. She never wanted to hang out at home. Not that her parents were mean or unusually strict or anything, but she had two little brothers. Keenan and Davy were nine and seven, respectively, and right at the worst possible age. A little too old to be cute, and a little too young to be anything but annoying.

But she'd refused to come to my place, and she wouldn't say why. In fact, she'd been especially gloomy and subdued for a few weeks now, nothing like her usual bubbly self.

Then again, the whole town was like that. Somber and quiet, and scared. Because now we had an official serial killer, and he'd claimed his fourth victim.

The media called him the Singing Woods Killer. Soon after Tricia Spinks turned up dead, like everyone suspected even while they hoped she wouldn't, another girl had vanished. Her name was Marie Caruso. Carson and I barely knew her, since she was a total band geek and neither of us went for music activities, but we couldn't help feeling her loss. She was sixteen, like us. Like the others, Tricia and Angeline. I knew I'd never forget their names.

And the horror still wasn't over. A few weeks ago, the Singing

Woods Killer struck a far more personal blow when he took Dana Moody, my boyfriend's sixteen-year-old sister. She was a sweet, quiet, funny girl, and we'd taken her right into our circle of friends like she'd always been there. Losing her had hurt in ways I couldn't even describe.

But it'd hurt Ian far more, of course. I hadn't seen him at all since last Thursday, when they found Dana's body after she'd been missing for a week and the police came and took him right in the middle of lunch period. No one had to ask why — we all knew what happened. He'd stopped coming to school, stopped leaving his house, and I couldn't really blame him. He was all that his parents had left.

As we walked toward Fravor Road where Carson lived, she kept scuffing her feet along the sidewalk with exaggerated strides, huffing to herself. I'd already asked her three times what was wrong, and that was just today. The first two times she'd said nothing, and the last she claimed she was on her period, which I knew she wasn't. I'd probably be pushing it if I asked her again.

But I was about to anyway when I noticed a familiar and extremely unwanted figure cutting across the street, heading toward us. My jaw clenched angrily. "Don't even try it," I yelled at the strawberry-blond-haired reporter who for some reason had fixated on me as his enemy, and kept hinting in his articles that I knew something about what happened to the murdered girls.

Carson startled and followed my line of sight. When she spotted Frank Kilgore puffing across the street, she stopped and went rigid, her hands clenching into tight fists at her sides. "That asshole," she seethed, watching him with fury sparking from her eyes.

I tried to pull her away. "Come on, just ignore him," I said.

"No. I've got something to say to him."

My stomach churned unpleasantly as I stood by my best friend, helping her to hold her ground, even though it was the last thing I wanted to do. Just being near this guy gave me cold chills.

Frank was close to laughing as he stepped onto the curb in front of us and slowed. "Madeline and Carson," he said, his empty grin fixed in place. "How about a nice quote for the New Tribune? I'll even let you amend your previous statements, because I'm feeling generous."

It was on the tip of my tongue to scream at him, to tell him I didn't make any previous statements and he was a filthy, disgusting liar.

But before I could open my mouth, Carson drew an arm back and punched him in the face.

"Oh, my God," I whisper-screamed as Frank reeled back with a shout, one hand cupped over his nose. "You said you wanted to *talk* to him!"

Carson flashed a wild, heated grin of triumph at me and took hold of my arm, giving it a quick tug. "Run, Mads!"

We both took off sprinting, our backpacks slapping our shoulders as Frank Kilgore spewed threats and curses at us, peppered with words that no teenager should probably hear. At the next corner we turned right and ran another three blocks, until Carson pulled in front of me and held an arm out as she slowed to a walk.

I kept pace with her, staring at my best friend with awed amazement. "I can't believe you did that," I panted. "I mean ..."

"It was *epic*, right? The look on his face!" She nearly doubled over with a laugh, grabbing my shoulder for support. "Come on, Mads. You know he deserved that."

"Yeah, I know. I just don't want you to get in trouble."

She flapped a contemptuous hand. "You really think a guy like him is gonna tell anybody that he got punched by a girl?"

That brought a grin to my face. "You're right. He wouldn't."

Carson's good humor lasted only until we got to her house. By the time we reached her bedroom and closed the door in defense against her brothers, she was moody and withdrawn again. She threw her backpack against a wall and flopped back on her bed, looking blankly at the ceiling. "I hate men," she sighed dramatically.

"I don't think they're all like Frank," I said.

"Yes, they are. They're all assholes, every last one of them." Suddenly she popped upright and fixed me with a stare so intense, I could almost feel it burning. There were wars in her eyes. She looked like she was about to tell me something so awful that it would break her just to say it.

But then she sighed and hung her head. "Listen ... I feel terrible. I think I'm getting sick or something," she murmured without looking at me. "Do you think you could ask my dad if he'd give you a ride home? I'm really sorry, Mads. I think ... I just want to sleep right now."

Her hollow, detached voice worried me a lot more than her saying she didn't want to hang out. "Carson, what's wrong, really?" I said. "Is there something you want to tell me?"

Her head snapped up, and her eyes blazed. "Just go. Please," she said as her voice broke on the word. "I'll see you in the morning, okay?"

"All right." I moved toward her cautiously, wanting to hug her and tell her that everything was going to be okay, whatever it was. But her body language screamed to stay away, so I turned and walked out of the room.

Mr. Mills said he didn't mind giving me a ride home. No one was supposed to walk alone around town right now, especially sixteen-year-old girls — and as the father of one himself, he had to be extra worried.

A few minutes later, I was buckling myself into the front seat of his Chevy sedan as he backed out of the driveway and pointed the car toward my house.

We rode in silence for a few minutes, but Mr. Mills kept flicking awkward little glances at me. Finally, he said, "Madeline ... do you mind if I ask you something about Carson?"

I blinked in surprise. Carson's father had always been friendly enough, but he never really got involved in anything we did except when he told Carson to be home by nine and not to let any boys 'paw at her,' his uncomfortable way of saying 'make out.'

"Okay, sure," I said with a small frown.

But he didn't ask me anything. Not for a long, strained moment. Just when I thought he'd decided against asking whatever it was, he said in a quiet voice, "Has she said anything to you about anyone ... not behaving themselves around her?"

I had no idea what he was getting at. "You mean, like, drinking and drugs? Or, uh ..."

His lips pinched, and he shook his head rapidly as the back of his neck turned red. "No. I mean, has she mentioned that someone's been —" He swallowed hard. "Touching her?"

This time I knew exactly what he meant, and I wanted to throw up. He was asking if she said she'd been molested. Oh, *God.* It was a horrible thought, but that would explain the way she'd been acting lately. Depressed, angry, withdrawn. She'd even stopped fixing her hair and wearing makeup, for the most part. But if it was happening, she hadn't said a word to me.

"Madeline?" Mr. Mills sounded absolutely terrified. "Did she say anything to you?"

"No," I whispered, shaking my head for emphasis. "No, she hasn't —"

That was when the absolute worst idea hit me like lightning, stunning me into silence. Mr. Mills wasn't asking me if someone was molesting Carson.

He was asking if she'd told me that *he* was molesting her.

"I'm so sorry, Madeline, but can I ask you a favor?" Mr. Mills said, his voice sounding small and metallic through the blood rushing in my ears. I was about to faint. "Can you ... if she says anything, will you ... please, will you let me know?"

The words were torn out of him like splinters. He sounded so terrible, so remorseful, and suddenly I hated him with more intensity than I'd known I could feel. This man, my best friend's father, was a monster.

I mumbled something that I hoped sounded like an agreement. But if Carson told me that her father was molesting her, a question that I planned to pry the answer out of her at the earliest opportunity, I wouldn't tell him. I'd tell my parents, and I'd tell the police.

Even though it was only five or six blocks, the rest of the ride to my house seemed to take years. And when Mr. Mills pulled into the driveway, I couldn't get out of the car fast enough, feeling like I needed a long, hot shower just to erase his nearness.

I never wanted to be that close to a monster again.

15

Tuesday, June 3, 5:30 p.m.

We're having a rare early dinner at the dining room table. Renata didn't have anything going on after school today, and Richard finished up a job an hour faster than expected and decided to call it a day. Now we're enjoying the chicken I started marinating yesterday, which I have to admit is better for soaking in the sauce overnight, with braised new potatoes and a snap bean medley. Real la-di-dah stuff.

Take that, Mrs. Alexis Kingsford Brown.

The conversation is light and friendly around mouthfuls of food. I haven't mentioned Frank Kilgore showing up here earlier, because I don't want to spoil the mood. I want to indulge in the happy-family glow for as long as possible, soak it all up and keep it like a candle to burn against the dark at the survivor's group tonight.

Everyone's plates are nearly cleared, and I'm considering whether I want break out Lexi's cake that might put my 'gourmet' meal to shame, when the house phone rings a strident and unexpected note. "I'll get it," I say, reluctant to leave the cocoon of family that's been spun around the table. "It might be Dr. Bradshaw. I left her a message earlier."

Richard nods with his mouth full, and Renata helps herself to another chicken breast. "This is really good, Mom," she says. "You should make it like this all the time."

"I think I'll do that," I say with a smile as I push my chair back from the table. "I'll be right back, guys. This shouldn't take long."

I step into the kitchen and answer the cordless phone on its fourth ring. "Hello?"

"Madeline?" The voice is female, vaguely familiar and terribly uncertain. Whoever it is, I can't place it until she adds in a trembling whisper, "Mads?"

Carson.

I close my eyes, feel the small of my back slam into the kitchen counter as my weight falls against it, my muscles slack with shock. It's been twenty years since I escaped the Singing Woods Killer, and almost that long since I've spoken to my former best friend.

That was her choice. Not mine. Over the years, I've grown less angry and more melancholy about the way she left things between us, especially considering what I'm almost certain was going on between her and her father. But I'm not sure I want to go through the effort to repair the bridges she burned. Not at this moment. Maybe never.

I have no idea why she wants to talk now, after all this time. But if it's not to apologize, I'm not sure I want to know.

"Are you there?" Carson says, in a voice that's light years away from the happy, brazenly confident young woman I knew. At least until those last few weeks, right before the Mills family left Dayfield and never looked back.

"Yes," I finally say. "I'm here. Carson ... why are you calling me?"

Her silence is wounded. "At least you still know who I am," she rasps, as if she's on the verge of tears. "Madeline, I'm so sorry. I know it's been too long. But I'm back in town, and I really need to talk to you. In person."

I turn my back to the dining room so my family can't see my face, which I'm sure is haunted and drawn. She's *here*, in Dayfield? I can't even begin to guess why. Her family had moved abruptly to Scranton, Pennsylvania, of all places, a few days after I came back from the woods with a broken memory and a brand new pile of issues. Just before my father's suicide. I'd spoken to her only once after the move, and that was the conversation to end all conversations between us.

"Please, Mads," Carson says, the ghost of friendships past on the other end of the line. "It's important."

"I don't know if I'll have time." I can hear the hurt in my own voice, the years of silence and questions long unanswered. "Maybe in a few days. I ... I just don't know."

I'm not sure why I'm even opening myself to the possibility of seeing her again. If I do that, it's only going to bring it all back.

"It has to be soon. Please." She drags a shuddering breath and exhales. "I'm staying at the Stardust. If you call the front desk, they'll put you through to my room. I *have* to see you, Mads."

Something about this feels off, and I think of Frank Kilgore asking me to call him. Saying there's something he has to tell me. "I'll try," I finally say, with no real intention of following through. "I have to go now. Thank you for calling."

My tone is automatic and emotionless, and I hang up before she can say anything else.

For a moment I stand there facing the laundry porch, drowning in my past. Flashing past images of Carson and me together, laughing, crying, staying up late and getting up early, acting crazy, sharing secrets, being young and dumb and completely secure in the knowledge that we'd be friends forever. Then the phone call that sent everything tumbling into oblivion — me locked up in Brightside, her an entire state away and spewing hatred at me out of nowhere.

"Everything okay, babe?"

Richard's voice from the dining room makes me flinch as it shatters the mosaic of the past. "Yes, fine," I say immediately, patting my face to make sure I'm not crying before I put the phone on the charger and head back to my family. "It was Dr. Bradshaw. I just had a question about my new prescription. It's all good."

The lie pops out before I know it, and I wonder why I said that. Maybe because I've never talked to either of them about Carson, since it was over between us before I met Richard, and I don't want to explain it right now. Hearing her voice after all this time has opened fresh wounds that I'd prefer to nurse in private.

My husband gives me a questioning look as I take my seat at the table, but then he shrugs and smiles. "Dinner was great," he says. "Right, Rennie-Bean?"

"Yeah, definitely." Renata spears her fork into the last of her second helping of chicken. "Oh, I forgot to say I'm going to be late tomorrow," she says. "We have soccer practice, and then we're supposed to have study group for history at Eve's. If that's okay."

Tomorrow. The anniversary.

My first instinct is to say no, to tell her it's not safe and to come home right after school. To not walk alone. But that time of terror is long past for this town. It's my reality, not my daughter's, and I can't force her to put her life aside in service of the echoes from my old trauma. "All right, that's fine," I make myself say calmly. "Do you have a ride home?"

"Yeah, Jenny's mom is going to pick us up," she says.

"Speaking of tomorrow." Richard pushes his empty plate back. "I'll probably be home late too, unfortunately. Ian and I have a planning meeting to go over the advertising budget for the summer."

Disquiet fills me as I stare at the table, trying to summon the will to say it's okay. But I can't quite get there. Tomorrow, the worst day of the year for me, I'll be alone with my thoughts. With my ghosts.

"Maddie? What is it?" Richard says, and then his mouth falls open and he slaps his forehead. "Oh, shit. Tomorrow is the fourth, isn't it?"

Renata blinks at her father's cursing. He rarely swears in front of her. "What's on the fourth?" she says.

I'm grateful that she doesn't know, hasn't ever put it together. It means that so far, I haven't allowed this terrible anniversary to corrupt my daughter.

"It's nothing," Richard tells her in a casual tone, and then reaches across the table to take my hand. "I'll reschedule the meeting," he says. "It can wait a few days."

"No, don't." I give him a resolute smile, hoping it looks more confident than it feels. "It's important for your business, isn't it? I'll be fine. I can just have dinner with Jan."

He frowns. "Are you sure?"

"Positive."

"Well ... okay." He gives my hand a squeeze and relents. "You should treat yourself," he says. "Take Jan to the Stone Mill, maybe."

"Maybe I'll do that," I say.

"The Stone Mill?" Renata pipes up. "If you go there, Mom, you should totally bring me home a slice of cheesecake. Seriously, it's to die for."

Richard snorts a laugh. "To die for? Seriously?" he says. "Looks like we've got a blossoming food critic, here."

Renata sticks her tongue out at him and giggles. "I gotta go read, like, a million chapters for history," she says. "Thanks for dinner. It was awesome."

I smile at the rare, unprompted compliment. "You're welcome. And I'll see what I can do about that cheesecake."

"Sweet! You're the best."

She runs off, and I watch her with a lingering feeling of contentment. We've done all right by her, Richard and me. It's all been worth it.

For just a moment I remember another time, another child, and I wonder if I did the right thing. It didn't seem like a choice then. But I've often thought that maybe it should have been, that I should have fought harder.

There's nothing I can do about it now, though. It's out of my hands.

I almost decide to excuse myself from the survivor's group tonight, to risk incurring the wrath of Dr. Bradshaw and stay home where it's quiet. Where it's safe. But I'm going to need the deeper kind of healing that comes with the pain of group sharing, if I want to get through tomorrow.

I'll go to remind myself that I *am* a survivor. I am strong. I am good.

And I am terrified.

16

Tuesday, June 3, 8:16 p.m.

Dallas Walsh is here.

I knew he would be, despite my hopes that he'd stopped coming to the group. He's so isolated now that this must be his only remaining connection to other people, and the group leader would never ban anyone from attending the meetings. No matter how belligerent or angry they got.

However, she will make them leave for the night if they get too out of hand.

The survivor's group is held in the basement of the Masonic temple, a large room full of long tables with a semi-enclosed kitchen along the right-hand side. Tonight the tables have been pushed to the back, the chairs arranged in curved rows facing a central seat for the leader. There's also a ground-level entrance and exit near the back of the room, to avoid guests having to walk through the temple on the way here. The Masons rent out the basement for a nominal fee for wedding receptions, family reunions, birthday and anniversary parties, and other events that usually feature a crowd expecting food, but this group uses the room for free.

The group leader, Delphine Pearce, is a compact woman who always seems on the verge of exploding from her small body in a shower of boundless energy. She sports her hair in a pixie cut, and her eyes actually twinkle like stars. Everything about her is genuine and deliberate.

At first glance she seems too fragile to control a group of disparate, broken human beings, most of whom are on various medications and some who may be prone to violence. But when she speaks, it's impossible not to heed her. And besides, she has Bear for backup if things get physically out of hand.

Bear is an ex-bouncer who survived a horrific bar fire that killed two dozen people. Sometimes he jokingly refers to himself as a cockroach, with a hard shell that saved him from the blast. A cockroach that stands at six feet ten inches and weighs two hundred and seventy-five pounds, most of it muscle.

Delphine starts the meeting, as always, with a brief welcome for old friends and new arrivals. She never calls anyone out by name, always lets each person introduce themselves if and when they're ready. After the welcome, as always, she tells her own story to help us feel comfortable with sharing ours. It's hard to hear, Delphine's story. She was the sole survivor of a plane crash that killed her husband and their five-year-old daughter. They were taking her to Disneyland for her birthday, and it was a dream vacation for all of them.

And to complicate things, Delphine is barren. She and her husband went through years of struggle before they were finally able to adopt a baby, and she only had five short, precious years with her miracle child before her family was torn from her.

When she's finished, there aren't many dry eyes left in the audience. But I see at least one pair that hasn't shed a single tear. They belong to Dallas, and he's spent every second since I walked through the basement door glaring daggers at me.

Delphine invites the group to start sharing, in their own time. It's a long moment before an older woman in the second row raises her hand tentatively, and at Delphine's nod, begins to speak in a halting tone. She gives her name and tells a story involving a carbon monoxide leak, at a time before most people knew anything about the odorless killer gas and how it can get into homes. She talks about how carbon monoxide takes smaller people first, because their little lungs fill up faster, and then her face crumples and she's unable to go on.

Most of us can guess how that story would have ended. My heart goes out to the woman, who's clearly lost more than one child and is barely coping with her reality.

One by one, others share their survival stories. A man who went on a hiking trip with a group of friends from college, whose backpack strap caught on a snarl of tree roots when the cliff they were camping on crumbled and sent his friends to their deaths. A couple who were at a bank applying for their first mortgage and ended up hostages in an armed robbery, where the gunmen killed four people and wounded six more. A woman who'd left a party early because she'd had a fight with her boyfriend, and said boyfriend later hitched a ride home with a drunk friend, winding up dead along with five others in a three-car collision.

Dallas's burning gaze never leaves me the whole time. And when he raises his hand after the car-crash woman finishes speaking, my heart drops into my stomach.

Delphine glances at me before giving Dallas the go-ahead, as if she wants my permission for him to speak. I'm not sure I have the right to give it, but I nod anyway. Only then does she make an open gesture at him.

He's noticed our silent conversation, and he's clearly not pleased with it.

"My name is Dallas Walsh," he begins in a voice made ragged by years of alcohol abuse. "My daughter —" He stops suddenly, pressing his trembling lips together, and swallows once. "My daughter, Angeline, was murdered by the Singing Woods Killer."

A few of the newer people gasp, and one woman sobs aloud. The others, the ones who've heard this story before, look on in sympathetic silence.

Dallas rests his elbows on his thighs and lowers his hands palms-out, his fingers opening and closing. His gaze drops to his lap. "It's not right," he says hoarsely. "Not right for a man to outlive his child. She's been dead now longer than she ever got to live, my Angeline, and ..."

He raises his head slowly, his eyes glistening and lined with red, and a single tear zigzags slowly down his whiskered face.

He's looking straight at me. I can feel the hollowness in him, the empty rage, like a coiled fuse burning toward a bomb.

And then, he explodes.

"Why are you here, you *bitch!*" he roars with spittle flying from his lips, standing so fast that his chair clatters to the floor. "You stupid, psychotic whore! I can't stand the sight of you. You never should've come back!"

"Mr. Walsh!" Delphine's voice is like a gunshot silencing the room. "I understand that you're hurting, but I will not tolerate any abuse toward other members of this group. I'm going to have to ask you to leave for the night." Her eyes flick almost imperceptibly toward Bear, who's been standing near the door, and the big man comes forward immediately.

Dallas's wild gaze roams the room, as if looking for support for his side of things. He finds none. Finally, he takes a step toward me and bares his teeth. "Do you know what it feels like, to have your whole world ripped away from you?" he says in a simmering growl. "I hope you find out. I hope someone puts you through what I've been through, and you lose the thing *you* care about most."

Then Bear is gripping the furious man by the arm, dragging him toward the door. "Time to go home now, like Miss Delphine told you," the ex-bouncer says, a clear threat in his tone. "You go on and get some fresh air."

I close my eyes until I hear the door open and shut, and see Dallas's snarling face branded into my brain as he passively threatens my daughter. I'm sick with rage.

Someone touches my shoulder, and I jump and look into Delphine's concerned features. "Madeline, honey, are you okay?" she says. "I'm so sorry about that. I had no idea he'd ..." She trails off and sends a troubled glance at the overturned chair, which one of the others is moving to pick up.

"I know you didn't. It's all right," I manage. I want to go home, right now, but if I step outside, Dallas may still be there. I need to wait until he's far away with his hate. "Do you mind if I go in the kitchen and get something to drink?" I say.

"Of course. Take all the time you need."

She hugs me when I stand, and I hope she can't feel me trembling. As I walk away from the chairs, toward the kitchen, I hear the murmurs and whispers start up, the shocked exclamations, the questions. Who is she, what happened to her, why is Dallas so mad?

I've decided against sharing my story tonight. I don't need to speak my memories, or lack thereof, when Dallas has churned them into a waking nightmare.

I find several bottles of flavored water in the refrigerator and drink one gratefully as I stand in the corner of the kitchen, out of sight from the group. Suddenly, I can't face any more survivor stories. I'm still too wrapped up in my own, and I'm no longer sure that my story is over.

Eventually I return to the group as Delphine is wrapping things up and thanking everyone for coming. She's brought donuts and soda, and most of the attendees are wandering toward the snack table, still engaged in various conversations. Only a few are headed for the exit.

That's where I'm going, too.

I say goodbye to Delphine, and she apologizes again and encourages me to attend more meetings. I know I won't, but I tell her I'll think about it. I don't blame her for Dallas's behavior. But I also can't take the chance that he won't explode like that again, and if there's a next time, I may not be able to keep my composure.

Then I'll be the one Bear drags to the exit with threats that sound like concern.

When I get home, Richard is waiting up for me. One look at my face tells him that things didn't go well, and he enfolds me in his arms without a word. I let myself cry, just a little, and tell him about Dallas.

He's furious and wants to call the police. I tell him there's no point, and eventually he agrees, though he's not happy about it.

However, he gets happier when we go to bed, and he makes me feel things that are a vast improvement over hurt and anger.

Now I just have to get through tomorrow.

17

Wednesday, June 4, 8:30 a.m.

Tomorrow has arrived, and I don't think it could have possibly started out worse.

I was so shaken at breakfast, just knowing what today is, that I asked Richard to drive the carpool. He said he couldn't, that his first job started early, but then he recanted at my stricken look and offered to do it. I told him to forget it, half out of spite, and he left the house angry.

And then, there was the drive to school.

I swore that I saw shadowy figures standing on every corner, behind every tree. Stewart Brooks, Dallas Walsh, Frank Kilgore, even Trevor Downes. My mind dwelled on the group meeting last night, on the way Dallas skated around a threat to take Renata from me, to make me feel his pain. And on Frank's words to me at the community center: *How's your daughter doing, Mrs. Osborn?* By the time we'd reached the school, I was so worked up that I made Renata stay in the car when her friends got out, and I told her to come straight home after soccer practice.

We fought. Screamed at each other, really. I trotted out the 'I'm your mother and you have to do what I say' line, and she told me I was being too clingy, that it wasn't fair, that she was old enough and it's just a study group and she was going anyway, and she didn't care what I said.

I was shaking so hard on the way back home that I had to pull over, and I cried in the car until I couldn't breathe.

My empty house feels like a tomb. I've showered for the second time this morning, but I still feel dirty and crumpled. I'm sitting on the couch, staring at the blank eye of the powered-down television. I know I was irrational with Renata, and she had a right to be upset. But to speak to me that way, as if I'm her jailer instead of her mother ...

I drop my head in my hands, unable to cry any more. How will I get through today? I remember that Carson is staying at the Stardust Hotel, waiting for my call, and consider that possibility. Seeing my old friend. Finding out what she wants to tell me, seeking answers to the questions I never got to ask.

Reminiscing about old times. No, I can't face that. Not today.

I'm reconsidering Dr. Bradshaw's offer for sedatives, and I remember that I didn't actually speak to her about the prescription and why the pills look different. Last night's lie was a double falsehood, since I didn't actually call to leave her a message in the first place ... or did I? Everything is so jumbled in my head. But I know I haven't asked her about the pills yet. Maybe I'll call her, and see if she can fit me in for an extra session today.

I'm halfway to my feet when I change my mind and sink back onto the couch. If I talk to Dr. Bradshaw, it'll just be more of the same. Discussing my past, examining my feelings, trying to chip away at the vast mental block that still encases my memories of that week.

I can't remember. I don't *want* to remember.

Growing slightly agitated, I stand and pace in front of the couch. Though I've been home for what seems like hours, the clock is still just dragging toward nine. There is so much of this day still ahead of me, and I have nothing but my own warped thoughts to comfort me until I meet Jan for dinner at five, after soccer practice. When my daughter will no doubt be out defying me with a study group.

I ache to see her, to apologize for this morning. I want to ask her to come with me, to get her own slice of to-die-for cheesecake at the Stone Mill, to laugh and talk the way we did over dinner last night.

But if I don't allow her to grow up and become her own person, nights like those won't happen anymore. She'll resent me, avoid me. Hate me with the kind of inexperience-fueled, false-dramatic rage that only a teenager can generate.

I have to distract myself before I implode. The book I've been reading rests on the side table with a bookmark halfway through, but I know that words alone won't hold my attention. I flop on the couch and switch the TV on, wavering between cable and Netflix. There's rarely anything good on cable, and I don't want to accidentally catch a news broadcast that might mention the anniversary, so I fire up Netflix and scroll idly through the listings.

But my mind wanders all on its own, and I'm not seeing the fifty-inch screen covered with neat rows of thumbnail tiles, or the remote in my hand. I don't feel the way my fingers dig into my kneecaps as my surroundings fade. I see the woods, the eerie light of dusk blazing faint coronas around tree trunks that reach up forever and blot out the sky.

I feel the terror of realizing that I'm no longer Madeline Osborn, or even Madison Grant.

I am victim number five, and I only have one week left to live.

18

Madeline—the past

I must've been the biggest fool ever born, I thought as I walked home beneath a bruised sky that matched my mood. The threat of rain had hung over the town all day, though the oncoming storm hadn't broken yet.

Carson and I had a huge fight at school today, because she still wouldn't tell me what was obviously eating at her, and I felt kind of offended. It wasn't like a knock-down, drag-out cat fight or anything, but we yelled at each other pretty good. And maybe it would've come to blows if Ian hadn't stepped in and calmed things down, forcing us to make up with each other. Which we did.

She was still my best friend, even if she drove me crazy now and then.

Ian had been back at school for a little over a week. Most of the time he seemed okay, but he was always quiet now. And he hated leaving me alone, even for a minute. He walked me to every single class, holding my hand the entire way, and if I brought lunch instead of buying, he just wouldn't eat. He refused to go through the cafeteria line without me.

It was achingly sweet. I couldn't even imagine what he'd been through when he lost Dana, but if he needed me as an anchor to cling to, I'd absolutely be there for him.

I was pretty sure I loved him. For real, not just the kind of love you pretend to feel when it's just a crush. This feeling ran deep, beyond how gorgeous he was or what kind of flowers he gave me or the pride of being a sophomore and having a boyfriend who was a senior. When I saw the rest of my life stretching out in front of me, Ian was there at every turn.

And that was the reason I was such a fool, because I could've asked Ian to walk home with me when Carson ditched me after a few blocks, claiming she felt sick and was going to throw up. I could've called my dad, who'd gone home after seventh period because he didn't have a late class today, and asked him to pick me up.

But I didn't do any of those things, and now I was walking alone while a killer stalked sixteen-year-old girls.

By then, my pride had gotten the better of me. I was still a little angry with Carson, and also pretty sure Ian's parents had picked him up from school early for some family thing. He probably would've come for me anyway if I asked, but I didn't want to interrupt them. And my dad ... well, it was just plain embarrassing to ride with him. Parent *and* teacher, the ultimate combination of lame. At least in the eyes of my friends.

Besides, I reasoned, it was three o'clock in the afternoon. People didn't get abducted in the middle of the day from nice neighborhoods.

Geary Street was just ahead. A right turn, then four blocks to Mrs. Vanderwall's, and then I could cut through the back yard and I'd be home, all of my insecurities and latent feelings of regret behind me. I'd probably call Carson later to see how she was feeling, and maybe Ian and I could hang out tonight.

I felt the first sprinkling drops of rain on my face just as I turned the corner, and heard the rumbling of thunder in the distance. Half a block later, the skies opened up all at once, as if someone up in the clouds had turned on a giant shower head.

"Oh, great," I said with a weak laugh, swiping rainwater from my face. But it didn't make much of a difference. I'd been instantly drenched when the storm started, and it showed no sign of slowing down. I gave into it, my head down slightly against the wind as the rain lashed against me, stinging my arms and slithering down my back.

At least it was a warm rain, but that didn't make me any less soaked.

I was less than two blocks from Mrs. Vanderwall's when I saw a figure in front of her house, headed in my direction. I couldn't make out much in the rain, but whoever it was, they were tall and willowy, with bright red hair. It kind of looked like Miss Shearman, the student teacher who'd been helping Coach Jenkins teach my gym class this year. I really liked her, and she wasn't even that much older than me. Practically a student herself. I wondered if she knew Mrs. Vanderwall.

I was focusing so hard on the figure obscured by the driving rain, trying to figure out if it was Miss Shearman, that I didn't see or hear the SUV that pulled to the curb a few feet behind me. I didn't hear the door open or the driver get out.

And when an arm wrapped around my stomach from behind me, and a hand pressed something soft and thick that reeked of bleach over my nose, I didn't realize what was happening until it was too late to scream, too late to do anything but pray that the red-haired person in the rain would see what was happening and save me.

But as I struggled weakly against my abductor's grip, peering into the rain-soaked afternoon in desperation for a savior, I realized the tall person with red hair I thought I'd seen was just a stop sign with somebody's scarf caught on it, fluttering violently in the wind.

There was no one to rescue me. The man who killed Angeline and Tricia, Marie and Dana, would take me to his secret place in the woods that the police had failed to find. He'd do terrible things to me for endless days, and when he was done, he'd dump what was left of me like garbage. My parents would be devastated. Ian, Carson, all of my friends would mourn me. Their pain would outlast my death.

I didn't want to go through any of that, to experience firsthand what the media and the police had only hinted the other girls had gone through, what my imagination had filled in with nightmarish paint strokes. I *couldn't* do that.

So I found a switch somewhere deep in my brain, and I turned it off. There was no Madeline Grant.

And if I didn't exist, the Singing Woods Killer couldn't hurt me.

19

Wednesday, June 4, 5:30 p.m.

Jan and I have a booth at the Stone Mill, which should be cause for a minor celebration. Most of the booths are usually taken long before the dinner rush starts. But I'm not in a celebratory mood, and not even the prime-cut steak dinner in front of me that looks like a magazine spread and smells like heaven can lift me from my funk.

Renata didn't come home after soccer practice. She'd gone to the study group after all.

I didn't expect her to, really. I know she's right, that I'm being too clingy and paranoid, projecting all my fears onto her. But I'd hoped that maybe she would come home for a few minutes, or call to apologize, and I would offer the same, and we would be okay again.

Fighting with my daughter always felt like scooping my own heart out of my chest.

"How did she seem today at practice?" I say to Jan as I stab at my steak, which is so tender I can cut it with a fork. I don't have to say who I mean, because I only ever ask about Renata. "Did she ... say anything about me?"

Jan smiles over her surf-and-turf. "She seemed fine," she says, and then adds quickly, "Maybe a little quiet."

I know she's trying to cheer me up by hinting that Renata feels bad about our fight. But I also know that her mother is the last thing on her mind when she's with her friends, and that's normal for teens. They're so desperate to grow up, to be independent and prove themselves, that even considering their parents during everyday activities is a betrayal of their impending adulthood.

"I think everything will be fine when she gets home," I say. "I'm sure we can still talk about things."

"Of course you can. Renata's a great girl." Jan spears a shrimp from her plate, pops it whole in her mouth, and moans with pleasure. "God, that's fantastic," she says when she swallows.

We eat in silence for a few minutes. The steak practically melts in my mouth, but as good as it is, I can't focus enough to really appreciate it. It's still the horrid anniversary, and right around now is the time of day it was at the spot where my memories start back up again. In my mind, the abduction and the bloody end of Stewart Brooks happened on the same day. The time between the rainstorm, the SUV and the stop sign that wasn't a person, and my desperate, agonizing flight through the woods from the madman chasing me, is simply a blink.

On that day twenty years ago, I closed my eyes on Geary Street and opened them in the woods.

"Jan, can I ask you something?" I say as my mind reaches back through time and seizes on that stormy afternoon. "It's going to sound completely random, and probably crazy."

She arches an eyebrow, her attention captured. "Let's hear it," she says.

I take a moment, because I'm not exactly sure *how* to ask. "The day I was ... taken," I begin slowly, reluctant to speak the word 'abducted' aloud. It's such an ugly word, a word with sharp teeth and nasty breath. "I thought I saw someone."

The tiniest flicker of something flashes in Jan's eyes, but it's gone so fast, I can't interpret it. "What do you mean?" she says. "Besides the killer?"

I give a careful nod, looking intently at her. Her voice seems off. There's a faint edge to it, as if she's anticipating something unpleasant.

But it's probably just the subject matter. No one enjoys talking about serial killers who've murdered people they know.

"Yes, on Geary Street," I say. "That's where I was, in case you didn't know. I was so close to home. Less than two blocks."

"Of course I didn't know." Her words are almost indignant. "Oh, Maddie, that's awful. I can't imagine how you must have felt, to be almost safe before ... it happened."

A little voice in my head whispers that she *can* imagine it, because she was there. But I know I'm being ridiculous, projecting a terrified girl's confused and fragmented memories onto a woman who's been my dear friend for years.

Still, I have to finish asking. I have to know.

"It was raining really hard," I say. "And the person I thought I saw was far from me, by Mrs. Vanderwall's house." It's hard to say the rest, but I spit it out anyway. "This person looked tall, with red hair. At first, I thought it was you."

Jan reels as if I'd slapped her, and tears form in her eyes. For a split second I think she's going to confess. But she says, "Oh, Maddie, do you really think I saw you being abducted?"

I can't formulate a response. She sounds so sad, so hurt, that I have to believe her shock is genuine.

"I didn't ... I never would have ..." She takes a shuddering breath, fumbles a napkin from a small stack at the edge of the table and dabs at her eyes. "If I'd been there, if I *had* seen you, I would've done something," she says. "There's no way I would stand back and watch *any* kid get abducted, especially one I knew." She gives a dainty sniff. "But I wasn't there. I've never been to your father's house."

The statement hits my brain like a bolt of lightning. I didn't mention that I used to cut through a driveway to get to my back yard instead of walking around to my own street. All I said was Mrs. Vanderwall's house.

I never said anything about my father's house.

"Okay. I'm sorry," I say after a pause, in what I hope is a normal voice. I don't want to draw attention to the possible slip Jan's just made. Not until I know what to think about this. "I remember thinking, when he had me, that it was actually a stop sign with a scarf stuck on it, fluttering around like hair."

Relief breaks across Jan's face. "That must be it," she says. "And *I'm* sorry, really. I shouldn't be upset, when you're the one who went through that horrific experience."

"It's okay. You're allowed to have emotions," I say with a smile. "Everyone does."

But now I'm trying to remember if there is, or was, a stop sign on Geary Street near the house where Mrs. Vanderwall lived. I'm picturing all the times we used that shortcut, Carson and I. And in not one of those times can I envision a stop sign anywhere in that area. The closest one I recall is at the corner of Geary and Sturgeon, the right turn on the walk home from school. Four blocks away from the shortcut, in the opposite direction.

For some reason, Jan is lying about this. Maybe she didn't see it happening through the rain, or she didn't know it was me until afterward, but she *was* there.

And now I have to decide whether I can live with that.

20

Wednesday, June 4, 9:00 p.m.

Renata should've been home an hour ago.

I'd bought her not one, but two slices of cheesecake at the Stone Mill and brought them back in Styrofoam takeout boxes, and then I'd made her favorite dinner. Spaghetti and meatballs, fresh grated parmesan, and just-lettuce salad. She never really got into vegetables the way I did, but she did love her ranch dressing, with a bit of lettuce to give the dressing some texture.

Eight o'clock came and went, and then eight-thirty. Now it was nine. I'd sent three texts to her phone and called twice, but she'd either turned her phone off or was ignoring me.

I'll just have to embarrass her and call Eve's parents.

Dayfield is just enough behind the burgeoning curve of technology that most of us old people, otherwise known as parents, still have house phones and are still listed in the actual printed phone book. I grab my worn, two-year-old copy from the kitchen drawer and set it on the counter, flipping through the white pages to the B section for Blanchard. There's Diane and Paul, a Deborah Blanchard that I believe is Eve's aunt, two F. Blanchards, and then Greg and Valerie Blanchard. That's them.

My cell phone is already in my hand, so I dial the number. After four rings, there's a click and a woman's voice says, "Hello?" over the faint babbling and giggling of teenage girls in the background. At least I'm nearly positive I have the right house.

"Hello, Mrs. Blanchard?" I say. When she confirms it's her, I continue. "This is Madeline Osborn, Renata's mother."

There's a strange little pause, and Mrs. Blanchard says in a puzzled voice, "Oh, yes. Hello. Can I help you with something?"

I'm stunned enough that I almost can't say a word. She sounds like she doesn't know why I'd be calling her. But I must be reading something into it that isn't there, or maybe she's tired and hasn't connected my call with my daughter yet. I know I'd be exhausted with a house full of teenage girls.

"I just need to speak to Renata for a minute," I say. "Would you mind putting her on the phone?"

This time Mrs. Blanchard's silence screams through me like wildfire. Something is very, very wrong.

"I'm sorry," she says, "but Renata's not here."

My vision goes white and an awful buzz clogs my ears. Damn it, I am *not* going to faint. There has to be a reasonable explanation for this, one that doesn't involve my daughter being nowhere she's supposed to be. One that has nothing to do with today's date.

I shove a finger in my mouth and bite down until I nearly scream. The pain drives my senses clear. "Did she leave the study group early?" I say in a voice I don't recognize, as if some other, calmer woman is speaking. Maybe she's on her way home right now, and I've just missed her.

But Mrs. Blanchard shatters that hope when she says, "No, she didn't come over with the rest of the girls. I haven't seen her since the last soccer game, actually."

A strange, high-pitched noise rises around me, and I realize the sound is coming from my own panicked throat. I swallow hard to stop it and force myself to speak again. "Is Jenny Kline there with them?"

She pauses, probably to check on the group. "Yes, Jenny's here," she says as the confusion in her tone is replaced by concern. "Do you want to talk to her?"

"Please," I say. "Maybe she knows where Renata went."

"Okay, just a minute." There's a clunk as she sets the phone down. I don't breathe again until Jenny picks up and says, "Hey, Mrs. Osborn. What's up?"

She sounds so happy and unconcerned that I can't imagine anything's happened to Renata. Her best friend would know, wouldn't she? "Hi, Jenny," I say. "I was just wondering if you know where Renata is, since she didn't go to the study group with you."

"Wait, she's not home?"

Those four syllables punch me in the gut and leave me breathless. The panic that's been swirling just beneath the surface threatens to erupt in a wordless, unending scream. But I don't have the luxury of screaming. I have to know what happened, where my daughter is.

"No, she's not," I finally say. "I called because I thought she was with you."

Jenny gasps, and my heart shivers. "She went home right after soccer practice," my daughter's friend says. "Well, not *right* after. We were all walking over to Eve's, and she said she didn't feel so great and was going home to shower and lie down. I offered to walk with her, but ... is she okay?" she finished in a trembling voice.

"I'm sure she's fine." Somehow I manage to speak the words with conviction and reassurance, despite not believing a single one of them. "Jenny, does Renata have a boyfriend or something? Maybe someone she hasn't told me about?"

"Oh my God, she's not okay, is she?" Jenny practically wails, near tears now. "No, she doesn't have a boyfriend. She was just going to go home. Did you try her cell?"

I forgive her immediately for asking such a patently stupid question. "Yes, I did. She's not picking up," I say. "Listen, Jenny, I have to go. Will you please call me right away if you happen to hear from her?"

"Absolutely. I'm going to start texting her right now," she says. "I really hope she's okay. She didn't seem that sick, really, just ... kind of sad, I think."

That's the ultimate blow. Now I can't help thinking that she *did* feel bad about our fight, that she *was* coming home because I'd asked her to. Only something had happened to her on the way.

And I'd gone out to dinner with Jan, oblivious, as if everything was just fine.

"All right, Jenny. Thank you. I have to go." I can't bear to hear any more of the worry in Jenny's voice, so I disconnect the call, and then instinctively grab the cordless phone to dial 911. The police can give me all the excuses and disbelief they want, but I *know* something is wrong. Renata is not where she's supposed to be.

My daughter is missing.

That word, *missing*, ricochets around in my brain like a bullet as I wait through three rings, and an operator answers. Male this time. "Nine-one-one, what is your emergency?"

"My daughter is missing," I say. "She's sixteen, and she's been gone for at least five hours. I need help, right now."

"Okay, ma'am. I'll send someone right over." There isn't a trace of doubt or disbelief in the operator's tone. "Can I have your name and address, please?"

"Madeline Osborn," I say, and rattle off the address.

I don't hear any typing. There should've been typing.

"Mrs. Osborn, can you stay on the line for just one moment? I'll be right back."

"No!" I shout to a series of clicks and a brief hiss of air. I can't believe he's put me on hold. If this has anything to do with the 'special' procedures the police station is supposed to follow with me, and something happens to my daughter because they're jerking me around, I'll ... I don't know what I'll do. But it won't be polite or restrained.

There's another click, and a new male voice comes on the line. "Detective Burgess."

"Detective," I grind out as a red haze drowns my vision. "Your police station had better stop 'handling' me. Damn it, my daughter is missing!"

"Mrs. Osborn, please, calm down —"

"Don't tell me to calm down!" I scream. "My. Daughter. Is. *Missing!*"

"I think I got it," he says, and I can't tell if he's being sarcastic or patronizing. "If you'll just take a breath and tell me what happened —"

"I will not take a breath, and I will not explain this over the phone, like I'm calling to report my wallet stolen!" I'm seething now, barely holding myself in check enough to stay coherent. "You will get someone over here right this minute to take my statement, in person, and to *find my daughter.*"

"All right. We're on the way," the detective says, and hangs up.

It takes all my effort not to throw the phone across the room and smash it against the wall.

Richard. I have to call Richard.

I dial his number from memory. It rings once, and goes straight to voicemail.

With a frustrated shout, I disconnect without leaving a message. I'm pretty sure that the voicemail picking up right away means his phone is off. How could he turn his phone off? I suspect Ian might've had something to do with that. Maybe he didn't want Richard's evil bitch of a wife interrupting their meeting.

I don't even know where they are. And even if I did, I can't drive to him, because the police are on the way.

Fighting to stay focused and functioning, minute by minute, I dial Richard's phone again. One ring, voicemail. I try three more times, and on the third try I wait through his message: *You've reached Richard with Osborn Outdoor Services. Please leave your name and number, and I'll contact you as soon as possible.*

"Richard, call me. It's about Renata," I say in a dead tone, and end the call.

Just as I return the cordless phone to the cradle with shaking hands, I hear the swell of an engine outside and tires humming to a stop on the asphalt driveway.

I break into a stumbling run for the living room, silently begging that it's Renata. She's been out riding around with a friend, and her phone died. She went for a walk, got lost, and decided to hitchhike back. She fell asleep in the park and someone's parent drove her home. Anything. I don't care why she wasn't here or where she's been, as long as she's safe.

But when I fling the door open, Richard is jogging up the steps, a half-smile lengthening to a full one on his face. There's a heartbeat of time when I hate him for that smile, for not knowing what I know. And most of all, for not being Renata.

Then I fly to him, already sobbing, and I see his expression crumple into fear as he squeezes me tight. "What happened?" he says, his voice rising to break at the end.

"Renata." I whisper her name, afraid I won't be able to say anything more. Finally, the rest of it emerges on the edge of a shriek.

"She's gone, Richard. Our daughter is missing."

21

promises to keep

What have I done?

I didn't mean to do it. I've stopped for so long, and I haven't even felt tempted in all these years. I was doing fine. Proving that my impulses couldn't control me.

But she's so beautiful, so young. We were alone. And she trusted me.

How could I resist?

I know who she is, of course. And I know what will happen, now that I've done it. I'll never be able to get through to her. Never live this down.

Unless I stop her from talking forever. I haven't gone that far yet.

But maybe I'll have to.

Her parents are going to be relentless. They'll never stop until they've found me and dragged me out, until they've ruined me. It's only a matter of time.

I can't wait long, can't let them find me. I'll have to make a decision soon. Do I let the girl live, keep her in my sights, and hope for the best? Or do I end her, like I did before?

The clock is ticking. For me, and for the girl. I wonder if she's strong enough to keep the promise I've extracted from her, the promise of silence.

I wonder if I'm strong enough to let her try.

22

Wednesday, June 4, 9:40 p.m.

Detective Burgess and Sergeant McKenzie are officially my least favorite people in the world. I want to scream in their faces, bash their heads together, *make* them stop acting like I've gone off the deep end and they wished I would just get it over with and drown, so I wouldn't waste any more of their precious time.

This is my time, my *daughter's* time. And they're the ones wasting it, with their prejudices and preconceptions. They shouldn't be grilling me.

They should be looking for Renata.

"You did mention that your daughter is sixteen?" Burgess is sitting in the arm chair angled toward the couch, where Richard and I are huddled together in an attempt to prop each other up. McKenzie has dragged a chair in from the dining room and set it next to his partner. "I'm just saying that teenagers take off all the time," he says. "Usually they come back when they're good and ready, and not a minute before. It's really not that late right now."

"My daughter did not just 'take off'," I tell him coldly. "She wouldn't do that."

"Yes, that isn't our Rennie-Bean at all," Richard adds. He's badly shaken, in the worst state I've ever seen him.

"You're sure about that," the detective says. "Have you spoken to her friends?"

"Of course I have!" My patience isn't just wearing thin, it's completely gone.

McKenzie leans forward slightly. "What about problems at home?" he says. "Is there any reason she might be upset or angry with either of you?"

I hate him for asking that. Renata's face flashes in my head, flushed and close to tears as she screams that it's not fair, she didn't do anything wrong, I can't stop her from being with her friends. "We had a fight this morning," I admit in a small voice. "But that doesn't mean she would —"

Richard touches my arm to stop me. "Do you know what today is, Detective?" he says. Not shouting yet, but there's an angry edge to his voice.

I'm so grateful that I want to cry. The police may not be taking me seriously, but my husband is. He understands why this can't be a random occurrence or some kind of mistake. This happened today for a reason. I *know* someone has taken my daughter.

Detective Burgess stares, unimpressed. "It's Wednesday, June 4," he says. "Are you giving me a pop quiz, Mr. Osborn, or is there some significance I'm not aware of?"

"You know my wife's history, obviously," Richard says. "But I guess you don't know it well enough. June 4 is the day she escaped the Singing Woods Killer, twenty years ago. The day he died. Maddie was sixteen that day, just like Renata is now." My husband's face is white with tension, his eyes red and glittering. "This isn't a coincidence. Our daughter did not run away. Someone has her."

The detective and his partner glance at each other, and a look passes between them. They *didn't* know about the date. Some of the tension and pressure in me eases, just a little, as I dare to hope they'll finally listen.

"All right," Burgess says as he produces a notepad and pen from somewhere. "McKenzie's going to put out an APB on your daughter, and get some uniforms to start canvassing the neighborhood. Do you have a recent photo of Renata that we can use?"

The dramatic one-eighty shift in the conversation drives everything home, all at once. She's really, truly missing. The police are going to circulate her picture and question people. Meanwhile, whatever bastard has my daughter —

It's him. You KNOW it's him.

— is terrifying her, probably hurting her, right now. She may be ...

I burst into loud, ugly sobs and drop my head into my hands. I can't face that possibility. I just can't. She *has* to be alive.

He keeps them alive for a week.

Through the tide of grief I can't fight off, I sense my husband shifting beside me. He's getting his wallet, handing the detective Renata's sophomore picture that was taken just last month. He always keeps a copy of her newest school photo in his wallet

"Thank you," Burgess says, and I know I have to focus. He's going to ask questions. I need to answer them.

I drag my hands away from my face in time to see McKenzie on his feet, Burgess handing him the picture. The brief glimpse of Renata's beautiful, smiling face nearly sends me off again, but I need to keep it together. For her.

McKenzie heads for the front door, already speaking into his radio. Richard and I are left with Burgess, who still appears stern and skeptical, but the lines of his face have softened.

"Mrs. Osborn," he says in a tone that's approaching kind. "Can you think of anyone who might have done something like this?"

Him. It was him! Stewart Brooks has my daughter.

I give a wet sniffle and attempt to wipe the tears away. Richard startles and leans forward, pulling several tissues from the box on the coffee table, and hands them to me. I blow my nose, pat my eyes.

"Dallas Walsh," I say, and my husband stiffens.

The detective raises an eyebrow and scribbles the name on his pad. "Any particular reason you believe that Dallas Walsh would harm your daughter?"

"He threatened me last night. Well, not directly, but ..." I release a shivery sigh. "Richard, would you get me a glass of water, please?" I say. He's already heard this story, and he was furious about it the first time.

It'll be easier for me to tell it again if he's not right here, getting angrier by the minute.

I don't want to end up with him arrested for assault.

My husband nods and stands. "Do you want something to drink, Detective?"

"I'm fine, thank you," Burgess says.

As Richard heads to the kitchen, I face the detective. "I attended a survivor's group meeting at the Masonic temple last night, and Dallas was there," I tell him. "You know his daughter, Angeline, was..."

"One of the SWK's victims," the detective fills in, an intense look on his face.

"That's right. She was the first, and I was the last," I say. "But I survived and Angeline didn't. Dallas has always hated me for that." I shudder at the remembered look on his face, the rage in his eyes. "At the meeting last night, he went off on me. Called me a lot of nasty names. And he said he wanted me to know what he'd been through. That he hopes I lose the thing I care about most."

Burgess is fully engaged now. "He wanted you to lose your daughter, the way he lost his," he says. "But it wasn't a direct threat."

"No," I sigh. "It was enough to scare me, though."

"Who else was at the meeting to witness Walsh's outburst?" The detective's pen is poised to write. "I'll need to take statements from them."

"Delphine Pearce. She's the group leader," I say. "She threw him out after it happened. And there was Bear ... you know, I don't actually know his real name."

"Gregory Vanderwall," Burgess says as he writes.

My breath catches.

He notices and looks at me. "Does that name mean something to you?"

"Yes. Well, no, it's just ... I don't think it has anything to do with Renata."

"Tell me anyway," he says. "Any detail, no matter how small, might help us find her."

I close my eyes briefly. He wants to find her. He believes me.

"There was a Mrs. Vanderwall who lived right behind my parents' house, but she's passed away since," I say. "When I was in high school, I used to cut through her driveway walking to school and back. I was near her house the day I was abducted." It's still hard to say that word. "I didn't know her that well, and I think she lived alone, but she was older. She could've had grown children, and Bear ... uh, Gregory would be the right age, I think."

Burgess nods and scribbles something. "Do you know what her address was, or her first name?"

"I think it was Tracy, or maybe Theresa?" I say. "I don't know the house number, but it was on Geary Street. Detective, you don't think that Bear would ..."

"I'm not going to think anything until I have more information. I just want to make sure I'm covering all the bases," he says. "All right, I can get the list of last night's attendees from Delphine. Is there anyone else you can think of that we should look into?"

I stare at him for a moment as a few things connect in my mind. He knew Bear's real name, and he called the group leader Delphine, not Pearce. Has he been to the survivor's group? I'd missed a year of meetings, so it was certainly possible.

I guess it doesn't matter, and I wouldn't ask about it. That would be rude. "There's one other person," I say. "Frank Kilgore. He's a reporter."

Burgess looks surprised as he writes it down. "That name rings a bell, for some reason."

"He writes for the New Herald," I say as my mouth twists in disgust. "He covered the original Singing Woods Killer for that paper, if you can call what he wrote 'coverage.' It was mostly lies. He used to harass me and my friend all the time when the killer was ... active."

"And your friend would be?" he says.

I swallow. "Her name was Carson Mills."

"Was? Is she ..."

"No, she's alive. I said 'was' because we're not friends anymore," I say softly. "She and her family moved away twenty years ago, but Carson is actually in town right now. I spoke to her yesterday."

Burgess scribbles and scribbles, and I wonder if he's going to question Carson. "What about Kilgore?" he says. "Why would he target your daughter?"

I tell him about the confrontation at the community center and he takes it all in, nodding and grunting. "All right, we'll find him," he says. "Walsh, too."

Dallas Walsh isn't hard to find, but I suspect Frank Kilgore might be. Now I wish I hadn't burned his business card.

Richard comes back to the living room then, holding two glasses of ice water. The ice clinks and shivers against the glass as he sits on the couch and hands me one. His eyes are rimmed with bright red, and I realize he must've been crying quietly in the kitchen all this time.

I take his free hand, and he gives me a faint smile. "Have you figured anything out?" he says to the detective.

"We have some leads now, at least," Burgess says. "Anything else you can think of, either of you?"

I don't want to say it, but I have to. "There's the man I saw in the back yard."

The detective draws a carefully blank face. "We haven't found anything on that yet, but we'll keep looking," he says.

I know he's lying. Of course they're not looking into him, because they don't believe he exists. I'd managed to convince myself that everyone else is right, that I was hallucinating or having an episode and that Stewart Brooks was never really there, because he's dead. But now I'm not so sure.

If I'm right, if I'm not crazy, then *he* has her. And his motive is the strongest of all.

He wants revenge.

Detective Burgess stands, tucking his note pad away. I can sense the slight change in him, now that I've climbed back on the crazy train, but at least I've given him possibilities that he'll actually investigate. "Okay, we have a lot of work to do," he says as he fishes a card from a pocket and hands it to me. "This is my direct office line, and my cell. Call me if you hear anything, or think of anything else. We'll also be here first thing in the morning for comprehensive statements, lists of friends and family —"

"The morning?" Richard interrupts. "If there's something else you can do, you should do it now!"

"Right now, we need to get out there and look for your daughter, Mr. Osborn," the detective says. "At this point it's only been a few hours. This time is crucial. The sooner we get started, the better the chances of recovering her."

"Yes. Of course," Richard rasps hollowly, his gaze dropping to the carpet. His shoulders heave once.

"We'll be back in the morning, or sooner if we find something," Burgess says. "Meanwhile, call me immediately if anything changes."

Richard sees the detective to the door, and I finally take a sip of the water. I want to tell the police that I'm going with them, to help look for my daughter, but I know what they'll say to that. This isn't my first time dealing with law enforcement that is not exactly on my side.

So I'll wait until they've gone, and then I'll go looking for Renata myself.

23

Madeline—the past

My head felt like someone had split my skull open and stuffed rocks inside it, and then closed it back up with a staple gun. My eyes were closed and I didn't want to open them. Was he gone? Did I really ... kill him?

Was I safe?

I knew I was in the woods, and it was getting dark. The light was so low that I could barely tell which shapes were trees, and which was the man chasing me. But I'd seen his face, before the light faded. I'd seen it so well that it was burned into my brain, like one of those wood etchings I did in art club with a soldering iron.

And I'd stabbed him with something. A tree branch, I think, and there was blood. So much blood. The smell of the blood mingled with the sweet, crisp scent of the woods still clogged my senses.

I'd pushed him off me, and he hadn't moved. He was dead.

Please let him be dead.

It had to be dark by now. When I looked, I'd see blackness, and I would be aware of the dead body right next to me. I didn't want to look. If I felt for him and he wasn't there, if I hadn't killed him, then I wouldn't have a chance.

Finally, I forced my eyes open and saw white ceiling tiles. Metal rails on both sides of me. A blanket covering my feet, a white wall with a mounted television beyond them.

I was in a hospital. Not the woods.

"Maddie?" That voice sounded so sad, so scared. Did I know that voice? "Oh, God, Maddie! She's awake. Wendell, she's awake."

Faces loomed over me, faces I recognized.

Mom. Dad.

I'm alive.

I killed him.

"Maddie, sweetheart," my mom sobbed, crumpling into a chair beside the hospital bed as she grabbed my hand. "Oh, thank God. My baby."

I tried to smile at her, but it hurt. Everything hurt. My mouth was drier than a desert. I turned my head, very slowly, to see my dad standing on the other side of the bed with tears streaming down his face. I'd never seen him cry before.

What happened to me? How did I get in the woods, with a man trying to kill me?

That man. It was *him*, the Singing Woods Killer.

He grabbed me on Geary Street. I remember now. It was raining, and I could see Mrs. Vanderwall's house. I was almost home, and then there was a man, and an SUV, and a bleach-soaked rag.

And someone else. Wasn't there someone else?

I wasn't sure I could speak. I licked my dry, dry lips with my dry, dry tongue and opened my mouth. "Him," I croaked. "He's ..."

"Wendell, get her some water," my mother said, still sobbing.

Something floated in front of my face. A glass with a straw. I wrapped my lips around the straw, sucked in cool, sweet water and felt it soothe my scratchy throat, my swollen mouth. Tears leaked from the corners of my eyes as I drank, but they weren't sad tears. They were relief. I could drink water, and I was in a hospital. With my parents.

Safe. I was safe now.

Some time passed. I'd forgotten what I was going to say, before the water, but my mom and dad didn't seem to expect me to continue. They sat with me, one on each side of the bed, and they cried, and I cried, until I wasn't sure why I was crying anymore. Except that everything still hurt.

It felt like something was wrong, besides all the pain in my head. The thin blue blanket covered me to just below my arms, and I was wearing a yellow hospital gown beneath it. I hated yellow. I wanted to ask for a different color gown, and at one point thought I did, but I wasn't sure if I actually said it out loud.

I guessed it didn't matter too much. Other things were more important.

Another while passed. Maybe several whiles. My parents seemed to be waiting for something, but I had no idea what. A doctor? The killer? Whatever made my head hurt this way, it felt like it'd done something to my thoughts too, broken them somehow. Nothing would connect the right way. Nothing made sense.

I tried to lift the blanket once, but my mother gave a startled cry and snatched it from my hand, smoothing it back into place. "Not yet, sweetheart," she said in a shaking, terrible voice. "Please, just try to relax."

So I tried to relax. I didn't know what we were waiting for, though.

Eventually I heard a door open, and then voices. Two of them, one male, one female. Another set of parents, maybe? Someone else's? But why would another person's parents be here?

One of the voices said, "You can have ten minutes. She's still very weak."

The other voice said, "Fine, thank you."

There were footsteps. My father walked around the bed to sit next to my mother on the side near the window, and someone else was coming to the side he'd just left. We must have been waiting for this.

I turned my head on the pillow and looked at the someone else. It was a woman with dark hair in a business-like suit, with a gold badge clipped to her waist, and also a gun. A police officer, a detective. She looked sort of familiar, and for some reason I thought of cop shows. Gruff men with bad personal lives drinking coffee.

Female detective. She'd come to my school. Wasn't her name Barbie? Or maybe Becky?

The detective was smiling, sort of, like she wasn't sure it was appropriate to smile. "Hello, Madeline," she said. "My name is Detective Brenda Westhall."

Her name is Brenda.

My name is Madeline.

I wasn't sure why I thought that. I knew my own name, didn't I?

Detective Brenda looked at my parents. "I just have to ask her a few questions at this time," she said. "I'll try to keep it brief. You can stay in the room, if you'd like."

"Damned right we're staying," my father said in a gravelly voice that didn't sound like him at all. A papa bear voice. "I don't see why you have to put her through this right now."

My mother sobbed some more. I wondered if she would ever stop crying.

"I'm sorry, Mr. Grant, but this is extremely important," the detective said. "As much as anything, it's to protect your daughter."

At that, my mother wailed loudly.

"All right, Judith. It's all right," my father said, rubbing my mother's back. "Ask your questions, then, Detective."

Brenda Westhall took a seat next to the bed and brought out a note pad and pen. "Madeline, I know this is going to be hard for you," she said. "Can you tell me how you got away from Stewart Brooks? Where he was keeping you?"

Stewart Brooks. I didn't know him. "Who's Stewart Brooks?" I said.

For some reason, this made my mother cry harder.

"Stewart Brooks is the man who abducted you," the detective said patiently. "We need to find out where he was keeping you, because there may be more victims. And maybe someone else survived, like you did."

Keeping me? I didn't understand. "He wasn't keeping me," I said slowly as my head started to pound again. "It was raining on Geary Street, and he grabbed me. And then he ... chased me through the woods. I don't know how we got there, but I got away." I whispered, staring at my hands. They'd started to shake. "I killed him, didn't I?"

My mother made a strange, choked sound.

"He is dead," Detective Westhall said with caution. "That's why I need you to tell me where he took you, since he can't. If he had other victims, they might still be alive. But they won't be for long."

"He took me to the woods," I said again. "Just the woods. I was running, and he chased me, and I killed him."

"So you were in the woods, all this time?" the detective said. "Did he tie you up somewhere? Maybe there was a cabin, or a cave?"

"All *what* time?" I could hear the panic in my voice. None of this made any sense. "We were on Geary Street, and then we were in the woods. That's it."

"Madeline ..." Detective Westhall folded her hands over her note pad and stared at me like I was crazy. "You were abducted a week ago. Stewart Brooks had you for a week."

A week? No, that couldn't be right. There wasn't a week between the rain and the woods. There was nothing there. Nothing at all.

He keeps them alive for a week. He does terrible things, and then he kills them.

Fear swallowed me whole, threatening to choke me. This was why my mother wouldn't let me move the blanket. She didn't want me to see what happened. What he'd done to me.

He'd done things I couldn't remember. At all.

"Madeline, please try to think," the detective said. "You're the only one who can help us find his place."

My mother shot to her feet. "She doesn't remember!" she screamed. "Can't you see that she doesn't remember? Leave my baby alone!"

Detective Westhall fixed a gaze on me, and I saw disbelief in her eyes, and something that looked like hatred. She thought I was lying.

Why would I lie about this? If there were other victims, other girls like me, I wanted them to be saved. I would have told her anything I knew, but I didn't know anything. There was no week. Just the rain, and the woods.

And someone else.

The detective rose slowly and placed a small white card on the chair behind her. "Please call me if she remembers anything," she said, looking at my father. Apparently she'd decided that he was the only sane person here. "It's very important. I'll come back tomorrow to see if she's improved."

"Don't you come back!" my mother yelled. "I won't have you harassing my daughter."

Detective Westhall glowered at her, and then at me. She turned to leave.

"Wait."

Everyone looked at me as the word crawled out. I tried to take a few breaths and to wet my still-cracked lips. "There was someone else," I said. "Someone ... else."

Red hair in the rain, by Mrs. Vanderwall's house. Was that it? No, that was a stop sign, a fluttering scarf. Or maybe it wasn't. Another person ... were they on Geary Street?

Or was there someone else in the woods?

"Who was it?" the detective said in an excited tone, ignoring my mother's continued protests. "Did you see another victim? Was Brooks working with someone?"

"I don't know," I muttered, suddenly more exhausted than I'd ever been in my life. None of this made sense to me, and I just wanted it to stop. "Maybe on Geary Street, I think. By Mrs. Vanderwall's."

Let the detective chase after stop signs. As long as she left me alone.

Detective Westhall shook her head, her mouth pinched and unhappy. "Please tell me if she remembers," she said, and then she walked away.

Once again, my parents and I were in the room, shedding tears. More whiles went by. A nurse came and fussed with machines, said encouraging things, and left.

We were waiting again.

Finally, my mother took my hand. Gently, so gently, as if I would shatter with a touch. "Madeline. Sweetheart." Her voice was thick and foggy, and her breath hitched like a bicycle chain ratcheting into gear. She glanced at my father, and he flinched as if someone had punched him. "There's something ... something you need to know," she continued. "It won't be easy."

Nothing was easy. Not anymore. I couldn't imagine that what she had to say would be worse than the things I already knew. I'd been abducted. There was an entire week missing from my life. And I'd killed a man.

But it turned out that there *was* something worse, and it came with my mother's next trembling, horrified words.

"Honey ... you're pregnant."

24

Wednesday, June 4, 10:55 p.m.

I'm driving through the park at a crawl, straining to see as far as the car's headlights will reach. I can't think of a single reason why Renata would be here, since her love for the park faded right around the time she decided she was too old for the swing set. But I'm desperate, and I'll look anywhere. Everywhere. Until I find my daughter.

Richard didn't want me to go. I'd finally convinced him that I couldn't just sit at our house, waiting for the police. I had to do something. Then he'd offered to go with me, but one of us had to stay home in case the police called, or Renata came back on her own.

I've already cruised past all her friends' houses, the school, Angelo's, the community center. There are more police cars out than usual, and I know they're looking for my daughter too. It's not that I'm ungrateful for their efforts.

It's just not personal for them. I have more to lose.

I have *everything* to lose.

There's one more place I haven't checked. Again, it's a place I can't imagine Renata would go even casually, let alone stay there for hours, but I'm not going to rule anything out. I'll scour every inch of this town.

And even if my daughter has never done it, I know a lot of teens like to hang out in the graveyard at night. I'd done it myself a time or two as a kid. Mostly with Carson, once with Ian. But I hadn't been near the place since the abduction, not even to visit my father's grave.

Stewart Brooks was buried there.

If he'd actually been buried at all.

As with most towns, the cemetery isn't far from the park. I've never understood why it's common to have the dead buried so close to where children play and families gather, but I suppose it's a matter of convenience. Wide open space is required for a graveyard, so you simply extend that space and leave part of it untouched, and call it a park.

The iron gates of the Woodlawn Cemetery are always open, another common practice I don't understand. Who decides to visit the graves of their loved ones in the middle of the night? The only people in a graveyard after dark are usually partying teenagers or wandering drunks, two categories of people that *shouldn't* be there. And besides, if you were never going to close the gates anyway, why install them in the first place?

I recognize that my brain is going off on tangents, trying to distract me from dwelling on the real reason I'm here. I can't let that happen. I need to stay focused.

My tires crunch on gravel as I roll through the gate and take the first right turn. The cemetery path is an oval that circles the entire grounds, bisected by three straight lines that divide the oval into sections. I'll drive around the outside, and then up and down each path.

Even though I can already tell there's no one here, certainly not my daughter.

As I circle the cemetery, my headlights washing over rows of tombstones in various shapes and sizes, I realize that I have no idea where my father is buried. Everything surrounding that time is so hazy, and soon after his death, my mother checked me into Brightside where I was occupied with other things that didn't involve visiting graves. I did go to his funeral, I remember that. And there was something strange about it, something to do with my mother.

She didn't cry. Not once during the calling hours, the funeral, the graveside service. She never shed a single tear for my father. I wonder now if she was in shock.

Maybe she should've been institutionalized right along with me.

I reach the far curve of the oval, where there's something different on the other side of the road, outside the circle of memorials bearing flowers and balloons and other mementos left by loved ones. Separate from all that are the metal marker poles with small, numbered signs, loved by no one. I know exactly what that small, desolate patch is. Pauper's graves.

That's where Stewart Brooks is buried.

Almost against my will, I stop the car and put it in park with the headlights washing over the marker poles.

I'm out of the car before I know what my own intentions are. I'm going to find his grave. I even know which number marks his final resting place. Cosmic coincidence and a cold, unfeeling state bureaucracy conspired to assign a number with undeniable meaning to this particular marker, immortalizing his crimes with indifference.

Stewart Brooks' grave bears the number 16, the age of his victims.

The markers aren't arranged in numerical order, and I have to peer at each one, moving slowly down the rows. I don't know what I expect to find here. Signs that the ground has never been broken, because there wasn't actually anyone to bury? A gaping hole in the earth, dug outward from six feet under? A note from the killer informing the world at large that he'd returned from the grave to finish what he started?

When I finally identify his marker, I do find something unexpected, but it isn't any of the things I've imagined. There's a bouquet of fresh flowers propped against the pole that's stamped with 16. As if they'd been placed there today, on the anniversary of his death.

What kind of sick person leaves flowers on the grave of a serial killer?

Cold sinks into me, right down to the bone, and I rush back to the safety of my car. I'm suddenly convinced that the bringer of those flowers is still here in the cemetery, lurking behind a tombstone, crouched low to the ground. Hunting me.

I shouldn't be out here. I should be home with my husband, letting the police do their searching. I need to be there in case my daughter comes home. There must be another way I can help to find her, something more deliberate than this random after-dark tour of the town that's accomplishing nothing.

I'm back at my house in less than ten minutes, still shivering from the experience in the cemetery. As I get out of the car and walk around, I happen to glance at the mailbox at the end of the driveway and see something sticking out at the top. The white corner of an envelope crushed in the lid, as if someone had hastily shoved in a letter and slammed the mailbox closed.

I know I already checked the mail earlier today. And the flag is down, so it's not that Richard decided to send a late-night letter.

Filled with unnamed dread, I head to the mailbox, grasp the tab, and hold my breath as I pull it open. Nothing explodes or jumps out at me. The letter that was jammed into the lid comes down with it, lying on its face. My hand shakes as I scoop up the envelope and turn it over.

On the front is my name, Madeline, in glued-on letters cut from magazines or newspapers. There's no writing and no other markings, no postage. Just my name.

A cry bursts from my throat, and my eyes fill with tears as I stumble toward the house, leaving the mailbox open. Part of me, the part that watched all those cop shows as a kid, demands that I don't open the envelope. I could destroy evidence, or there could be poison inside. But I can't just leave it alone. I have to see.

I tear the envelope along the seam as I walk up the porch steps, and remove a single folded sheet of paper. It's bulky and crinkled, with dark shapes showing through from the inside. More cutout letters.

The front door opens as I stand in front of it beneath the porch light and slowly unfold the paper. Richard is there, a worried question on his face. He must have heard my car drive in. "Maddie, what —"

"Shh," I tell him, as if I won't be able to read while he's talking. My throat is tight, my fingers numb, and finally I get the paper opened to read the message.

This is exactly what you deserve.

Your daughter has one week.

I shove a fist in my mouth as tears fill my eyes, and Richard snatches the paper from me. Within seconds, he lets out an animal growl. "Where did you get this?"

"The mailbox," I whisper.

"I'm calling the police," he says, and turns back into the house.

I don't follow him. I can't move. To know in my heart that my daughter's been kidnapped is one thing, but to get that note. To have something physical that proves all my worst fears have come to pass.

I'm completely undone.

Suddenly Richard is there, putting an arm around my waist, guiding me gently inside without a word. I don't resist. He settles me on the couch, and then takes out his cell phone. When he turns away, I realize he's speaking angry words to someone, but I can't understand them. I'm trapped in a nightmare. I know exactly how Dallas Walsh feels.

My whole world has been taken from me.

But I'm going to get it back, my world. My daughter. I have a week. It's more time than Dallas had, and I know who's done this, no matter what anyone else says. It was him. I stopped him before, and I can stop him again.

I *will* protect my child. I will save her.

The way I couldn't the first time.

25

Madeline—the past

Drenched in sweat, exhausted and hollowed out, I lay on the bed staring at the ceiling, and all I could think was: *It's over. It's finally over*.

There was a nurse next to me with a tiny, white-wrapped bundle. She offered to give it to me, but I said no. I couldn't hold the baby. Not even once. If I did that, I might get attached. I could feel myself wanting to take it, to complete the bond that had been developing for nine months.

But I resisted. I didn't know anything about the infant I'd given birth to, and I didn't want to. Even knowing that a nice couple in Pennsylvania was already lined up to adopt the baby was too much information. One of the orderlies had let that slip, and I'd been furious.

I knew what they thought. I was a monster, needlessly hating an innocent child. But that wasn't true. I didn't hate the baby.

I loved my child. And I knew that the worst possible fate for her would be to grow up with me, a too-young, broken mother, with the knowledge that one of your parents was a serial killer. That kind of shadow was far too heavy for any child to bear.

This way, the baby would never know any of that.

They wheeled the bundle away, and I fell into a deep, exhausted sleep. By the time I woke up, night stained the window. Someone had changed the stained sheets and my bloody gown. There was a fierce ache *down there*, the only reminder of what had happened just a few hours ago.

I found myself wanting my own mother, before I remembered that I hated her. She'd abandoned me to go through this alone, because she couldn't bear the shame, or any of the repercussions of my ordeal. Not the pregnancy, not the bizarre disorder that had fractured my mind, apparently when I'd cracked my skull on a rock in the woods.

I hadn't seen her in months. She was never going to come here again.

I'd been awake for maybe fifteen minutes when Dr. Carrington bustled into the room. He was a medium height, medium build, older man with a caring but distracted manner, and he'd been my primary doctor since I arrived at this place. The Brightside Retreat for Teens and Young Adults. What a terrible, misleading name. There was nothing bright here, and it wasn't anything like a retreat.

It was a prison. The only thing missing were the bars on the doors, but there were plenty of them on the windows. In case one of us 'guests' at the 'retreat' decided to try jumping out one of them.

I'd considered it, many times. But I'd decided that the fall from the third floor wouldn't kill me, and I'd just end up crippled *and* locked in the nut hatch.

"Hello, Madeline," Dr. Carrington said briskly as he picked up my chart from the end of the bed and looked through it. "The nurses tell me that you're recovering nicely. We should be able to get you moved back to your room in the morning."

I stared dully at him. I didn't want to go back to my room. I wanted to get out of this place. "Will I get to go home now?" I said, hating the pleading tone in my voice. "I thought, after ... the delivery ..."

"Well, we'll just have to see about that," Dr. Carrington said.

That's what he always said. We'll have to see about that.

And what he meant was no.

I closed my eyes so I wouldn't end up crying. What I saw behind my eyelids was a tiny body held in two gloved hands, smeared with dark fluids, little fists clenched and waving, little mouth opening to release little cries.

The baby. She was so tiny, so perfect. So helpless.

That quick glimpse was all I had, before I'd closed myself off to the very idea that I was a mother at just barely seventeen. A mother to the child of a monster. I knew I'd spend the rest of my life trying to forget that image.

Dr. Carrington replaced my chart and bestowed a wan smile on me. "I'll have the cafeteria send you up a plate," he said. "We've got you on a saline IV to keep you hydrated, but you should try to eat something. You'll need to regain your strength."

For what? I almost said. There was no point in getting better, not for me. I was never getting out of here. My mother didn't want me, the doctors couldn't fix me, and now I was an empty shell of a human being with no purpose. I'd spent nine months growing a child for someone else to love and raise, and now that was over.

As they said in the movies, my work here was done.

"Thank you," I made myself say to the doctor. "I'll try to eat."

"I'm glad to hear it," he said, and then left me alone in the room.

With my thoughts.

With the tiny, ghostly cries of an infant who could've been my world.

I had nothing left.

26

Thursday, June 5, 5:45 a.m.

I wake with a gasp, half-remembered nightmares shrouding my mind in a deeper darkness than the one still settled over my bedroom. My sheet is tangled around my legs, my skin tacky with sweat, my breathing shallow.

Then I remember the real nightmare I'm living, and the shadows fall from my mind.

My daughter is missing.

I'm wide awake in an instant. Richard is in the bed beside me, snoring gently, and muddled resentment swims through me for a moment. How can he sleep when Renata has been kidnapped, after that horrible note I found in the mailbox last night. How could *I* have slept?

Then I remember. He took sleeping pills last night, because he was so agitated and distraught that he could barely sit down, let alone get any rest. I remember that I had some half-formed idea for us to sleep in shifts, one of us waiting for Renata, the other restoring enough energy to take over. I'd lain down with him, to help him relax, and I'd somehow drifted off to the peaceful rhythm of his breathing.

I decide to let him sleep as long as he can, and ease carefully out of bed. I really have to pee. But before I do anything else, I slip out of the bedroom and walk down the hall, and open Renata's door. I'd give anything to see her shape in the bed, covered by blankets, one foot sticking out and hanging over the edge the way she always sleeps. Anything to make all of this not real.

But her room is silent. Her bed is empty.

I'm not dreaming.

I use the bathroom, grab a change of clothes, and head downstairs. After I get a pot of coffee started, I step into the first-floor bathroom to get out of the clothes I'd slept in last night and shower the night sweats away. Soon I'm at the small table in the kitchen by the window, with a cup of coffee I'm not sure I'll drink, watching the sun stain the horizon outside.

It's too early to do anything but sit here and wait, and I can't stand it.

For the next hour or so, I mentally run through all the ways I could've prevented this, could've kept my daughter safe. By not going out to dinner. By being a firmer parent and insisting that she come right home after practice yesterday, no matter how much she complained about it. By installing a tracker on her somewhere, her clothes, her purse, her backpack. An extreme measure, one I never would've considered except in hindsight.

By moving away from Dayfield, back when I knew I was about to get married and start a family. I never should've stayed here, never should have raised my daughter around the ghosts of my past.

At some point I get up, open the fridge and stare into it, with the vague idea that breakfast is a thing that should be eaten in the morning, even though I don't intend to eat anything. My gaze lands on the Styrofoam containers with the cheesecake slices from the Stone Mill, the ones Renata was supposed to enjoy last night.

I spend the next ten minutes crying.

Around seven, as the light of day brightens the kitchen window and my coffee sits cold and untouched in front of me, I decide it's late enough to call Detective Burgess. His business card is sitting on the kitchen counter by the cordless, and I pick up the phone and glance at the numbers on the card.

But first, I dial my daughter's cell phone. I have to try, even though it hurts so much to hope as the phone rings and rings and rings, and finally informs me that the person I'm calling is not available.

I choke back a sob at the impersonal recorded message. My daughter is *not available*.

Squaring my shoulders, I dial the detective's office number and start pacing. Through the kitchen, into the dining room, toward the living room. After three rings, the call is answered with a single, gruff word: "Burgess."

The detective sounds like he's barely slept, just like me. Once again, I'm surprised and heartened that he seems to care. "Detective, it's Madeline Osborn," I say.

"Yes, I know. I have caller ID." He drags out a sigh. "I was going to head to your place around nine for the interview, but real quick, I'll tell you what we have so far. Okay?"

"Thank you," I say, still pacing aimlessly, heading toward the front door. "Did you find anything — oh, my God," I finish in a strangled tone as I glance through the side windows.

There are news vans parked outside my house. Four of them, circled like vultures at the curb. I can't believe they're here, and so soon. My daughter hasn't even been missing for twenty-four hours.

"What?" Burgess says. "What is it?"

"The media. Four vans, in front of my house," I say as I turn away, sickened that they'd stalk my home like this. No one's come to the door, so they're probably waiting for someone to walk outside before they accost us.

Detective Burgess curses profusely. "How the hell did they find out already?" he snaps, but I can tell he's not asking me. "All right, I'm going to send a few squad cars over to get rid of them," he says. "Can you hold for a minute?"

I agree, and he clicks away. I don't mind waiting if it means getting those people out there away from my house, from my life.

It's not long before the detective comes back on the line. "They'll be out of there in ten minutes," he says. "I'm also going to have a car stationed at your house, twenty-four-seven, until ..."

He doesn't finish the sentence, but I know what he means. Until we find my daughter. One way or another.

She has six days left.

"So unfortunately, there's nothing on the envelope or the note," Burgess says. "No prints, no hairs or fibers. The letters were cut from common, modern magazines and newspapers, so that's no help either. We did pick up Kilgore, though. Found him at a hotel, late last night around 2 A.M. He's still in custody and insisting he had nothing to do with it, but he doesn't have an alibi."

My stomach churns sourly. If they didn't find him until two in the morning, he could've been the one to put the note in the mailbox. Could it really be him? "Okay," I say shakily. "What about Dallas Walsh?"

The detective pauses, and then says, "We haven't found him yet."

"What?" I blurt. Dallas was supposed to be the easy one. If he's not home, he's at one of the two bars in town, or wandering around to drunkenly berate anyone unfortunate enough to come within ten feet of him. My heart speeds to a frantic pace. "He must have her, then," I rasp. "He's got my daughter."

"We don't know that yet," Burgess says firmly. "We weren't able to interview many people last night, because it was so late, but I've got officers already starting the rounds at the school, with the parents closest to you. We're going to need that talk with you and your husband so we can fill out the rest of the interview list."

"Yes, of course. You can come now," I tell him. "I'll wake Richard, and —"

"McKenzie and I will be there at nine," he interrupts, and I can hear the ragged exhaustion in his voice. "Mrs. Osborn, I know you hate being told to calm down, but ... please try," he says. "We know she's still alive, and we have a definite deadline. And if I don't get at least a little bit of rest, I'm going to be useless in this investigation."

What he says makes sense, and my attitude softens. "All right," I say. "I'll try."

"I appreciate that, Mrs. Osborn."

"Call me Madeline," I say, finding a smile somehow. "People who've stayed up all night trying to help me get to use my first name."

He gives a brief chuckle. "Okay, Madeline," he says. "And I'm Tom."

"Thank you, Tom."

I hear muffled sirens and glance outside again to see squad cars pulling up behind the news vans. "It looks like the cavalry's here," I say. "I'll let you go, and Richard and I will be ready by nine."

"See you then," he says. "Madeline ... we're going to find your daughter."

Tears prick my eyes and spill out rapidly. "Thank you," I whisper. "It means a lot that you'd say that."

"I mean it." His tone is far gentler now. "See you at nine."

We end the call, and I head back to the kitchen with a rumbling stomach. I'm still not sure I can eat anything, but I should probably try. I need to regain my strength, just like Dr. Carrington used to tell me.

Maybe Dallas Walsh has my daughter, but I still think it's *him*.

And I'm the only one capable of believing that.

As I reach toward the charger to replace the phone, I realize there's another important call I have to make. It's Thursday. I'm supposed to teach a class this afternoon, but there's no way that's going to happen. I need to ask Selma if she'll arrange a cancellation and make the calls for me. I can't face talking to each of my students, trying to explain why I have to cancel today.

It's still early, and Selma won't be in the office yet, but she has a machine. I'll leave a message and give some vague reason for cancelling. It's easier than actually telling another person what happened to my daughter.

I find the administrative number for the community center in the phone book and dial it. The phone rings twice, and there's a click.

But instead of an answering machine, a woman's voice says, "Dayfield Community Center, director's office."

"Selma?" I say with complete surprise.

"Yes, this is she. Can I help you?"

I haven't told her who I am yet. "It's Madeline Osborn," I say. "I have a pottery class —"

"Oh, Madeline, good morning!" Selma says brightly. "How are you doing? I hope that reporter hasn't been bothering you again. Mike's keeping an eye out for him."

"Thank you," I say weakly, dizzied by the normality of the conversation. Of course, she has no idea what happened. "Selma, I'm going to have to cancel my class this afternoon. I was wondering if you'd be able to notify my students?"

There's a slight pause before she says, "Yes, it's no problem. I have your class list on the books. Are you feeling okay, Madeline? There's a nasty summer cold going around, you know. I hope you haven't caught it."

I fight against a wave of sorrow so strong, it nearly knocks me off my feet. If only this was something as simple as a cold. And before I know it, I blurt out, "No, it's Renata. My daughter. She's gone missing."

"Oh, dear God in heaven!" Selma gasps. "Oh, Madeline, you must be absolutely terrified. Of course I'll make the calls for you. Have you any idea where she might be?"

"None," I manage to say. It doesn't matter that I've told her. The media will break the story first thing, if they haven't already, even without any supporting details. "The police are looking for her. They're coming to interview me and Richard soon."

"My God. You poor child," Selma says, and the warmth in her voice makes me shiver. "I'll pray for your daughter's safe return. Is there anything else I can do for you, dear?"

I swallow the lump in my throat. "I don't think so," I say. "But thank you. For handling the cancellations."

"It's no trouble at all. You call me anytime if you need something, or even if you just want someone to talk to," she says.

"Thank you," I whisper, close to tears again and wondering why the smallest kindness from anyone seems to undo me.

I say goodbye, replace the phone and head upstairs to wake Richard. We'll need each other to get through this interview, to get through the hours and days of however long it takes to find our daughter. And we *will* find her alive.

Even if I have to ruin every other life in this town in the process, I'll get my daughter back.

27

Thursday, June 5, 9:00 a.m.

Burgess and McKenzie arrive promptly at nine, as promised. The first thing they ask Richard and I to do is write down a list of names and contact information for everyone we know, everyone we can think of that Renata knows, any family in the area.

I list all of Renata's friends from school, any parents' names I know. All of her teachers I can remember. Jan Shearman, my friend and her coach. Selma Ferguson at the community center — most of the kids in town know her, since the school holds a lot of events at the center. Richard tells me to include Ian Moody, and it reminds me that I never got a chance to ask my husband about the meeting last night, and why I couldn't reach him.

He probably just didn't answer the phone because he was driving, though.

On impulse, I add Brenda Westhall to the list. She left the police force right after the Singing Woods Killer case, and she's not my biggest fan, because I wasn't able to help her find Stewart Brooks' lair. But as far as I know, she still lives in town.

Then it's time for family. Richard has no one here but me and Renata, since he moved into town alone right around the time I was released from Brightside. As for me, the only relative in the area is my mother. My father was an only child, and his parents had passed away before he met Mom. My mother has a brother and sister, and her father is still alive, but her family lives in Ohio.

I write 'Judith Grant' at the bottom of the list of names. I have to get my phone out and look up her number in my contacts. I call her so rarely that I might as well not have her number at all — it's just brief, strained chats every few months, updating her on how Renata's doing, how Richard's business is going, and which holiday or birthday do we have to suffer each other's company for next.

Sometimes I believe that my mother really was replaced by an imposter after my abduction and my father's death. That despite my condition, my brain isn't actually lying about her. She'd become a completely different person.

Finished, I hand the clipboard holding the list to Burgess, and he scans it slowly. "Brenda Westhall?" he says after a minute. "She was a cop. A detective."

"Yes, she worked on the original case," I say. "Renata doesn't know her, but I do, and she had a pretty big grudge against me."

He quirks an eyebrow. "You have a surprising number of enemies in this town, Mrs. Osborn. Madeline," he says. "Why is that?"

I shrug. "I suppose that's what happens when you're officially labeled a mental case, and everyone knows you've been hospitalized for it."

"My wife is not unbalanced, Detective," Richard says, taking my hand. "She has a physiological condition, but it's not a psychosis, and it's controlled with prescription medication."

"So I've heard. Capgras Syndrome." Burgess smiles slightly at my look of surprise. "I have done my homework, you know," he says. "If I thought you were unbalanced, I'd be talking to your psychologist instead of you. And speaking of her, why isn't she on this list?"

I frown. "Dr. Bradshaw isn't my enemy, and my daughter doesn't know her."

"Maybe not, but I want everyone you know. Please," he says, handing the clipboard back to me.

"All right." I scribble down 'Dr. Gillian Bradshaw' and find her number in my contacts.

Burgess takes the list again. "Most of these are Renata's friends and their parents, is that right?" he says. "Walk me through the names who aren't in that category."

I tell them about Jan and Selma, who they are, what they do. "Ian Moody is Richard's business partner," I say. "He's also my ex-boyfriend, but that was a long time ago."

"No matter how long ago it was, he's still an ex. That gives him possible motive." The detective marks a hasty star by Ian's, Brenda's, and Jan's names.

My brow lifts at that. "Why Jan?"

"She's very close to your daughter, and she may have been the last adult to see her before she was kidnapped," he explains. "Is there some reason she should be excluded from suspicion?"

I'm actually starting to think just the opposite, and I can't believe I'm suspicious of Jan. But I didn't even think about the point Detective Burgess — Tom — has just made. She *was* the last adult to see Renata.

"There is something ..." I begin, not sure I want to say this. There's no way to be sure it even happened. My memory isn't reliable enough, and I still don't know if I actually saw a person or a stop sign that day.

But there was what she said about my father's house. And I'm *nearly* positive there are no stop signs in that area.

Tom leans toward me. "Anything and everything, remember?" he says. "Tell me."

Richard looks confused as I prepare to throw potential suspicion at my closest friend. "Okay, but there's no evidence," I say. "It's a memory, and I'm not sure it's real. The day I was abducted, I saw ... I thought I saw ... someone else on Geary Street. Tall with red hair, like Jan. If there was actually a person where I thought, they would've seen Stewart Brooks take me. It happened almost right in front of them. If it was really someone."

"And no one ever reported seeing you abducted, right?" Tom says.

I nod and swallow. "It was raining so hard, and ... I was confused. *Am* confused. My memories from that time are jumbled, and most of them are missing completely. But still." I take a deep breath. "I actually confronted her about it last night. We had dinner together, and I told her what I thought I'd seen that day. She immediately denied seeing me abducted, even though that's not what I asked her." My hands were trembling. "And I told her the person I saw was near Mrs. Vanderwall's house, but she said she'd never been to my *father's* house. I didn't mention that my father's house was right behind Mrs. Vanderwall's and our back yards connected."

Tom has his note pad out, and he's writing something down. "I'm going to consider Jan Shearman a person of interest, along with Ian Moody and Brenda Westhall. And I'll question Gregory Vanderwall to see if he knows Shearman," he says. "Now, Selma Ferguson. Who is she, again ...?"

"She's the director of the Dayfield Community Center. All the kids know her," I say. "I teach a pottery class there ... oh, God. Trevor."

Both Tom and Richard stare at me.

"Trevor Downes." I'd managed to forget about him and his creepy questions. "He also teaches a class at the center. Internet for seniors. But he's obsessed with serial killers, especially Stewart Brooks. He's always asking me horrible questions about my experience, about the killer, things like that. On Monday, he asked me how it felt to murder someone."

Richard slips an arm around me and draws me close. "Oh, babe. You didn't mention that," he says. "If I knew he'd been harassing you, I would've done something about it."

I shake my head. "He's only been disgusting and annoying. But if his obsession went any further ... maybe he ..."

Tom is already adding Trevor Downes to the list and starring his name. "Is that everyone here who isn't a friend or the parent of a friend?"

"All but one." I point to Judith Grant. "That's my mother. We don't get along, but she loves Renata."

He nods and puts a check next to her name. I wonder what it's for, but I decide not to ask. I'm actually not against the police harassing my mother.

"Okay, I think we're set for now," Tom says. "I'm planning to get through this list by the end of the day, so —"

The phone rings in the kitchen. My heart scrambles madly, and I leap up and run to answer it. *Please, please be Renata.*

"Hello?"

"Madeline, it's Carson. I *have* to see you."

All at once, I'm furious. "I don't have time for this," I hiss into the phone. "My daughter is missing, and the police are here right now."

"Oh, God. Mads, I'm so sorry," she says, her voice completely miserable.

"Don't call me that," I snap.

I've hurt her, but I don't care. "All right," she says. "But we have to talk. Can I —"

"You didn't want to talk twenty years ago. Why start now?" I half-shout, and then hang up the phone, slamming it back on the charger cradle.

As I'm standing there, seething, a hand rests on my shoulder and I jump. "It's just me, Maddie," Richard says behind me. "Who was that?"

I turn to him, tears already forming in my eyes. "Someone from my past. And she should've stayed there," I say, just before I start sobbing.

My husband holds me, soothes me, but it's not going to help. There's too much hurt in me. I can't take any more.

I'm losing the battle in my head, when the one I need to fight is outside it.

28

Madeline—the past

My mother visited me today.

It's been two months since the baby, and she didn't even ask about it. She wouldn't answer me when I asked about being released, either. I knew the reason I was still here was that *she* kept refusing to sign the release papers, and because I was a still a minor, I didn't get a say.

She didn't want me to come home. She was afraid of me.

But in less than ten months from now, I could check myself out.

I don't even know why she came. She didn't say much of anything, just sat in the visitor's room looking out the window while I tried to find things to talk about. The only real reaction she had was when I asked about Carson, if she would ask her to visit me. Ian came here sometimes, when he could get away from the job he'd taken after he graduated, and he insisted that he still wanted a relationship with me when I got out. I wasn't sure that would work, for his sake more than mine, but I appreciated his continuing friendship. Especially since he was my only visitor besides my mother.

That's why I mentioned Carson. Because I was lonely.

And I was shocked at my mother's response.

"Your little bitch of a friend left town. Her and her awful family," she'd snapped at me. "I don't know where they went, and I don't care. Good riddance to bad rubbish."

She might as well have slapped me. My mother *loved* Carson, treated her like a second daughter. Why would she say that about her?

After my mother left and I went back to my room, Wanda came in to check on me. She was my favorite orderly, always smiling, always making jokes. And she'd really listen when you talked to her. She was the only one at Brightside who seemed to genuinely care about the inmates. I mean guests.

Wanda knew how I felt about my mother. That was why she came in to talk.

She listened as I told her about the visit, my mother's indifference, and her bizarre behavior when I mentioned Carson. Then I had an idea. "Wanda, is there any way you could help me find her?" I said. "Carson, I mean. She's my best friend, and it'd really help me to talk to her."

Wanda's brow furrowed. "Well, I don't know, Madeline," she said slowly. "You're supposed to limit your outside contacts, and —"

"Please," I begged, and put on the biggest pleading smile I could manage. "It would be so productive. Dr. Trenton is always telling me that I have to work on my social skills, and this is totally social."

I could tell she was going to relent when her eyes sparkled like that. "Okay, let's do it," she said, standing from the chair next to my bed where she'd been sitting. "Come on."

Grinning, I followed her to the nurse's station. I waited as she slipped behind the counter and pressed a button on the computer, making it beep. "Do you know her parents' names?" she said.

I nodded. "Lisa and Stephen Mills."

When I said her father's name aloud, a chill ran down my spine. I'd never gotten to ask her about the terrifying conversation with Mr. Mills in the car, when he asked if anyone was molesting her. When he hinted, without trying to, that *he* was molesting her, and he didn't want her to tell me.

Wanda typed something in, each key on the keyboard making a loud, sproinging click sound. "You don't have any idea where they moved?" she said.

"No. My mother just said they left town."

"Okay, we'll work around that." Wanda dragged the mouse and clicked something. "I don't see them in New York. Let's try a few nearby states."

After a bunch more typing and clicking, Wanda said, "Bingo. Stephen and Lisa Mills, Scranton, Pennsylvania." She pulled a note pad from under the desk, picked up a pen and scribbled something down, then tore off the top sheet and handed it to me. "Here you go," she said.

It was a phone number with an area code of 570. Carson's number.

"You're the best, Wanda," I said. "Thank you."

"No problem. Let's keep this between us, though," she said with a wink. "Go ahead and call your friend."

I smiled as I walked down the hall and around the corner to the 'guest phones,' which was just a bank of phones along the wall with dividers between them, and tables and chairs in front of them. We were allowed to make pretty much any calls we wanted to, but the phone lines were live-monitored by the security staff, in case one of the less-stable 'guests' tried to order twenty pizzas or threaten the President or something.

This was the happiest I'd felt since I was brought to Brightside. I was going to talk to my best friend. I imagined being on the phone for hours, catching each other up on our lives, hearing about her annoying brothers and her new school and how much we missed each other, and how we'd get together once I got out of here.

I wouldn't ask about her father, though. That wasn't something we should talk about on the phone.

No one else was using the phones, so at least I'd have a little privacy. I sat down at the last station on the end, dialed the number from the paper, and waited.

It rang four times, and then a woman's voice answered with, "Hello?"

It was Mrs. Mills. I knew her voice. "Hi," I said, but for some reason I got stuck on saying her name and it wouldn't come out. Instead I just said, "Is Carson there?"

"Yes, she is. Just a minute."

I didn't hear Mrs. Mills put the phone down, but the faint background noises changed as, I assumed, she walked through the house. I guessed they must've gotten a cordless phone. They didn't have one before. I heard the mutter of a television, a boy's voice shouting something, a soft tune that sounded like a music box. Then a muffled question, and someone responding from a distance.

Seconds later, there was another, "Hello?"

This one belonged to Carson.

Warmth and good memories flooded me with that single word. "Hi, Carson," I said. "It's me, Madeline."

She didn't say a word. Not 'oh my God' or 'how did you find me' or even 'hi, Mads.' Her silence was broken by a click, as if she'd just closed the door to whatever room she was in.

Then she said in a low, menacing tone, "I don't want to talk to you."

I could've sworn I heard my heart shatter, the broken pieces raining all over my dissolving picture of our happy reunion.

"What?" I managed to say. "Carson, I don't —"

"Leave me alone!" she whispered harshly. "You *ruined* my life."

I didn't even realize I was crying until I felt the tears dripping from my jaw, splashing the top of my shirt. "What are you talking about?" I said, my voice rough with shock. I hadn't done anything to her. I didn't even know she'd left Dayfield.

"Lose my number, Madeline. Don't call me, and don't look for me." I heard her breathing hard, and something in the background snapped. "I never want to speak to you again."

She hung up.

I sat there with the receiver in my hand until the phone started blaring its piercing off-the-hook alarm. Slowly, I replaced the handset and folded my hands in my lap, staring at nothing, a single thought pulsing in my head.

What just happened?

But there was no one to answer my question.

Carson had abandoned me, too.

29

Thursday, June 5, 11:50 a.m.

I can't stand sitting around the house and doing nothing while my daughter's life is in danger.

We have police officers here constantly now. Two in a squad car in front of the house, one guarding the porch. The one right outside is Jeremy, but he'll be replaced with another officer when his shift ends at five. Jeremy is the only one I've spoken to, because it's his job to stop anyone who wants to come in the house and ask me or Richard if we want them there.

I'm grateful for him, because Lexi from next door and Heather Meyers from across the street have both tried to stop by and I don't want to talk to either of them. They aren't feeling sympathetic or supportive. They just want some good gossip to spread around.

As I'm sitting listlessly on the couch, and Richard is banging around in the kitchen making a lunch neither of us will eat, my cell phone rings. I've stopped believing that every ringing phone could be Renata, so I'm not in a hurry to answer. And I'm even less interested when I look at the screen and see my mother's name.

But I suppose I have to speak to her. She'll have seen the news by now, and she'll know that her granddaughter is missing.

I answer the phone, and my mother doesn't say hello. She says, "Why didn't you tell me about Renata?"

Pure anger is my first reaction, but I tamp it down and reply as calmly as I can. "I've been a little busy, Mom," I say. "Talking to the police. Because my daughter is missing."

"So I've heard," she replies, giving my cold tone right back. "There was some detective here asking me questions, insinuating that *I* had something to do with it. He just left."

I allow myself a little smirk and say a silent thanks to Tom Burgess. My mother deserves a bit of discomfort now and then, since she made the easy choice to abandon her troubled daughter rather than trying to help her through the darkest time of her life. "Yes, well, they have to question everyone," I say. "It's standard procedure."

"I don't like hearing that my granddaughter's been kidnapped from the police," my mother says. "I should have heard about it from my daughter."

"Really, Mom?" I say. "If you care so much, why are you still sitting on your ass at home and calling me? Why didn't you jump right in your car and drive over here, and give me a little actual support for once?"

Her hurt silence only makes me angrier. "That's not fair," she says. "You know how much I love Renata."

"Yes, I do know that. But you don't love me."

"Madeline!" she gasps. "That's not true."

I clench a fist. "Well, it feels that way from here, Mom," I say quietly. "You've barely been able to look at me since ..."

Since Dad died. I can't say it.

But she knows what I mean.

She's quiet again and I think, for one brief moment, that she's finally going to apologize for treating me like a stranger who's also inconveniently the mother of her granddaughter for all these years.

Instead, she changes the subject abruptly. "That Carson Mills was here yesterday, looking for you," she says. "I hope you're not speaking to her again. I never liked that girl."

Yes, you did! I want to scream. Did she somehow forget that Carson practically lived with me since kindergarten, that she always called us 'her girls' and treated my best friend like she was my sister? Once again, I find myself thinking that this woman isn't really Judith Grant. She's a duplicate, an imposter.

And it's not my condition making me think that.

"I'm not speaking to her, but I'm thinking about it," I say, deciding to try a different approach. Asking my mother anything plainly always leads to vague remarks, flat-out denial, or subject changes. So I'll try to side-step some information from her. "Any reason why I shouldn't talk to her? I mean, if you really think so, I'll take your word for it."

"Oh, so *now* you want to listen," my mother says, but I ignore her blistering sarcasm. "Yes, there is a reason. She's a liar."

I'd hoped to find out something useful, but now I'm just completely confused. "What's she lying about?"

"Everything," my mother hisses. "You should stay away from her."

Well, it just might be Carson's lucky day. Maybe I'll hear her out now, just because my mother thinks I shouldn't. "All right, Mom. I will," I say, and then hear the kitchen phone ring and Ian move to answer it. That's probably Jeremy from outside. "I have to go now. I'll try to—"

"Madeline, please." I can hear the tears in my mother's voice. "I'm so worried about Renata. Can't you just take a few minutes and tell me what's going on?"

I'm relenting, even though I don't want to. I really do know that she loves my daughter. But I also know that I can't tell her everything about the note, and the one-week deadline, and the horrifying similarities to my own abduction and near-murder. She might break down completely if she hears that, and I don't want that to happen. Despite everything, she's still my mother.

"The police are looking for her," I say as Richard walks out of the kitchen, headed for the door. *Ian's here*, he mouths at me, and I frown and get up to leave the room. I don't want anything to do with Ian right now. "They have a long list of people they're interviewing, and they also have a few suspects," I continue, walking into the dining room.

"Suspects?" my mother says shrilly. "You mean they've arrested people they think have ... hurt Renata?"

"Yes, that's what suspects are." I regret my sarcastic tone and dial it down immediately. "They're questioning Frank Kilgore, the reporter, and they're looking for Dallas Walsh."

"Angeline's father?" She sounds confused, stunned. "Why?"

"Because he's angry and wants to hurt someone."

I move from the dining room to the kitchen when I hear the front door open, and then Ian's voice. "That's all I know right now, Mom. I'm sorry," I say. "But I'll tell you if they find out anything else. They *are* going to find her, okay?"

"Are you sure?" my mother whispers.

"I'm positive. But I really do have to go now," I say.

"All right." She hesitates, and then says, "I'm so sorry, Madeline. I love you."

It's been so long since I heard her say that, I've forgotten when the last time was. And I know it's only a ploy to appease me, so I'll keep her updated about Renata. But I decide to accept it, and to give it back, for my own sake. Not hers.

"Love you too, Mom," I say. "Talk to you soon."

I hang up and slide the phone in my pocket. Behind me, I hear snatches of Richard and Ian's conversation in the living room, parts of it heated.

What are they arguing about?

Frowning slightly, I move into the dining room, closer to the two of them. They're speaking in loud whispers, as if neither of them wants me to hear what they're saying. Ian is a few feet inside the door, and Richard's in front of him with his back toward the dining room, blocking me from his view.

"... don't know what you're talking about," Richard says. "You must — mixed up — old records."

"I can read, Richard!" Ian is a little louder, a little clearer. "The numbers aren't wrong."

"Why would I — would be ruined!" comes from Richard. I wish I could hear everything he's saying, but his part of the conversation is uneven, rising and falling. "We'll look at — later. It's — big mistake."

"I don't think so. I double-checked everything." Ian's voice rises to an almost normal volume, laced with frustration. And then he catches sight of me.

"Madeline," he says. "Are you ..."

He doesn't finish the sentence, but what I am is incredibly confused. He's not glaring at me, not turning around and storming off at the sight of me. He looks like he's going to cry.

He looks the way he did in high school after Dana died. When he was so worried that he wouldn't let me out of his sight.

Richard whirls when Ian speaks my name, his eyes widening. "Hey, Maddie," he blurts, seeming incredibly guilty for a few seconds. As if he's hoping I didn't hear what they were talking about. "Who was that on the phone?"

"My mother," I say dismissively, unable to stop looking at Ian. I don't know what's changed, but he's not angry with me anymore. Does it have something to do with whatever he and Richard were arguing over? It sounded like work stuff, but I have no way to be sure. I'd missed most of it.

"Hello, Ian," I venture carefully. He came by the nickname Dark and Stormy because his emotions changed like the weather, flashing from hot to cold, passion to indifference, in seconds. This new, concerned Ian might be gone in the next breath.

"Madeline," he says again. He steps past Richard, and my husband actually glares at him. Now I really want to know what they're fighting about. "I was going to ask if you're okay, but that's a stupid question. Of course you're not okay." A hand goes to the back of his neck, and I know he's flushing with embarrassment, the way he does whenever emotions are part of the conversation. It's something I used to adore about him. "Can I do anything to help?"

Yes, I think, you can tell me what's going on with you and Richard, and why you're suddenly being nice to me. But I say, "Not at the moment. Thank you, though."

He takes another step toward me, looks like he's going to say something else. But Richard interrupts. "Ian was just telling me about a problem we're having at work. It sounds like a big mess," he says. "I'll have to handle it at some point, but I was about to say that I can't right now. He'll just have to deal with it himself until we find Renata," he adds with a pointed look at Ian.

Ian's eyes flash with fury, but he doesn't say anything.

I bite my lip. This could be an opportunity for me to do something I've been considering for the past few hours, something I can't do with Richard around. And I can't tell him about it, either, because he'll try to stop me. But if he leaves ...

"Whatever it is, it sounds important," I say, choosing my words with care. I have to make my pitch perfectly, or he'll turn it down. "Maybe you should go deal with it. I'll be fine," I say quickly, holding up a hand as he opens his mouth to refuse. "The police aren't going anywhere, and I have a whole bunch of phone calls to make. There's nothing more either of us can do, and we should both try to find a little distraction before we stress ourselves completely useless."

Richard's frown of refusal changes to a considering look. "I don't know. Maybe ..." he says slowly.

"It's okay, honey. Go on," I say. "If anything happens, I'll call you right away."

I can see the moment he relents as relief slides across his face. I think he actually wants to go and take care of whatever this is, probably for the same reasons I mentioned — to distract himself — but he didn't want to ask me if he could leave. He needed me to tell him he could.

"All right. I guess I should." He walks over to me, puts his arms around my waist and kisses me, slow and gentle. Part of me feels like he's warning Ian off, telling his partner to stop being friendly to me. Almost marking his territory. But that's ridiculous. "I'll be home in a few hours," Richard says as he pulls back. "This shouldn't take long."

I nod. "I'll be here," I tell him. "Love you."

"Love you too, babe."

Richard turns and walks past Ian. "Come on," he says briskly. "I want to get back home as soon as possible."

But Ian doesn't follow him right away. Instead he looks at me, and there's a pleading apology in his eyes, so strong that it takes my breath away.

Something's definitely happened to change his mind about whatever he was mad at me for.

I wish I knew what.

Without a word, Ian turns and walks outside after Richard, closing the door behind him. I wait until I hear my husband chat briefly with Jeremy, then car doors opening and closing, and the engine of my husband's truck start up.

Then I go to the kitchen, get the phone book out, and look up Brenda Westhall.

I have to do something to find my daughter. I'm absolutely convinced that no matter who's taken her, even if it's not the impossible, dead-and-unable-to-kidnap-anyone Stewart Brooks, this guy is playing his game. Following his patterns. He knows where he kept the girls, what he did to them, how he killed them. Where he dumped them. And that's what he's doing with my Renata. Forcing her to complete what the killer started with me, but was never able to finish.

The key to getting my daughter back lies in the black hole of memory in my mind. Somewhere in there are the answers, the location of the Singing Woods Killer's lair. I know I'll find her, if I can only remember what happened to me during that missing week. I *have* to remember.

So I'm going to start kicking the hornets' nests of my past, and the first one lies with former detective Brenda Westhall.

30

Madeline—the past

I was finally going home. Well, not home, exactly, but away from Brightside. To a new home, a place of my own. I'd turned eighteen and checked myself out. I was scared, exhilarated, and kind of sad, all at the same time.

I stood outside the gates of the mental hospital — excuse me, 'retreat' — with Wanda beside me, and my pitifully small suitcase at my feet. It was a cold spring day, the brisk wind whipping through my hair and slicing at my thin jacket, but I didn't mind. This was freedom, and I'd take anything the weather wanted to dish up.

"I'm going to miss you, Wanda," I said.

"Aw, sweetie." She turned and folded me into a hug. "I'll miss you, too," she said. "You're one of the good ones. A miracle recovery."

I wasn't so sure about that. Recovery from mental illness, I'd learned, was like a mountain you could never quite climb. Some days you were so far up that you could see the summit, and you were convinced you'd make it to the top if you could only have a few more good days to get there. But before that happened, you'd lose your footing and slide back down. Sometimes only a few steps, or halfway, but sometimes it was all the way to the bottom, where the shadows of other mountains blocked your path and you had to feel your way out of the dark. Then the climb would start all over again, and it seemed longer than ever.

But today was a good day. I could see the summit, and the flag on top said FREEDOM.

"I don't know about miracles," I said with a snort. "But I'll take being one of the good ones."

Wanda smiled. "You always will be," she said.

I watched the circular visitor's drive in front of us with mingled anticipation and dread. My mother was picking me up. When I'd told her last month that I was checking myself out a few days after my eighteenth birthday, she hadn't offered to let me stay with her, and I hadn't asked. I figured I'd sort out the details later. Ian had his own place, and he'd said I could stay with him as long as I wanted. I thought maybe I would for just a few days. I didn't want to impose, and I still wasn't convinced we'd be able to pick up right where we left off in high school, like he thought we could.

So I'd planned to crash with Ian in the short term, find a job, and rent something small for myself.

But then my mother surprised me last week when she called to say that she'd found a one-bedroom apartment, paid the security deposit and three months' rent for me ahead of time, and bought me a used car.

Maybe, in some absent, backhanded way, she still loved me after all.

A car pulled onto the drive, a dark blue sedan with rust along the bottoms of the doors. It wasn't my mother's; she drove a clean, newish-model silver Audi A3. The sedan pulled off to the curb on the far side and stopped. The engine turned off, the driver's side door opened.

And out stepped Detective Brenda Westhall.

I hadn't seen her since my first few months at Brightside, when she'd come in once a week to hassle me about whether I'd remembered anything. With every visit, she'd grown more and more agitated, until finally she'd stopped coming altogether. I thought she'd given up on finding the Singing Woods Killer's lair.

But if that was the case, what was she doing here now?

Brenda stepped over the curb and onto the sidewalk that bordered the drive, headed toward me and Wanda. She looked so much older, like she'd aged ten years instead of two. And instead of a pants suit or black slacks with a white dress shirt, what I'd come to think of as detective clothes, she wore jeans and a baggy sweater. No badge, no gun.

"Madeline Grant," Brenda said as she stopped around ten feet back. "I heard you were getting out today. Thought I'd stop by to wish you good luck."

The wind gusted, carrying the sour smell of alcohol all the way over from Brenda. I glanced at Wanda and saw her frown. She'd smelled it too.

"Thank you," I said cautiously, not knowing what to expect.

Brenda snorted. "I don't mean it, you know," she sneered. "Did you ever remember anything, Madeline? Did you even *try?*"

"All right, that's enough," Wanda said firmly. "Stop harassing my patient."

"She's not your patient anymore, is she? She's a free woman." Brenda took a wavering step forward and pointed an unsteady finger at me. "You're lying. You have been, all this time," she said. "No one could *forget* a week of being tortured and raped—"

"You need to leave, right now." Wanda's voice was loud and authoritative as she grabbed the CB clipped to her waistband. "I'm calling security."

Brenda raised both hands and backed up, fixing me with a sardonic smile. "Someday, I'm going to get the truth from you," she said. "You're going to confess. And I know your secret." Her smile turned into a leer. "It's not rape if it's consensual, is it? You loved that sick bastard, and you were trying to protect him. That's why you 'can't remember'," she spat, using air quotes for emphasis.

I reeled and stumbled with the unexpected onslaught. Where was this coming from? I couldn't even imagine ... no, that wasn't right. Not even close.

Brenda Westhall was insane.

Wanda was furious and looked about to take a swing at the drunk woman. Before she could, Brenda flapped a hand and stomped back to her car, yanking the door open. "I'd think about coming clean, little Madeline," she said. "Before something bad *actually* happens to you."

With that, she plunked down in the driver's seat, slammed the door shut, and drove away.

I clamped a hand to my mouth, breathing hard through my nose, pretty sure I was going to be sick. I'd known the detective was frustrated that I couldn't tell her anything, but this ... how could she say things like that? How could she even *think* it? The idea was monstrous.

But she'd planted a seed of doubt in my mind, and it was starting to grow. I couldn't actually remember what happened, not a damned thing. No matter how hard I tried. That lost week, it could've been anything.

Maybe it had been consensual. Maybe I'd...

The world grayed out for an instant, and then Wanda was there, holding me up. "Whoa, easy there, sweetie," she said as she supported me, helping me straighten. "Listen, don't pay any attention to that crazy woman. Believe me, I know crazy, and she's it."

I gave a weak laugh. "Takes one to know one, right?"

"Exactly." Wanda's smile grew serious. "I'm not kidding, though. All those things she said, she was just pulling them out of her ass. Don't let her get to you, okay?"

"Okay. I won't."

Just then my mother's Audi pulled onto the drive, circling slowly toward me. My heart constricted at the thought of getting into that car with her, of enduring an awkward ride to an apartment I'd never seen, a place she'd secured for me out of guilt.

Wanda must've sensed my tension, because she squeezed my hand and grinned. "You're going to make it, sweetie," she said. "Trust me, I'm a professional."

I hugged her tight and said goodbye, then picked up my suitcase and climbed into the car with my mother. I'd already tucked the encounter with Brenda Westhall into a dark corner of my mind, where I'd probably stumble over it on bad days when I'd fallen into the shadow of the mountain. But for now, the summit was still in sight.

"Hello," my mother said as she pulled from the curve and navigated the circle drive away from the hospital. No 'how are you,' no 'congratulations,' not even my name.

I sighed and leaned my head against the window. "Thanks for picking me up, Mom."

She didn't say 'you're welcome,' either.

Brightside was situated in a rural stretch of unincorporated township, more or less central to four different towns, including Dayfield. It was a fifteen-minute drive back to Dayfield, and another ten through the center of town to the residential east side, where two turns and a pothole-ridden driveway brought us to a parking lot in front of an apartment building.

Neither of us had spoken the whole time.

My mother parked and got out, and I guessed I was supposed to follow her. I climbed from the car, dragged my suitcase out, and turned to look at my new home. It was called Pine Ridge Apartments, according to the awning over the entrance. A tall, shapeless, industrial gray building with five stories, a flat roof, and small balconies with iron bar railings at every other window.

The place had a lot of similarities to Brightside.

Mom was standing by the back of the car, staring at the building. I walked over to her, and she faced me with an unreadable expression. Wasn't she going to say anything?

Finally, she pointed to a dull red Toyota Corolla with a small rust stain on the hood and a larger one on the roof. "That one's yours," she said, handing me a bulky envelope that jingled faintly. "Keys to the car and your apartment. You're on the third floor, number 315. It's furnished. The phone and electric are activated. There's also a debit card in there for your checking account. I deposited five thousand in it to keep you going, until you find a job." She stopped and swallowed once. "The car's in my name, so you don't have to worry about the insurance. Let me know if you want to switch it over to yours."

I stared at her, holding the envelope in numb fingers. "You're not coming in, are you?"

"I ..." She swallowed again. But instead of finishing whatever she was going to say, she gave me a stiff hug, and then walked back to the driver's side door. "My number is programmed into your speed dial," she said. "Call me if you need anything."

With that, she got in the car and started the engine.

I had no choice but to cross the parking lot alone, go into the building alone, find my apartment alone. I wished I'd had the guts to tell her that I *did* need something.

I'd needed my mother.

The apartment wasn't that bad. It was clean, carpeted, and didn't stink. There were four rooms — a living room with couch, chair, and television set; an eat-in kitchen with table and chairs, microwave, and a few dishes in the cabinets; a bedroom with a bed and dresser; and a bathroom with ... bathroom stuff, including a full-sized tub with the shower.

Plenty of space for me, considering I'd spent most of the last two years in a single room with a walled-off toilet and sink.

Later that night, I'd more or less settled in when my doorbell rang. *Mom*, I thought as I stood from the couch, but the brief hope died and I slowed down as I approached the door. It wouldn't be my mother. Maybe it was the landlord, or a neighbor welcoming me to the building.

Maybe it was Brenda Westhall.

There was a peephole in the door. I stepped up quietly and looked through it, and smiled with relief at the familiar face I didn't actually mind seeing.

Ian.

I opened the door, and he grinned like a kid at a birthday party. He had a hand behind his back. "Maddie, it really is you," he said. "I can't believe it. I'm so glad you're out of that place." He brought his arm around and thrust a bouquet of flowers at me. Daisies and carnations and baby's breath. "Can I come in?"

"Sure," I said, my pulse racing just a little as I took the flowers and stepped back. "Thank you, Ian. These are beautiful —"

He cut me off by catching me in a fierce embrace, the second I closed the door behind him. Surprise stole my breath as I hugged him back, feeling his solid warmth.

Then I burst into tears.

Instead of letting go, he hugged me tighter and massaged the small of my back. "It's okay, Maddie," he murmured softly. "Everything's going to be okay now. I promise."

I couldn't tell him why I was really crying.

He was giving me what I should've gotten from my mother. Happiness, welcoming warmth. Love.

When my personal storm subsided, I found a tall glass for the flowers, and we sat down and talked. It turned out Ian lived in this building, too. He'd found out I was moving in from the landlord, and he'd come straight over when he got out of work. He was on the second floor, in 265.

He ordered dinner for us. We ate, watched a movie, and enjoyed each other's company, talking about anything and everything. At the end of the night, he gave me a chaste kiss and went back to his place, without even trying to get invited to the bedroom. He was giving me the space I needed to readjust.

And I'd started to think maybe we could make this work, after all.

31

Thursday, June 5, 12:30 p.m.

When I walk out of the house, I tell Officer Jeremy I'm going for a drive. He seems dubious, but he doesn't try to stop me. I get into my car, and as I'm buckling the seat belt, my phone rings. It's Detective Burgess.

I answer, and he says, "We've taken Trevor Downes into custody."

My heart wrenches. "Did you find her? Did you find my daughter?"

"Not yet. We're satisfied that she's not on the grounds at his home," Tom says.

That doesn't sound satisfying. "Where do you think she is, then?" I say. "What made you arrest Trevor?"

"He's not under arrest. He's being questioned." The detective makes a thick sound. "We found what can only be described as a shrine in his basement," he says. "Dedicated to the Singing Woods Killer. It's extremely unpleasant."

I close my eyes, imagining what 'extremely unpleasant' looks like. "But there's no sign of Renata," I say. "Right?"

"At this point, no. And Downes does seem to have a solid alibi for the time frame of the disappearance. We're checking on it now." Tom blows out a breath. "It's unlikely that he's the one, but we're going to make damned sure before we let him go. Even if he's not, I almost want to arrest him anyway."

My vision of 'extremely unpleasant' gets worse when I hear the fury and disgust in his voice. Whatever Trevor has in his basement, it must be beyond awful.

"But we've had to release Frank Kilgore," the detective says after a minute. "The hotel security cameras show him going into his room around noon on the day in question, and he doesn't leave it until my officers arrived at 2 A.M. There's also no evidence suggesting he was involved in the kidnapping."

I'm not sure how I feel about that. I know Frank is cunning, maybe even dangerous, and I've always suspected he had something to do with the missing girls twenty years ago. He'd known too much about the case. But I can't prove that, and I guess cameras don't lie.

All I have is evidence that he lied and manipulated his way into Brightside, took pictures that he had no right to take, and printed a story that never should've seen the light of day. A story about my pregnancy, the victim giving birth to the serial killer's baby. I don't know how many people read that story, but I'm glad the New Tribune isn't exactly the most popular or reputable paper. Hopefully, most people thought it was a sensationalized load of crap, like just about everything else they printed.

Frank is a complete scumbag, but that doesn't mean he's kidnapped my daughter.

"Okay. Thank you, Tom," I finally say. More than ever, I'm determined to go through with my plan to dredge up my past, to break through the walls in my mind that are keeping me from the truth about my dark, missing week. I know Detective Burgess and the rest of the police are doing their best, and I appreciate it, but it's clearly not getting them anywhere.

And my daughter is running out of time.

"We're about halfway through the interview list, and we should be finished up sometime this afternoon," Tom says. "So just hang tight, Madeline. I'll update you as soon as we find something out."

I thank him again, and we end the call. I wonder if they've gotten to Ian yet, if maybe that's why he's done such an about-face with the way he's been toward me. It could be just an act so no one will get suspicious of him.

Putting the mystery of Ian aside for the moment, I start the car and drive to Brenda Westhall's address.

The ex-detective lives across town, on a street that borders the Singing Woods. Instead of cringing away from the sight this time, I stare at the tall, gloomy trees in the background, willing them to speak my secrets to me as I pull into a blacktop driveway behind a battered little Ford that sits in front of a closed one-car garage. But the trees are as silent as my missing daughter.

I'm still in the car, and I try Renata's phone again before I get out. It rings and rings, and a recording tells me that my daughter is unavailable.

She won't be for long. I'm going to find her.

I get out and head for the front door of the small white saltbox with green trim and red shutters. Other than the car in the driveway, there's no indication of life here, but I ring the doorbell anyway. I'm shaking as I wait for someone to answer, wondering if it'll even be Brenda. Maybe she's married, maybe she has a family.

Maybe she's peeking through a window right now, deciding that she's not going to speak to me.

Maybe she has my daughter in there.

Eventually I hear shuffling steps that stop on the other side of the door. The click of a lock drawing back, the knob turning.

The woman who peeks out cautiously at me should be not-quite-fifty, but looks seventy. Her dark hair is loose and unwashed, shot with gray, framing a face with deeply grooved lines and a permanent scowl. Her sunken eyes narrow as she takes me in, and then lets out a snort of disgust.

"Go away," she spits at me, and slams the door in my face.

I jam the doorbell again, pound on the door. "Detective Westhall, I need your help. Please," I shout. "My daughter's been abducted."

She's not going to talk to me, I think, just before there's a reluctant sigh and the knob turns again. The door creaks open onto soupy gloom. "Come in," the unseen woman says.

I step through quickly, deciding not to ask what changed her mind in case she changes it back. "Thank you," I say as I look around, trying to see where she's gone.

"Close the door," a voice says from somewhere to my left. As I reach back and swing it shut, a lamp flickers to life, pushing back the shadows.

The small living room is cluttered and dusty, furnished with a faded couch and chair that don't match, the lamp on a rickety side table, a scuffed coffee table holding a remote and a dirty bowl and spoon, and a flat-screen TV on a stand. Little puffs of dust swirl around my feet as I walk slowly onto the dulled carpet. There's a false fireplace on the back wall, the mantle stuffed with a striking and eclectic assortment of angel figurines, from chubby cherubs to elegant porcelain sculptures to pagan-esque winged shapes made with twisted sticks.

And on either side of the fireplace are several waist-high stacks of newspapers and magazines, from yellowed with age at the bottom to brand new at the top.

My throat tightens, and I wonder if she's also got a handy supply of scissors and glue.

Brenda, who'd been standing by the lamp, flicks a glance at me and crosses the room. "Take a seat," she says as she scoops the bowl and spoon from the coffee table and heads for what I presume is the kitchen. "I'm going to have a beer. Want one?"

"No, thank you," I say. It's barely after noon, and I'm not big on drinking, anyway. Especially beer.

She shrugs. "Suit yourself."

She vanishes into the kitchen, and I settle carefully at one end of the couch. I hear the bowl rattle in the sink, the snick and hum of a fridge door opening, metal cans bumping together. Brenda comes back with two cans of Milwaukee's Best, one in each hand, and places one on the coffee table before she drops into the chair and cracks the other. "That one's for emergencies," she says, cackling as she sips from the can. "So, what do you think of my place?"

I'm stuck for an answer. *It's nice* is going to sound like a polite lie, and *maybe you should vacuum* like a patronizing insult.

"Don't answer that. I know it's a shithole." Brenda flaps a hand at me and takes another swallow. "You said your daughter was abducted," she says. "When?"

"Yesterday." It already seems like a lifetime ago, the eternity I've spent without Renata. "Right on the ... twenty-year anniversary."

"Of the day you killed him." She cocks her head and gives a twisted smile. "You think it was him, don't you? The Singing Woods Killer, back from the grave."

I want to say yes, even though she's mocking me. Instead I say, "I'm not crazy, Detective Westhall."

"It's not Detective anymore, is it?" she snarls. "Thanks for that, by the way. I didn't actually like my job or anything."

Irritation flashes through me. "I didn't make you quit."

"No, you couldn't have, because I *didn't* quit. I was 'asked to resign'," she says, making air quotes around the words, the way she did years ago at Brightside with 'can't remember.' "And yes, it *was* your fault. Because you wouldn't tell me what happened, so I never found that bastard's lair, and ... everything went sideways. The whole goddamned thing," she mutters, staring off into the distance.

I've had enough of this. "I didn't tell you because I *couldn't*," I half-shout. "Why can't you get that through your head? *I don't remember.* It's all gone, and I need it back! That's why I'm sitting here, listening to you blame me for your shitty life!"

I hadn't meant to go that far, but it's out there now. And I'm tired of being polite.

"Hey, now. Where'd those claws come from, kitten?" Brenda smiles darkly and tips the can back, swallowing fast. "So you want me to help you remember," she says. "Where was this motivation all those years ago, when *I* needed to know?"

"My *motivation* is sixteen years old, hurting and scared out of her mind, with some psycho's clock ticking down on her life," I say, pinning her with a cold stare. "All those years ago, I was just a kid myself. My father was dead, my mother abandoned me, and I gave birth to a baby at seventeen, alone in a mental hospital. But I'm sure you know all that." I'm silently daring her to refute me. "You just didn't care."

Brenda stares at me with dead eyes. "What, exactly, do you want from me?"

"I don't know. The truth, or at least as much of it as you can give me," I say. "Whoever's got my daughter, they know a hell of a lot about the Singing Woods Killer. They're following his patterns. And if I don't remember what *I* know, I'm never going to get her back."

I'm shocked when sympathy softens Brenda's face, peeling some of the years back. She doesn't say a word, but she leans forward and sets the beer can on the coffee table, then stands and walks from the room, down a darkened hallway to the left of the fake fireplace.

A door opens, and a wedge of light spills into the hall. I hear her shuffling and rustling around. Something creaks, and she grunts and huffs for a few seconds.

Then she's in the hallway, headed toward me, carrying a battered brown file box that's stuffed tight with folders and papers.

She drops the box on the couch next to me, steps back and folds her arms. "Go on, take it," she says. "That's everything we had on the SWK case. All the notes, all the reports and photos, copies of the evidence. Maybe something in there will jog your memory."

"Thank you," I say softly, knowing she wants me to leave now. I stand and lift the box, surprised at how heavy it is. It's got to weigh fifty pounds, at least.

Brenda moves to the front door and opens it. As I cross the room, she says, "You and I do have a few things in common, you know."

I raise a questioning brow.

"I had a baby at a young age, too. He was beautiful, but I had to give him up." Her gaze is unfocused, glistening with memories. "I was never able to conceive after that."

My heart sinks. That's a terrible thing for any woman to go through. "I'm so sorry," I say, and mean it.

She nods, as if accepting and dismissing my sympathy. "I hope you find your daughter," she says.

"So do I."

I walk outside and hear the door slam behind me as I head to my car. This is a start, at least. I do feel bad for everything that's gone wrong for Brenda Westhall, and while I'm not sure I can forget the way she treated me, maybe I can forgive her.

I'm concentrating on opening the car's back door and maneuvering the heavy box onto the seat, so I don't see the piece of paper that's stuck under my windshield wiper until, keys in hand, I grab the handle of the front door. A scream curdles in my throat when I spot it, and I let go of the car and move forward cautiously, until I can make out what it is.

Another magazine-letter note. No envelope this time, so I can read the message without having to touch it.

Six days left.

Tick-tock, Madeline.

My hands shake as I fumble my phone from my pocket and call Detective Burgess.

32

and miles to go

She's not taking the hint. I've tried everything.

It's her fault that it's come to this. If she'd just left, taken her special brand of crazy somewhere else, then this thing with the girl never would've happened.

I was better. I swear it. But I'm getting so confused lately, remembering things from the past and mixing them all up in my head with the present. It's hard to keep my stories straight. Now I've dragged the girl into it all, and I didn't mean to. I didn't want to.

She made me do it.

Of course, she's not going to see it that way. She thinks *I'm* the crazy one, the psychopath, the cold-blooded killer. But it wasn't like that. Not at all. I only wanted to be loved back.

Then there was panic, and screaming, and I had to make it stop.

I just had to make it stop.

I should've known something was wrong with her, when she said that turned her on.

I'm really stuck in this now. I can feel them closing in on me. They'll find me soon, and then what am I going to do?

They're going to find out everything.

33

Thursday, June 5, 1:45 p.m.

Detective Burgess isn't pleased with me.

After I call him, I wait in my car, convinced that Brenda is watching me from the house. I'm shaken, trying to figure out if she had enough time to come out here and put the note on my windshield while I was here. She'd left my sight twice in the house, but I'd heard her moving around inside the whole time. She couldn't have done it.

But what if she has an accomplice? Someone hiding in another room, or maybe the garage, who left the note while we were talking. It's not impossible.

I'm working myself up, and I've got to stop. I need to stay calm.

It's not long before Burgess and McKenzie arrive in the unmarked sedan with the light bar. There's a squad car right behind them, lights flashing. As I get out of the car to meet them, Brenda's front door bangs open and she storms out, glaring fire at me.

"You called the police?" she shouts as she stalks toward me, ignoring the sudden door slams, the shouts from Burgess and the uniformed cops. "You've got one hell of a nerve coming here, asking for my help, and then trying to turn me in!"

"Stop right there, Westhall! Get your hands up!" Burgess shouts.

She does, and I cringe at the naked hatred on her face. This is not going the way I imagined it would.

As Burgess and McKenzie jog up the driveway, I point to my car, to the note still wedged beneath my wiper. "That's why I called them," I say to Brenda. "It's about my daughter. A threat."

"Well, *I* didn't put it there," she snaps. "You know I didn't. I've been in the house the whole time."

Burgess comes up beside me, and McKenzie heads for Brenda, taking his handcuffs from his belt.

"You've got to be kidding me." Brenda gapes at him. "Is that really necessary?"

"Hold up, McKenzie," Tom says, giving me a warning look that I take to mean I should stay out of this. I don't have a problem with that. "Westhall, I'd like my unit to search your house," he says. "If you'll allow that, I won't cuff you."

She rolls her eyes and lowers her hands. "Knock yourselves out, boys. Door's open."

Two officers in uniform enter the house, and a third officer wearing a windbreaker with CSU on the back heads to my car, carrying a briefcase. He must be collecting the evidence.

Tom sighs deeply and folds his arms. "Why did you come here, Madeline?" he says. "I haven't even questioned Westhall yet."

"Excuse me. You were going to question me?" Brenda says in a shrill voice. "I have nothing to do with this!"

McKenzie takes the ball. "We have to question everyone who may have a grudge against the victim," he says, the handcuffs still in his hand. "Come on, Westhall. You were on the force, and you know the procedure."

"Fine," she huffs. "But you're wasting your time. I don't have enough energy to hate her that much anymore."

"You're really not helping your case here," McKenzie says.

Brenda snorts. "What case? You've got nothing, rookie."

"I've got probable cause and a threatening note."

"All right, enough," Tom says, fighting a smirk. "Let's not play the veteran-rookie game, shall we? I think we can clear all this up with a few questions." He shakes his head and turns to me. "As for you. I know how you're feeling, but —"

"No, you don't," I say, trying not to think about the latest note, and how whoever has my daughter was less than twenty feet from me. And I failed to stop them. "You have no idea how I'm feeling."

His face twitches slightly. "Madeline, you need to let us do our jobs," he says. "Please don't do anything like this again. Promise me."

I can't promise. I *won't.* But I have to say it, or I'll find myself under virtual house arrest with the police following my every move, until it's too late for my daughter.

"All right. I promise," I tell him.

His expression says *why don't I believe you?*, but he nods in confirmation. "Go on home, and try to relax," he says.

Luckily, going home is exactly what I intend to do, so he can't be suspicious about that.

I just won't relax.

I back out of Brenda's driveway, maneuvering carefully past the sedan and the squad car, and head back across town. Within a few blocks, my low fuel light comes on and the car chimes to alert me. I know there's still enough gas to get me back to my house, and to the nearest gas station after that, but I decide to stop and take care of it now. I can use the breather, the chance to do something normal for a few minutes.

I'm in the main part of town, and there's a Sunoco on the next block. I pull in and drive up to a pump, dig through my purse and get my wallet out. When I get out to slide my debit card, I wince a little at the gas prices. They've gone up thirty cents in the past few days.

Or maybe they haven't. Maybe I just wasn't paying attention. Everything before now has blurred together, become a brief, compressed block of Pre-Abduction, the time before Renata was taken from me. Now that it's Post-Abduction, time expands like taffy, every minute lasting hours while I'm helpless to save my daughter.

Rising gas prices are meaningless in post-abduction time.

I decide to fill the tank, so I don't have to bother with it again for a while. I watch the numbers climb without seeing them. Beyond the gas pumps, the door to the convenience store jingles periodically as people go in and out. People buying coffee or soda or snacks, who suddenly find themselves a quart low on oil and don't mind paying an extra dollar or two, who need cigarettes or beer, whose daughters haven't been kidnapped.

Then a voice shouts from the direction of the jingling door: "Madeline! Hey, I need to talk to you!"

I stutter on a breath as I look up and see Frank Kilgore half-jogging toward me, waving something in his hand.

Only it's not Frank. It's an imposter. A charlatan, a fake.

And the thing he's waving is a gun.

I yank the fuel nozzle out of my tank, spilling gas down the side of the car, on the ground, on my shoes as I jam it back into the pump and snap the car's fuel door closed. The gas cap isn't on, it's dangling beneath the fuel door on its plastic safety strap, but I don't care. The car will still run.

Jerking the door open, I slide in and toss my wallet on the seat with my purse.

"Madeline, wait!" the imposter Frank screams.

I slam the door, twist the key and drive off without fastening my seat belt for possibly the only time in my life. I am *not* waiting around for the man who isn't Frank to shoot me.

When I've put at least four turns and twelve blocks between myself at the gas station, I pull over to the curb, shaking and gasping. Slowly, my senses fade to normal levels and I grip the steering wheel in both hands and rest my forehead on the curve. A sob wrenches itself from my throat.

I've realized what actually happened back there, and I'm horrified.

Why now? I can't deal with the symptoms of my condition resurfacing, not when so much is at stake. Not when my life, my *daughter's* life, hinges on my ability to keep a clear head, to be a sane person who knows that no one goes around impersonating random people just to screw with someone's head. That the thoughts generated by Capgras aren't real, could never be real, no matter how real they seem.

I've got to speak with Dr. Bradshaw. There's something wrong with my medication.

I call her right then, sitting sideways in the driver's seat with the door open and my feet on the road. A few cars driving by slow down, as if they're going to stop and help, but I wave them by. They can't help me.

After three rings, I get a recorded message: 'You've reached the office of Dr. Gillian Bradshaw. I'm in a session right now. If you are a current patient, please press one to leave a message. If you are a new patient looking to schedule a consultation—"

I press one and wait for the beep.

"Hi, it's Madeline," I say. "Please call me as soon as you can. I'm having a problem."

I hang up and scrub a hand down my face, pocket my phone and walk down the length of the car to screw the gas cap on. I close the fuel door, get back in, and buckle my seat belt. I am not insane. I am a normal, rational adult who obeys the rules of the road, and who doesn't see imposters running at me, waving guns.

What *did* Frank have in his hand?

This time I drive home with no interruptions and pull into the driveway. Richard's truck isn't here, and I'm glad, because I want to look at the contents of Brenda's file box alone. I haul it from the car and head from the house. Officer Jeremy offers to help, but I wave him off and tell him I'm fine as I wrestle the box inside and deposit it on the dining room table, where I'll have plenty of room.

Two hours later, I'm thoroughly sickened but no closer to recovering my memories.

There's so much in here. Files on potential suspects, police reports from people calling in with tips, articles about the case clipped from newspapers, transcripts of 911 calls from people who found the bodies. Maps of the Singing Woods marked with circles and Xs and arrows and pinpoint holes where thumbtacks were stuck through. Pages and pages of notes in close, blocky handwriting that I assume is Brenda's.

Crime scene photos of the victims. I look at those by accident, not realizing what they are until Dana Moody's bruised, bloody, dead face stares at me from the center of an eight-by-ten glossy, and I slam the folder full of pictures back in the box and spend the next five minutes crying myself breathless.

After that, I decide to focus on Brenda's notes. They're a mix of fact and speculation with some plausible theories and a few wild ones, including her unfounded suspicion that I'd cooperated with the killer and was lying about my memory loss. That I'd slept with him on purpose. The detail she went into on that one turn my stomach.

Then, in the middle of a page of notes concerning a theory that the killer had an accomplice, most of them crossed out or written over, I find a name printed in bold letters, scribbled darkly in ink and heavily circled.

Jessica Forrest.

The name holds no meaning for me, and it's not connected to anything else in Brenda's notes. It's just there, as if in the middle of trying to puzzle out this case, the detective had suddenly thought of something completely random and unrelated, and made it stand out on the page so she'd remember to check on it later.

But I'm intrigued, so I start searching the rest of the documentation, looking for more information. And I find there's nothing else. Jessica Forrest, whoever she is, never gets mentioned again.

As I'm trying to organize the files and loose papers in some sort of chronological order, so I can review the whole case from the beginning, my cell phone rings. I suspect it's Detective Burgess, who probably wants to make sure I actually went home and remind me again to leave police business to the police.

It is Tom, but he's not calling for the reason I expected.

"We have Dallas Walsh," he says. "A squad car picked him up six blocks from Brenda Westhall's place on a drunk and disorderly call. And we've found a fingerprint on the new note that's a match to him."

He has her. That drunk, belligerent, hateful old man has my daughter.

"I'm coming to the station," I say, and hang up before Tom can tell me no.

34

Thursday, June 5, 5:30 p.m.

I'm sitting in a hard plastic chair in a hallway at the police station, where people with guns and badges and clip-on name tags in various combinations of suits and uniforms keep walking past me in both directions. Sometimes they run. It's a busy place, filled with light and noise and activity, but there's a kind of chaotic rhythm to it all.

Around the corner, Detective Burgess is in an interrogation room, questioning Dallas Walsh.

He wouldn't let me drive myself here. When I'd rushed out of the house, my purse trailing from my arm, Jeremy stepped in front of me and told me not to get in the car. I'd almost exploded at him before he explained that he was going to drive me to the station himself, that Minks and Valjean — the two officers in the squad car — were going to stay at the house and wait for another car to arrive, and we could leave right then.

At least Tom didn't try to stop me from coming here. He knows enough about me now to understand that I wouldn't let him stop me.

If Dallas has my daughter, I want to know immediately. I want to look into that bastard's eyes and curse him for what he's done. Tell him that Angeline would be ashamed of what he's become.

It's a low blow, and I know it. But words are all I have.

I tried to call Richard, to tell him where I am, but his phone went straight to voicemail again and I didn't bother leaving a message. I'm too wound up. I've been waiting nearly an hour when Tom comes around the corner. His shirt's untucked, his tie loosened, and his hair is damp and sticking to his temples. There are dark hollows under his exhausted eyes, and when I look into them, I see the answer to a question I don't have to ask.

They haven't found my daughter.

"What did he say?" I ask as I start to rise, but he waves me back down and sits in the chair beside me. "Tom, please. Did he take her? Does he have Renata?"

"Not according to him." Tom leans forward, propping an elbow on his thigh as he runs the other hand through his hair. The motion leaves damp spikes leaning at crazy angles and it makes me think of cop shows, gruff coffee-guzzling detectives, Brenda Westhall. He hasn't told me how it went, questioning her, but I'm focused on Dallas now. Leaver of threatening notes. Crazy old man I tried to feel sorry for, actually *defended* in front of my daughter.

If he touched her, after that little speech I gave about being nice to him, I'll never forgive myself.

"Walsh claims that he didn't create the notes," Tom says, the set of his jaw suggesting he doesn't believe that in the least. "He says he found the first one shoved under his front door, with directions saying that if he put the envelope in your mailbox, he'd get five hundred dollars. He says that after he did it, the cash was delivered in the same way, with another note telling how to make five hundred more."

"That's insane," I whisper. If he's telling the truth, then whoever's abducted my daughter is extremely careful and deliberate. If he's right, there's a far more complicated plan than simply snatching a sixteen-year-old girl off the street and holding her somewhere.

"Yeah, tell me about it." Tom shakes his head, as if to clear it. "He doesn't have an alibi, but that's not surprising. I've got officers at his home looking for these mystery letters and envelopes of cash. Walsh thinks he might have gotten rid of the letters and the envelopes, and just kept the money. How convenient."

"But she's not there," I say. "My daughter isn't at his house."

It's not a question, but Tom answers anyway. "There's no one in the house. That's the first thing they checked for," he says, and frowns. "But Dallas Walsh owns five acres of land. Most of it's wooded."

All the breath goes out of me as I envision my baby, my kind and intelligent young woman, alone in the woods in God knows what kind of physical shape, terrified out of her mind. I can't take this.

"Let me talk to Dallas," I say.

"Absolutely not." Tom is firm, unshakably resolute. "There's no way I'm allowing the mother of a kidnap victim to speak to a suspect. Even if I thought it was a good idea, which I don't, I'd lose my job for that. And probably end up in jail."

"All right," I say. I'm disappointed, but I do understand. "Can I at least see him? You have one of those two-way mirror windows in the interrogation room, don't you?"

He flashes a tired smirk. "Don't believe everything you see on TV," he says. "We do, actually, but most stations don't." He pauses, tips his head back and closes his eyes as he mulls over my request. "Okay, I suppose you can see him," he says. "McKenzie is in there with him now. I don't know what good it's going to do you, though."

I don't know either, but I feel like I have to do this.

Tom leads me around the corner and to the end of a short hallway. To the left is a dented metal door, and then a large, thick window set into an industrial metal frame. The window looks tinted, and a fine diamond-pattern mesh runs through the glass, but I can see easily into the room behind it.

Dallas is seated at a thick table, in a chair that's bolted to the floor. His hands are cuffed to a metal ring embedded in the table. He leans forward slightly, head bowed, as McKenzie stands across from him shouting something. The sergeant's words are muffled sounds, even at the volume he's using.

"You want to hear them, don't you?" Tom says.

I nod. "Yes, please."

"I really can't imagine why," he says with a sigh, and then gestures. "Press the speaker button and hold it down. It's just to the right of the window."

I find a metal plate mounted to the wall with a circular grated vent and a small, red plastic button beneath it. I press the button.

"—know you threatened Madeline Osborn at that meeting!" McKenzie comes in mid-shout, his features set and furious. "Why *wouldn't* we believe you had something to do with her daughter's disappearance?"

A rattling wheeze emerges from Dallas. "I wouldn't hurt anybody's girl," he says as he raises his head slowly. His ruddy, rough-whiskered face glistens under the light of the interrogation room. "I just wanted her to leave. Leave town, that's all. Every time I look at her, I see my baby, my Angeline ..." He hitches a deep, phlegmy sob. "I just wanted that woman out of my sight!"

I release the button as a shudder moves through me. "He didn't take my daughter," I whisper, hugging myself.

"Madeline, you can't know that," Tom says gently as he puts an arm around my shoulders and steers me away from the window. "He left those notes, and that's plenty of evidence to formally arrest him. We're going to search every inch of his property, too. We'll bring her back to you."

I nod slowly, knowing there's nothing I can say now. They have their suspect, and they're going to squeeze him until he pops. But they won't find anything inside him. Dallas Walsh is an empty shell, incapable of anything beyond boozing and bluster.

He doesn't have Renata. And it's going to be up to me to find out who does.

"I think I'll call Richard and ask him to bring me home," I say. "Will you tell me if you find anything, please?"

"Of course," Tom says, all warmth and reassurance. "It's only a matter of time now."

He's right, but not in the way he thinks. It's just a matter of time until Renata's clock winds down and she meets the violent end that was meant for me.

I won't let that happen. I will not fail my daughter.

I'm going to remember everything.

35

Thursday, June 5, 7:01 p.m.

Richard and I are at the Rainforest Café, a place with meaning for us. He brought me here on our first date. But since I was still getting over the bizarre, unexpected breakup with Ian at the time and wasn't ready to try another relationship, he'd insisted that it wasn't really a date.

"Think of it as a test drive," he'd said. "You can take this gently used, late-model Richard in fair condition with optional extras out for a spin, and at least you'll get free coffee and refreshments out of it, even if you decide you're not in the market."

I thought I'd die laughing. He'd won me over pretty quickly after that.

Now, he'd brought me here to try and shock me out of my stupor. I'd been so upset when he picked me up at the police station that I could barely speak.

I had to admit, it was working. I was already starting to relax, to breathe easier.

He'd ordered us both lattes and a huge plate of assorted fresh-baked cookies that we'd never get through. I know I have to tell him about Dallas, and about the box of files I'd gotten from Brenda that was still strewn all over the dining room table. He hadn't been home yet when I got hold of him.

I'll be ready to talk in a minute.

I cup both hands around my mug and sip at the latte, closing my eyes as the warm, sugary liquid slides down my throat. It tastes wonderful, and I feel guilty enjoying it. I shouldn't enjoy anything while my daughter is still missing.

Richard is patient, as always. He doesn't say anything, doesn't needle me with questions he must be dying to ask, until I'm calm enough to speak.

Finally, I say, "The police have Dallas Walsh in custody, and they think he did it. But they can't find Renata."

To my husband's credit, he doesn't explode, though he looks like he wants to. "Are they sure it was him?" he says.

"No, they just strongly suspect. He has a motive, no alibi, and five acres of wooded property." I take another sip of latte. "And they found his fingerprint on one of the notes."

"Wait a minute," Richard says in a strained voice. "*One* of the notes?"

I explain quickly about my visit to Brenda Westhall, the box of files, the note on the windshield. I tell him that the files are at our house, and that I've looked through them, but I don't say why yet. "Dallas admits to leaving the notes," I say. "But he claims someone else gave them to him, anonymously, and paid him to deliver them."

"You've got to be kidding me." Richard rams his fingers through his hair, agitated and jumpy. "So now our daughter's abduction is some kind of big conspiracy with creepy notes and secret payoffs? *Why?*"

I shrug. "Detective Burgess thinks he's lying about that," I say. "I don't know if he is or not, but I don't think he took Renata."

Richard scowls. "Why not? He's got a motive, you said it yourself. And that paid-delivery thing sounds like a pile of desperate bullshit, made up by a drunk."

"You should have seen him, Richard," I say softly as I set my mug down, not meeting his eyes. "Dallas Walsh is broken. He's been broken for a long time ... just like me." A memory floats through my brain, and I almost smile. "It takes one to know one."

"What?" My husband reaches across the table and takes my cold hand in his big, rough, warm one. "You're not broken, Maddie. You're the strongest woman I know."

If I was so strong, I'd be able to break this mental block that's keeping me from my daughter.

But I don't say that to Richard.

Instead, I stare out the window at the community center across the street, dark and silent except for the parking lot lamps and the security lights along the front of the building. First date at the Rainforest, wedding at the community center. This place is the cradle of the beginning of our lives as husband and wife.

I got lucky when I found him — or rather, when he found me. Richard has been the most steadying influence in my troubled life, and I don't even want to imagine where I'd be now without him.

I know we'll get through this, together. We'll have our family back.

It's only a matter of time.

36

Madeline—the past

Today was our six-month dating anniversary, and I'd finally decided that I had to tell Richard about my past.

He was different from anyone I'd been with. Not that I had a wealth of dating experience, since my handful of other boyfriends had been in high school. I counted Ian among them, even though I'd dated him beyond high school.

I'd been with Ian for two years, actually, not counting the two-year interruption of my stay at Brightside. It was Ian before, and Ian after. He didn't abandon me while I was locked up, the way everyone else had, and I'd loved him fiercely. For that, and more. I truly thought he was the one.

Until he'd completely snapped, out of nowhere. One day we were blissfully happy, madly in love, spending all our free time together and talking about the future, where we'd live, what kind of house we'd buy, how many kids we'd have.

The next day he'd bagged up all my stuff and thrown it into the hall outside his apartment. And when I'd tried to confront him about it, he'd screamed at me. Called me a bitch, a traitor, a backstabbing sicko — or maybe it was psycho — and a lot of other names I didn't understand. He wouldn't explain any of it. I'd retreated to my own apartment, where I hadn't actually stayed for months, and a few days later Ian moved out of the building.

I'd thought my heart would stay broken, maybe forever this time. And then Richard came along.

I knew him, more or less, before the first time he'd asked me out. I was working as a waitress at Fresno's, the little diner on Owego Street, and Richard was a regular customer. He came in for lunch Monday through Friday, from noon to 12:45. You could practically set your watch by him. He always sat at the same table, which happened to be in my section, and he always ordered the same thing. An All-American Burger, medium well, with a lightly toasted bun and double fries, coffee and a blackberry lemonade to drink. He also left me a generous tip, every time—five dollars on a fifteen-dollar ticket.

Richard had been coming to Fresno's for six months when Ian left me, and by then we were friends, though it was a very casual basis. He knew I had a boyfriend, but not what his name was or where he lived. When I told him about the breakup, I left out most of the details, but he definitely noticed how devastated I'd been by it. He didn't immediately pounce on newly single me. He talked less and listened more, brought me small gifts, offered to drive me home after a long day on my feet.

When he finally asked me on a date, I said no at first. I didn't think I was ready. But then he said it wasn't really a date, and something about wouldn't I like to test-drive a gently used Richard, and I couldn't say no.

I never regretted that choice.

Tonight we were at the Stone Mill, a fancy new restaurant that had just opened on Main Street. We'd enjoyed a wonderful dinner and our decadent desserts were on the way.

If I didn't tell him now, I'd lose my nerve and never say anything. But he had to know the truth about me, before things got more serious than they already were.

I was pretty sure I'd fallen in love with him.

"Richard ... I have to talk to you about something," I said. We were in a booth, and the soundproofing was good enough that I couldn't make out anyone else's normal-volume conversations around us, so it was unlikely we'd be overheard.

I didn't want that to happen, regardless of how Richard ended up reacting. Enough people in this town already thought I was crazy.

"Uh-oh. This sounds serious," he said with a smile. "Whatever it is, Maddie, you can tell me."

"I know I can. It's just ... hard." I let out a sigh. "There's some personal history I have to tell you about. It's not fair if I don't."

He took my hand, and a warm shock ran through my body. "If this is about the Singing Woods Killer, you don't have to talk about it," he said. "I already know."

"You do?" I whispered. "For how long?"

"Since I moved to Dayfield, since before I met you," he said, rubbing a thumb in circles on the inside of my palm. The movement made me shiver deliciously. "I don't care, Maddie. I mean, I *do* care, but only about you and how you feel. I know people say you're crazy because you were in that mental hospital, but I'm not buying it. You're perfectly sane, and ... well, you're just perfect."

I wanted to cry with relief. "Thank you, Richard. That means a lot to me."

"*You* mean a lot to me," he said.

"You too." I smiled at him. "I'm glad you know," I said. "But there is something specific I want to tell you, if that's okay."

"Of course it is. I want to know everything about you," he said. "Even the unhappy stuff. I can't imagine going through anything like what you did. What it's like living with those kinds of memories. I really admire your strength."

I laughed, surprising myself. I didn't think I had it in me to laugh about what happened. "Actually, I don't have any memories of the ... experience," I said. "I remember someone grabbing me, and then running through the woods. But I guess there was a whole week between those things, and there's just nothing there."

"Really. You blocked it all out?" he said.

"Not on purpose," I said with a smirk. "Apparently my brain did me the favor of erasing whatever happened to me."

"Well, I'm glad you don't have to carry a burden like that," he said. "If you ask me, your brain is really smart."

For some reason, that struck me as hilarious. Of *course* my brain was smart. That was its only job. I laughed so hard that a few people at nearby tables shot me dirty looks, but it was okay. Because Richard was laughing right along with me.

"So, is that what you wanted to tell me?" he said when we'd calmed down a bit. "About your amnesia?"

"No. Unfortunately, there's more." I folded my hands in my lap, knowing this was the point of no return. Richard would either stay with me, or decide that my brand of crazy was too much hassle. But he had to know before I ended up having an episode around him, because if that happened, he'd definitely leave.

"When I was escaping the killer, I suffered a serious head injury," I began slowly. "It left me with a ... condition, called Capgras Syndrome."

He blinked. "Sounds French."

"I think the name is, yeah," I said. "It's really rare." Then I took a deep breath and explained what it was, what it did to me, how it affected other people. I told him about my mother, how my condition scared her out of my life, but I didn't mention the episode with my father. That was still too raw. I mentioned the medication I was on and how it seemed to be working most of the time, but not always.

And I waited for him to abandon me. At least he'd do it politely.

He sat there processing it all for a minute. Eventually he said, "So you'll usually know who I am, but sometimes you might think that I'm someone else who looks just like me?"

"Yes, that's about it," I said. "Weird, right?"

He waggled his eyebrows. "Actually, I think it could be really interesting for our sex life."

For the third time in a single conversation, I burst out laughing when I thought I'd never laugh again. And that was when I knew.

Richard was perfect for me.

37

Friday, June 6, 6:45 a.m.

My daughter has been missing for two days.

I've been up since four, unable to sleep for longer than twenty minutes at a time. Helpless as I feel during normal times, there's less than nothing I can do to advance the search for my daughter in the small hours of the morning while the rest of the world sleeps. So I think, and I pace. I dial her phone, again and again, chipping another piece from my heart every time it rings and she doesn't answer. I read all the evidence from the original case, again and again, until it's meaningless.

My memories remain locked in the vault of my mind, taunting me with hope I'll never reach.

I'd gotten the final update on the interview list from Detective Burgess last night. None of Renata's friends, or their parents, had any useful information. The police have cleared Ian's and Jan's alibis, and I suppose their questioning is the reason Jan hasn't called me once since my daughter was abducted, not even to offer sympathy or support. My mother, of course, is not a suspect, and they've released both Frank and Trevor. So that leaves Dallas Walsh.

At least, that's what the police think. I don't agree. And I can't convince them to stop chasing this lead, so I'll look for a better one on my own.

Richard is still asleep. People handle grief in different ways, and the way he's chosen is sleeping pills and oblivion. I almost envy him the luxury, but what I need is the opposite of blissful ignorance.

I need painful knowledge.

I'm just starting a pot of coffee that I probably won't drink when the kitchen phone rings. Tom only calls my cell now, so I think it must be either Officer Jeremy, who's come back for the day shift at six, or Dr. Bradshaw finally returning my call.

It's Jeremy. When I answer the phone, he says, "Ian Moody is out here, and he'd like to come in. Do you want him there right now?"

I'm surprised he's here so early. It's just after seven, and I know Richard had planned to go to the job site for a few hours today, but that was supposed to be at nine. After all the strangeness that just happened with Ian, I'm not sure I should bring him in while my husband is still sleeping.

But maybe, if my ex hasn't gone back to hating me for no reason, I can find out what he and Richard were arguing about.

"Yes, that's fine," I tell Jeremy. "He can come up. Thank you."

Jeremy acknowledges me, and I hang up the phone and head for the front door, rushing a bit. I don't want Ian ringing the doorbell. When I reach the foyer, my hip bumps the sideboard and the bulky purse I left on it last night slides halfway off. I shove it back, grab the knob, and open the door just as Ian is raising a hand for the bell.

He looks startled, and desperately sad. "Madeline," he says, very quietly. "Is Richard awake?"

"No, not yet."

His expressive green eyes spark with anger. "Good. May I come in?"

Now I *really* want to know what's going on between them.

I step aside to let him pass, and then close the door behind him. "I just started some coffee," I say tentatively, still not sure if his feelings toward me are running hot or cold at the moment. "Do you want a cup?"

"I'd love one." The sadness in his expression is approaching misery.

I start for the living room, and he follows me. "Madeline, there's something I need to tell you—"

"What the *hell* are you doing here?"

That thrumming, angry voice belongs to my husband. He's on the landing halfway down the stairs, a dagger-filled glare fixed on Ian.

"Richard!" I gasp, shocked at the intensity of his rage. I've never seen him this angry.

But Ian ignores the apparent threat. His jaw firms, and he lifts his chin in a quick jerk toward my husband. "You know damned well what I'm doing," he says.

"Get out of my house, Ian." Richard starts down the stairs, fists clenched at his sides. "I told you, I will *not* let you upset my wife any more than she already is."

I want to tell him that I can decide for myself whether I hear what Ian has to say, but I'm too stunned by his behavior. This is nothing like Richard.

Ian stands his ground for a moment longer, but then he's backing into the foyer, keeping a wary gaze on Richard. He hits the sideboard, and my purse slides completely off and thumps to the floor.

"Shit," Ian mutters as he bends to pick it up. "Sorry." He fumbles with the strap for a few moments, and finally manages to drop the purse back in place.

Richard reaches my side and his anger deflates, all at once. "I'm sorry. I didn't mean ..." he mutters, swiping a hand down his face. "Jesus, it's too early for this. Can we please just talk about it at the job site?" he says to Ian. "I'll be there at nine."

"Yeah, sure. No problem," Ian says, though the rigid lines of his body suggest that it's still a very big problem. "See you then."

He slips out the door and closes it with a near-silent click.

Richard puts an arm around me. I stiffen for a few seconds, still reeling from his outburst, but then I relax into him with a drawn-out exhale. "I'm so sorry about that, babe," he says. "It's the stress. It's really getting to me. And ..."

I look up at him. "And what?"

"Honestly? I don't trust Ian right now." It seems like it pains him to say that. "Will you sit down with me for a minute? I'll explain why."

"Of course," I say. "Do you want coffee? I just made some."

"That sounds fantastic."

He drops on the couch, still barely awake, and I go to the kitchen and take out two mugs. Fixing the morning coffee for the two of us is as natural as breathing, and the ritual briefly comforts me. Cream and sugar, one and one for me, three and two for him, add coffee, stir. I pick up the mugs — mine in the left hand, his in the right — and walk back to the living room to sit beside him.

Richard takes the coffee and sips gratefully, and then releases a sigh toward the ceiling. "So, there was a problem with the books at work," he says. "That's why I went in yesterday. Ian claimed there were discrepancies and said I'd done something wrong. He'd decided I did it on purpose."

I frown. "Why would you do that? I mean, why would he think ..."

"That was pretty much what I said, when he told me that," he says. "Why would I screw over my own company? But he was insistent, accusing me of stealing. From myself, apparently." His lips pressed together firmly, and his gaze clouded. "When I reviewed the records yesterday, I did find issues. And I tracked down the real problem."

"What happened?" I say.

"It was Ian. *He's* the one siphoning funds." Richard pales suddenly, looking like he might throw up. "I haven't told him that I know yet, because I think I found out what he's spending it on, and ..."

"Oh, honey. What is it?" I take his hand, horrified that he has to go through something like this in the middle of the worst personal crisis of our lives. This means I'm probably right about Ian's sudden mood change. He's trying to throw suspicion away from himself, maybe even hoping to get me on his side because of our past relationship.

How could he possibly think I'd take his side over my husband's?

"God, I don't know if I can even say it." Richard gulps hard, and his eyes gloss over with tears. "I think he's using the money for ... girls," he says, his voice cracking on the word. "Girls that are ... not old enough."

My aching sympathy turns to horror. I can't believe that, not from

Ian. Yes, he's brash, and possibly emotionally unstable. He's had very few long-term relationships and hasn't dated in a few years, as far as I know, so he's probably lonely. But underage girls? Ian isn't a pedophile.

How do you know that?

My mind whispers the question, and I don't have an answer. And suddenly my heart turns to ice as I think of my daughter, and Ian's inexplicable rage toward me all these years.

I think of Dallas Walsh, hating me for surviving. And how Ian's sister was also murdered by the Singing Woods Killer.

"Richard," I croak through numb lips. "You don't think he would —"

He shudders and closes his eyes, and I know that's exactly what he's been thinking.

"We have to tell Detective Burgess, right now," I say breathlessly, bolting upright as I reach for my phone on the coffee table. "If he —"

"Maddie, wait." Richard takes my hand and pulls it back gently. "I'm not completely sure about this yet," he says. "The police have already questioned him, and I don't think they'll bring him back in if we tell them we have a 'feeling' about it. Do you?"

I have to admit he's right.

"Let me look for proof," he says. "That's why I'm going into work today. I could still be wrong, but if I find anything that even suggests I'm right, I'll call the detective myself."

I don't like waiting even a moment longer than necessary when there's a possibility that we can find Renata. But if we pull the trigger too early, and the police refuse to question him further, he could get away with it. And then we may never find her.

"All right," I say shakily. "Please let me know right away if you find something." I'm still stunned that Ian would do something like this, *be* something like this, and I can't quite believe it. But I know why I'm resisting the idea.

I don't want to think I'd been stupid enough to date a pedophile for so long.

I leave Richard to get ready for work and go back to the files on the dining room table, poring over them in detail once again. While I have to admit there's a possibility that Ian might be guilty of this, and maybe had something to do with Renata's abduction, I can't do what the police are doing right now. I can't fixate on a single potential and ignore the rest.

I'm still going to do anything and everything to enter the black hole in my head, so I can find my daughter.

38

Friday, June 6, 8:30 a.m.

When Richard leaves for the job site, I call Dr. Bradshaw's office again. I still want to ask about my prescription, but I've had another idea that I want to run by her as well. Something we've never tried that might help me recover my memories.

This time she answers and greets me by name. "Madeline, I'm so sorry that I didn't return your call yesterday," she says, sounding flustered. "My new receptionist somehow managed to erase all my messages and didn't tell me about it until this morning. I'd been going through the caller ID, trying to piece things together, and I'd just seen your name right before the phone rang, when you called. Have you found anything yet about Renata? I know exactly how much of a nightmare this must all be for you."

She finally pauses for breath, just when I think I won't be able to get a word in edgewise. "No, we haven't found anything yet. But the police have a suspect," I say, not wanting to get into the details about Dallas Walsh. I know she won't ask for specifics, anyway. She's very good at not pushing too hard on people who are already under tremendous strain. "That's not why I'm calling, though," I say. "I think there's a problem with my new prescription."

"Really. Why do you say that?"

"The pills are different. At least, they're different from the last time I had this strength." I tell her about the size and shape of the tablets, the lack of markings. "Also, I've had a few episodes," I admit. "Nothing intense, and so far I've snapped out of it quickly and been able to recognize them as episodes. But it's worrying."

"It certainly is," Dr. Bradshaw says with real concern. "I don't recall any changes in formulation for pimozide, even at the higher dosage. Maybe there was some kind of mix-up at the pharmacy." There isn't much certainty behind those words. "I'd like you to switch back to the lower dosage for now. You still have some of the old prescription left, don't you?"

"Yes, I had two weeks' worth left when I switched over," I say. I haven't taken today's morning dose yet, so I'll do that with the lower-dosage pills when I finish talking to her.

"All right, good. Go ahead and take one and a half tablets of the old pills, and I'll call the pharmacy to get this straightened out and order you a replacement prescription," she says. "I can't believe they'd be so sloppy, dispensing the wrong medication for a controlled substance like this. They really have no idea how drastically this sort of thing can affect people."

I nod, and then realize she can't hear me moving my head. "It really does," I say.

"And for you to go through this now ... it's just inexcusable on their part." Her voice wavers slightly. "I want you to bring that new prescription, the yellow pills, to your next session so we can have them tested. In fact, if you're able, I'd like you to come in for a session later today. I have an opening at five, but if that doesn't work for you, I can move other patients around. You're a top priority right now."

My eyes well up at her show of concern. "Thank you," I say. "Actually, five o'clock will be perfect." That gives me most of the day to wait for whatever Richard finds out about Ian, and to keep sifting through the files for possible leads. "Dr. Bradshaw, there's something I'd like to try at the session, if you're willing. I think it might really help me."

"I'm certainly in favor of things that will help," she says. "What are you thinking?"

I take a deep breath. "Hypnosis."

"Oh, Madeline. I really don't think that's a good idea." She seems distressed over not being able to agree. "I assume you're considering this to deal with your memory block, to try recovering your lost time?"

"Yes, exactly," I say. "Renata ... everything that's happened is so similar to what I went through. If I can just remember that week, I can find his lair. Find my daughter."

Dr. Bradshaw's silence lasts just a little too long. "Madeline," she says gently. "Stewart Brooks is dead. You know that. He hasn't taken your daughter."

Yes, he has! I nearly scream it before I get control of myself. Part of me is convinced, has remained convinced all along, that it's him. It's probably the crazy part of me. But when it comes to saving my daughter, I refuse to dismiss any possibility, even a serial killer who's come back from the grave.

I just won't share that theory with anyone else.

"You're right. I'm sorry," I say. "But I'd really like to try hypnosis. I need those memories for my own sake. For closure."

I hope that throwing out psychological terms will persuade her, but she remains unconvinced. "Hypnosis is only proven to be successful as a relaxation technique," Dr. Bradshaw says. "There's no evidence to suggest that it's an actual, useful tool for recovering hidden memories. In fact, it can be dangerous."

I frown. "How is it dangerous?"

"If a subject isn't responsive to hypnosis, the technique can actually push subconscious memories deeper into the mind," she says, as if reciting from a textbook. "In some cases it's even recovered false memories, complete fabrications that harm the subject further. I don't want to see that happen to you, Madeline."

I can hear the subtext in her words: *You're already confused enough as it is.* I won't be able to convince her to try. At least, not over the phone.

But I'm determined to make this happen, and I think she'll have a much harder time refusing in person. I'll convince her at the session tonight.

"That does sound unpleasant," I say. "Maybe it's not such a good idea, after all."

"I'm sorry. I truly am." I can tell that she means it, that she's disappointed to be unable to help. "You can still come in for a regular session, if you want to."

"Of course. I'd like that," I say. "See you tonight."

We end the call, and I go upstairs for my meds. I open the cabinet in the master bath and see the new, wrong prescription, but not the old bottle. Frowning slightly, I pick up a few other pill bottles that I know aren't the right ones and read the labels, just in case. Ibuprofen, aspirin, multi-vitamins. No one-milligram pimozide.

I check around the bathroom, under the sink, behind the toilet, even in the shower. I rifle through the small trash can filled with mostly paper refuse, but it's not there.

How could I have lost it, when I haven't taken those pills for days?

Getting upset, I grab the new prescription bottle and head back downstairs with a quick scan of the nightstand as I pass through the bedroom, in case I'd left them there for some reason. I haven't. But I may have stuck them in my purse at some point. I'll check it and toss the new bottle in, so I won't forget it when I see Dr. Bradshaw tonight.

In the foyer, I grab my purse from the sideboard and bring it to the living room, where I can have a good rummage through it. I sit on the couch, set the purse and the incorrect prescription on the coffee table, and start digging.

Almost immediately, I find something that doesn't belong in my purse, but it's not my old prescription. It's a small book, a journal of some kind, with a folded piece of paper wrapped around it and secured with a rubber band, and it's certainly not mine. I've never seen it before in my life.

My hands shake as I hold the little book and stare at it. Is this another threatening note? Am I destroying evidence by holding it? If it is a threat, Dallas Walsh didn't deliver this one. But I don't understand how it could've gotten into my purse. It's never out of my sight unless I'm home, and with a constant physical police presence outside, no one could have possibly broken in and put it there.

Then I remember this morning. Ian bumping the sideboard and knocking my purse to the floor, then fumbling with it forever as he picked it up.

He put this book here. I'm sure of it.

And if it's a threatening note, I don't want to wait for the police to process it to find out what it says. Besides, there's no mystery about who delivered it. Ian's the only one who could have.

Before I can talk myself out of it, I yank the rubber band off, take the piece of paper and set the book itself on the coffee table. Then I unfold the paper.

My heart stops as I read what's written on it.

MADELINE,

This book is why I left you ... but it's all wrong, every single word in it. I know now that you never wrote this, that it's all fake. I have proof.

I can't tell you how sorry I am for ever believing this in the first place. Please forgive me.

I still love you.

-Ian

THIS IS the reason for his drastic attitude change. This book, whatever's written in it, and whatever proof he's talking about. I'm not quite sure what it all means, but there's only one way to find out.

I tuck the note into my purse and pick up the book.

When I open the cover, the first thing I see is my own signature. Not Madeline Osborn, but Madeline Grant, in what looks exactly like my handwriting. I flip quickly through the pages and see more of my writing in dated entry format, like a diary. There are quite a few entries in here.

But I'd never kept a diary. Not even while I was in the mental hospital, where it was a 'suggested activity' that I'd refused. This had my name, and my handwriting, but it wasn't mine. Not at all.

Who would do such a thing, write an entire diary in someone else's name?

And why did Ian have it?

I know those questions won't be answered anytime soon, but I have to read it. Somewhere in here is the reason Ian broke up with me. I need to find it.

It's not long before I realize that the fake diary is filled with reasons for Ian to leave, and to react the way he did. I would've reacted exactly the same way if the tables were turned. My stomach churns harder with each entry, my hands shaking as I turn the pages.

This book is a diatribe of hatred and manipulation directed not only at Ian, but at Dana.

Whoever was pretending to be me had written awful, unspeakable things about his murdered sister.

The dates of the earliest entries are a few weeks before my sixteenth birthday, all in blue ink. The first few are innocuous enough, typical teenage thoughts about school, teachers, making weekend plans with Carson, being excited about my upcoming birthday party. Everything is fairly vague, but there's just enough detail to suggest that whoever wrote this knew me, knew my life.

It's completely disconcerting to read this. Nothing is incorrect. It's so flawless that I actually *could* have written it, but I know I didn't.

I didn't write this.

Did I write this?

I have to physically shake off the disquieting thought. That's just not possible. I couldn't have written an entire diary without remembering it.

The first unsettling entry is dated a few days before my birthday. It says that Ian is coming to my party, and that I plan to seduce him. It hints that I have some sort of agenda for snaring him, but doesn't spell out whatever it's supposed to be. It's followed by a few more normal-sounding entries.

Then, the day after my party, the diary gloats about my plan succeeding, that I've captured Ian. And that I'm going to peel his life away from him, piece by piece, until I'm the only person he can trust and depend on and he'll *have* to stay with me forever.

It's a classic description of psychological abuse, written in a teenage voice with a teenager's vocabulary and thought patterns.

And the fake diary keeps getting worse, and worse.

I'm portrayed as obsessively jealous, willing to go to any lengths to make sure Ian pays attention to me and no one else. There are snide comments about his friends, his family, how they're all wrong for him and I'm the only one who understands him. The only one he needs.

And the first of many truly horrific entries is where 'I' say that I hope the Singing Woods Killer takes Dana, because Ian pays too much attention to her, and that attention should be all mine.

There's so much more, pages and pages of sickening, twisted vitriol. I'm only pretending to like Dana so that Ian will love me more, but I actually can't stand her. Tricia Spinks deserved to get murdered because she talked to Ian once.

I'm so glad that Dana is dead.

When I see that, I have to run to the downstairs bathroom, and I barely make it to the toilet in time to vomit. It's horrible enough reading it for myself, but I'm also imagining Ian seeing those words, believing I'd written them. How badly that must have hurt him.

The rest of it is more jealous obsession, and the entries grow increasingly erratic and paranoid. I'm apparently convinced that Ian is sleeping with every female under the sun, and I want the Singing Woods Killer to take them all. Every girl, every woman who's ever laid eyes on my precious boyfriend should die a horrific death.

The dates stop a few days before my abduction, but the 'diary' doesn't end. There's a gap of two years, and then more entries that start when I was released from Brightside. The exact night I was released, actually. These are written in black ink. The first entry after the gap talks about Ian coming to my apartment, and how I still have control over him, and how I'm going to start targeting any other women that may have gotten involved in his life since I've been gone. And it goes on from there, until just after the breakup.

In the final entry, 'I' simply say that I'm going to kill him for leaving me.

When I finally put the little book down, my veins are filled with ice and I'm bathed in cold sweat, shaking so hard that my teeth are chattering. I'm stunned that Ian never called the police, or even tried to have me re-committed. He'd only broken it off with me, without ever mentioning the diary.

He must have truly loved me, to let me off so easily after reading this.

I have to call Richard. He's got to know the real reason Ian's been acting so strangely, that it's not because of the business. Whatever my husband found in the records, there has to be another explanation, because it's not Ian. I need to stop him before he turns Ian in for something he didn't do.

Richard doesn't answer. I'm still in too much shock to get angry, so I leave him a message and then fire off a text that says the same thing. *Don't turn Ian in. Call me.*

I hesitate, and then open my contact list. I'm almost sure that I have Ian's cell phone number in there, even though I never use it. I think Richard entered it there for emergencies, in case I couldn't reach him for some reason.

There it was. I call the number, holding my breath. But Ian doesn't pick up, either.

I leave him a voice message and text him. *I got your note. Please call.*

I'm not sure how long I sit there after failing to reach either of them, wondering what to do next. I don't know where the current job site is, so I can't go there and talk to them. There's no main office for the business, no receptionists for answering questions and scheduling appointments. Osborn Outdoor Services is just Richard and Ian, with varying numbers of part-time, seasonal employees when there's too much work for the two of them.

The ring of the kitchen phone startles me. I jump up to answer, hoping it's Jeremy and that he'll say Ian's outside again.

I'm disappointed when Jeremy asks if I want a different visitor.

Carson Mills is at my house.

I open my mouth to tell him no, she can't come in, but then a horrifying thought occurs that I can't shake.

What if Carson wrote the diary?

She certainly knew enough about my life to fake being me. She wasn't around when I got out of Brightside, but she could've found out when I was released, and learned that Richard lived in my building. She may have even had a contact to get the information in the second half, like the landlord or another resident. The post-hospital entries are slightly less detailed, so she wouldn't need to know much.

And why would she do this? To get back at me for whatever it was she thought I'd done to ruin her life, by ruining mine. By creating a huge, terrible avalanche of lies to bury me under. My mother did say she was a liar.

Maybe the reason Ian knows the diary is a fake is that Carson told him she wrote it. And she needs to talk to me so badly because she's ready to confess what she's done.

It all seems to make sense.

"All right," I say. "Let her in."

39

Madeline—the past

It was the happiest day of my life. Or at least, it should have been.

But having my ex-boyfriend at my wedding put a bit of a damper on the occasion.

I knew that Richard was going to be working with Ian. A few weeks back, my fiancé — now my husband, as of an hour ago — had been finalizing the plans for his new business, the one he'd start after our honeymoon. He told me that he'd taken on a partner, a man who'd started working for the town DPW with him six months earlier and was willing to quit the job for the business. Richard needed someone else because he already had too many clients lined up for him to handle alone.

I'd been thrilled for him, happy that his business was going to be so successful.

And then he told me that his new partner was Ian Moody.

I failed to hide my reaction. I must've looked like he'd informed me he changed his mind and wanted to start a whorehouse instead, or something equally shocking, because he immediately started apologizing without knowing why he was sorry. And I had to explain to him that Ian was the ex-boyfriend I'd been telling him about when I worked at the diner, the one who'd broken my heart so thoroughly for no reason.

But I'd never mentioned Ian's name, and Ian never talked about me at work. So Richard had no idea he was my ex.

He was horrified. He said he'd find someone else, that he'd have to delay the business launch and maybe lose clients but he'd work it out. I told him not to do that. I didn't want him to start all over again, especially since it would mean ruining his reputation before he even got started. He'd already been working with Ian for months at the DPW, and they must've gotten along, since Richard had asked him to be his partner. I didn't really mind, because it wasn't like *I'd* have to work with Ian five days a week.

I did mind when he showed up at the wedding, though.

I'd confronted Richard about it after the ceremony, just before the reception at the community center started. Once again, he'd been crestfallen and falling all over himself to apologize. He'd invited Ian to the wedding a month ago and had simply forgotten to un-invite him after he found out Ian was my ex. He'd been caught up in so many preparations for the wedding and the business launch that it just slipped his mind.

I wasn't angry with Richard. But I did wonder why Ian had actually showed up. He didn't *have* to come, just because he was invited.

And yet, here he was. Drinking the free booze, eating the food, glaring hatefully at me every time I crossed his line of sight.

Maybe he just wanted to make me feel bad on my wedding day, because of whatever mysterious reasons he'd kicked me out of his life so abruptly.

It was working.

I tried not to let it bother me as I danced and laughed and circulated among the guests. My mother wasn't here, so that was a plus. Jan Shearman was. She's been my maid of honor, and her latest boyfriend — a biker, not usually her type —had come as her plus-one. The boyfriend wasn't the dressing-up type, apparently, as he'd worn jeans, a faded t-shirt and a leather vest. But he did add a necktie to the ensemble. And Selma Ferguson, the director of the community center, was here too. She was one of Richard's clients for his new business, the biggest one.

Most of the other guests were either from the DPW, or people I'd worked with at the diner, along with a few scattered friends. It was a nice gathering, a happy gathering, and I wouldn't let Ian's presence cast a cloud over the celebration. I was officially married to a wonderful man, and my life was going just fine without him.

A few hours into the reception, I noticed someone slipping into the room to hover near the doorway, looking around nervously. It was a woman with blonde hair, in jeans and a sweatshirt, and she seemed lost. She wasn't exactly dressed for a wedding.

I headed toward her, thinking I could help point her in the right direction. Maybe she was here for a class, or to use the pool. As I approached her, I realized that she looked familiar. Stomach-dropping familiar.

It was Carson Mills.

I stopped mid-step, my head spinning with confusion and the beginnings of anger. Why was *she* here? This made two people at my wedding who'd shut me out violently with no explanation given, and as far as I was concerned, that was two too many.

She finally spotted me and froze, like a rabbit who'd just seen a cat. And then she spun and bolted out the door without a word.

What the hell?

Arms slipped around my waist from behind, and I caught a quick breath and squealed as Richard lifted me and spun me around. He set me on the floor and stepped in front of me, kissing the rest of my breath away.

"Hey, babe," he said with a wide grin. "It's finally time to cut the cake. You ready?"

"Yes," I beamed as I took his hand and walked back to the reception, deciding to ignore the fact that my former best friend, who lived a whole state away, had just crashed my wedding for a micro-second.

It was the first day of the rest of my life, and she didn't belong in it anymore.

40

Friday, June 6, 9:45 a.m.

I haven't seen Carson Mills in twenty years, except for that brief glimpse at my wedding, but I don't have any trouble recognizing her. She looks the same as she did in high school. She seems to have simply matured without aging, the adorable teen evolved into a gorgeous woman.

But all the happiness, the energy that used to crackle around her like a personal lightning storm, is gone. Her beauty is melancholy, her motion deliberate and weary.

My ex-best friend is sitting in my living room, on my couch, apparently unable to look at me. I've taken the upholstered chair. I haven't told her my suspicions about the diary yet because I want to hear it from her. I want a confession.

I won't accept an apology, even if she offers one. There isn't a sorry big enough.

When she finally lifts her head and engages me, the faintest of smiles touches her lips. "Believe it or not, it's good to see you, Mads. I mean Madeline," she says.

I don't believe it. I also don't feel like being nice, pretending this is some kind of social visit between old friends. It's far from it. "If you don't mind, can you just tell me why you're here?" I say. "I'm a little busy. My daughter's been abducted."

She recoils from the vitriol in my tone. "Yes, of course," she whispers, her eyes swimming with tears.

I'm furious that she'd cry for me, for my daughter, after what she's done.

Carson shivers briefly and reaches for the purse on the couch beside her. "There's something I have to show you," she says. "It may explain everything."

"Is it a diary?" I can't resist saying.

Her features knit with confusion. "What? No," she says. "It's ... let me just show you."

Before she can get whatever it is out, my cell phone buzzes. I take it from my pocket, look at the screen, and see it's Detective Burgess. "Excuse me, I have to take this," I say as I stand and walk into the dining room. I don't want Carson to hear anything that has to do with my life, which she's no longer a welcome part of.

I'm afraid Tom may be calling to say that they've taken Ian back in for questioning, and that I'll somehow have to convince him to let him go. But when I answer the phone, the detective leads out with something that shocks me rigid.

"Frank Kilgore is dead," he says. "He's been murdered."

My head spins itself blurry, and I drag one of the dining room chairs out from the table and drop into it before I can fall to the floor. "What? How?" I stammer, even though those aren't the questions I should be asking.

The right questions are *who*, and *why*.

"He was shot to death. We found him in the alley beside his hotel," Tom says. "No suspects yet, but I'm wondering if it may be related to your daughter's kidnapping."

"So am I," I murmur, and then tell him about what Frank said, or what I thought he'd said, at the gas station, about needing to tell me something.

"Why didn't you mention this before?" Tom says sharply.

I close my eyes. "Because I was having an episode," I say with difficulty. "My condition. I thought he was an imposter, and ...

nothing I see or hear can be trusted when I'm experiencing symptoms."

Tom relents and softens his tone. "All right. I've got people searching his hotel room and his vehicle right now," he says. "If we find anything relevant, or something that looks like it might involve you, I'll let you know. It might be something that only make sense to you, so I'll probably need you to go over the evidence we gather."

"That's fine. Just tell me when you need me." Pushing the shock of Frank's murder aside for the moment, I decide to preemptively bring up Ian in the hopes I can stop something awful from happening. "Tom, have you heard anything from my husband this morning about Ian Moody?" I say.

"No, I haven't. Should I expect to?"

"I don't know. Maybe." I give him the briefest possible version of the situation, leaving out the gruesome fake diary. "If he does get in touch with you, can you ask him to call me? I think there's been a terrible misunderstanding here somewhere."

Tom hesitates before he replies. "I'll try, but I will have to take any evidence that's presented seriously and follow up with it, even if you believe it amounts to nothing. I hope you understand that, Madeline."

"I do understand." At least I'm confident that even if they question Ian again, they'll find him innocent. But I still hope it doesn't come to that. "Thank you for the update, about Frank," I say. "Honestly, I don't know how to feel about this."

"How about feeling hope that we find something to lead us to your daughter's kidnapper?"

"Yes. I still have that," I say.

When I hang up the phone and return to the living room, Carson is watching me with unbridled sympathy. I'd almost forgotten she was there. "Was that about your daughter?" she says. "Is there ... any news?"

I'm angry that she's asked that, as if she ever cared about Renata, but I can't sustain the emotion for long. The impact of Frank's murder is sinking in fully, and I only have room for terror. The kidnapper has killed someone and will kill again.

My daughter could be the next victim.

I collapse into the stuffed chair, massaging a temple. For reasons I don't understand, I decide to tell her what I've just learned. "Frank Kilgore has been shot to death," I say.

Carson gasps, nearly choking. "That reporter?" she blurts. "The one who used to harass us, who wrote all those awful things about you?"

"Yes. The one you punched," I say.

I don't even realize I'm smiling at the memory until Carson smiles back. "That really hurt my knuckles, you know," she says. "I had bruises for days."

I actually start to laugh, but I stop myself. There is no joy in this meeting, or in Frank Kilgore's death. It's irrefutable proof that the danger to my daughter is real. That whoever is doing this has a complicated plan that's being executed step by step.

It's proof that Dallas Walsh isn't the kidnapper. I hope Detective Burgess has realized that.

I've already been around Carson too long, so I decide to just come out and say it. "Carson, I know you wrote the diary. I know you broke up me and Ian for revenge. But I never did anything to you. Not then, and not now."

She gapes at me, like I've just suggested she's secretly Charles Manson or Ted Bundy. "What diary?" she cries. "You and Ian ... what are you talking about?"

I actually revel in her miserable confusion, until I realize this is exactly what she did to me while I was in Brightside. Hurled a bunch of vague accusations I didn't understand, left me with her anger and no idea where it had come from. And I'd just said I never did anything to her.

Maybe I'm wrong about the diary. Maybe I should give her a chance.

"Okay, never mind that now," I say. "Let's start over. Tell me why you're here."

She stares for another moment, and then slowly picks up a cell phone that's sitting on the couch beside her. That must be what she was getting out of her purse. But instead of showing me whatever it is she wanted me to see, she whispers, "This is about your father."

My mind goes completely blank. "My father?" I echo dumbly. "What ..."

She's going to tell me it wasn't suicide, after all. She'll say that he was murdered, and she knows who did it.

"He's the reason my family moved away from Dayfield." Tears slip silently down her face, one after another. "I tried to tell you, Mads. I tried so many times, but I just couldn't. And then it was too late, and I hated you *so* much, but it wasn't ever you I hated. It was him."

I don't understand. At all. "Why did you hate my father?"

"Because ..." She sobs loudly, and clasps a shaking hand over her mouth. It takes a full minute for her to regain her composure and lower her arm. "Because he raped me."

No.

No. I refuse to believe that. She's lying, just like my mother said. "That's not true," I say. "*Your* father raped you. He talked to me about it in the car, that day you told me to leave and he drove me home. He was interrogating me, making sure you didn't tell me what he'd done to you. Why would you blame that on *my* father?"

Her jaw drops the whole time I'm speaking. "Madeline," she says in a surprisingly calm tone. "I know who raped me. Do you really think I can't tell the difference between your father and my own? It happened one day after school, when I was —"

"No!" I don't recognize my own high-pitched, panic-stricken voice. "My father couldn't ... he would never ..."

Carson stands slowly, her phone in her hands. She swipes at the screen a few times as she walks toward the chair, and then turns the phone around to show me what's on it.

"His name is Benjamin. He's nineteen," she says, so gently that my heart breaks.

This time I'm the one putting a hand to my mouth and sobbing into it. I feel like I'll never stop crying.

Finally, I pull myself together enough to whisper, "Can you forward me a copy of that? There's someone else who needs to see it."

Carson agrees. I think she must know who I mean.

And it's high time *she* told me the truth.

41

Friday, June 6, 11:55 a.m.

I spend an hour with Carson, and it's almost exactly what I envisioned would happen when I called her from Brightside all those years ago. We talk like crazy, reminisce about everything, laugh and cry and make plans to get together for real.

But our true happy reunion will have to wait until I have my daughter back. Carson heads back to the Stardust, where she's staying for another week, and I promise to keep her in the loop about Renata.

Meanwhile, there's someone I need to confront.

Twenty minutes later, I'm pulling into my mother's driveway behind her latest Audi. I never bothered remembering the model of this one, or the three before it. I haven't told her that I'm coming. I want her to be completely blindsided when I show her what I got from Carson.

I want real remorse. An explanation, and an apology.

It takes her five minutes to answer the door when I ring the bell. She sees me, and a range of emotions flicker across her face — surprise, hope, worry, fear — before she closes her expression. "Have they found her?" she says. "Have they found my granddaughter?"

I shake my head. "Not yet. Can we talk?"

My mother looks uncertain. If she dares to refuse, I'm going to barge in anyway. This confrontation is happening now.

"Of course," she eventually says as she moves back from the door. "Come in."

I walk inside, refusing to look at all the elegant furnishings and artful surroundings. After my father died and she had me committed, she'd sold the house I grew up in and bought this small but luxurious Cape Cod that was really only big enough for one person. As if she'd decided, even then, that she'd never allow me to live with her again.

I've only been here a handful of times. I hate the place.

She leads me to the breakfast nook by a sunny kitchen window, and I take a seat. "Would you like something to drink?" she says, still standing.

I shake my head. "Please sit," I say with forced politeness.

She lowers herself regally into the opposite chair. "What can I do for you?"

What can I do for you. As if I'm some kind of customer, instead of her daughter.

"You can explain this," I say as I take out my phone and swipe to the photo that Carson's forwarded to me. A young nineteen-year-old man, who is practically the spitting image of my father. There's no mistaking it.

I turn the screen toward my mother. "This is Carson's son, Benjamin," I say. "Want to guess who his father is, or are you going to make me say it?"

My mother's eyes roll back in her head, and she slumps face-first onto the table.

I have no sympathy. She knew, she *had* to know. This is why she told me Carson was a liar, why she demanded that I not listen to her.

This is why she didn't cry at my father's funeral.

She knew he was a monster.

When my mother starts making small, moaning sounds, I stand up, go to her kitchen, and pour a half-glass of water from the sink. Then I walk back to the breakfast nook and throw the contents in her face.

She bolts upright, spluttering and gasping. "Madeline! Was that really necessary?"

"Yes, it was." I sit back down calmly, fold my hands on the table, and stare at her. "Tell me everything."

My mother starts in a halting voice. Soon she's crying openly, talking about affairs and 'younger women,' as if Carson was a potential rival for my father's affections instead of his sixteen-year-old *student.* Every word that comes from my mother's mouth is self-pity, when it should be righteous anger.

"Mom, stop!" I finally shout. "He didn't have an affair with Carson. He raped her!"

Her mouth drops open, and her entire body shudders violently. "I know," she whispers. "God help me, I know."

"Then why didn't you *do* something about it?" I cry shrilly.

She shakes her head, her lips pressed tightly together. "I only found out about Carson after ... after he killed himself," she says. "Before that, he really did have affairs with younger women. Actual affairs between consenting adults, though they were still far too young for him." She swipes uselessly at her tears and her ruined makeup. "Oh, he'd sleep with them for a few weeks, and then he'd come back to me. It would be months, years, between these women. But ... Carson ... she was like a daughter to me. For the longest time after I found out, I refused to believe it. It was easier to blame her, to pretend she'd seduced him. She always had crushes on older men, so the idea fit with the reality I created for myself. I couldn't admit ..."

"That you'd married a monster?" I say almost gently as I recall having almost the exact same thoughts about Ian.

My mother nods miserably. "I was afraid ... that he'd done it to you, and you never told me," she rasps. "I just couldn't bear the idea that I'd allowed something like that to happen to my *daughter.* So instead of reaching out to you — foolishly, selfishly — I shut you out." She stares at the table. "And I never figured out how to let you back in again."

I don't know if I can actually forgive her, but I can understand her. That's what makes me reach out and take her hand. "Thank you for telling me the truth," I say.

She nods again, her mascara-soaked tears dripping onto the ash-blond table and leaving inky black splashes. "While we're on this subject, Carson isn't the only child that your father ... forced," she says, her mouth twisting around the word.

A lump forms in my throat. "Who else?" I say.

"I don't know." She shakes her head. "I found out that he'd been sending money every month, for years, to some girl in Pennsylvania as a bribe, so she wouldn't tell anyone what he'd done. Her name was ... Jennifer? No, Jessica. Jessica Forrest," she says.

I barely hear her last sentence. There's a balloon inside me, expanding and pushing, filled with the name of the girl my father had been paying hush money to. Jessica Forrest.

The name that's marked in bold letters and heavily circled in the middle of Brenda Westhall's notes on the Singing Woods Killer case.

"Mom, I have to go," I blurt, standing hard enough to scrape the chair legs on the floor with a loud shriek. "I'm sorry, but I have to go *right now.* I don't have time to explain, but I promise I'll call you later and fill you in. It could be about Renata."

Her expression is instantly serious. "Go."

For once, I do what she tells me.

42

before I sleep

It's all over for me now.

I sit here in the cool, musty darkness, and I wonder where it all went wrong. How I could have failed so completely. How *she* managed to outsmart me so thoroughly.

When she came here to Dayfield, when she moved back into my life and flaunted her presence, laughing at me the whole time, I thought she only wanted more money. I thought I could pay her off, and she'd leave.

I was so wrong.

She wanted to destroy me, and she has.

As if it wasn't enough that she drove me back to my old patterns. I'll never forgive myself for that, for what I did to the girl. At least she's gone now, moved away. But I think that forgiveness is the last thing I'm ever going to worry about, where I'm going.

That's not all *she* did. No, that isn't even close to the tip of the iceberg. She's fooled everyone into thinking that she's a nice, normal person. A good friend. Good at her job. Probably kind to children and animals or something.

She's an absolute madwoman, a monster. Always has been, always will be.

She came to me just this morning. After my own personal nightmare seemed to be over. She reminded me of what I'd done, the life I'd taken. And she told me a secret, a horrible secret. She told me that the money was never for her silence.

She told me exactly who was responsible for what's happened.

I'm responsible. I did this.

All those years ago, when I met her, everything that was going on then, it all confused me. I knew what I wanted was wrong, but I couldn't seem to help myself. When I took that girl out into the woods that night — she was so young, far too young — I didn't know that *she* was already following me. That she'd watched as I started to love the girl, as she resisted me, as she started screaming.

As I strangled her to make her stop.

Then *she* came to me. I nearly killed her too, out of sheer panic because she'd seen me. But she soothed me, seduced me. She helped me get rid of the body, so that no one would ever know what I'd done, what I never meant to do. The accident I'd had.

She was hot for me.

She was mine.

She stayed in my cabin. Stayed there and waited for me, let me do whatever I wanted with her, whenever I wanted to. And I learned more about her life. How she lived with her stepfather and his vapid wife, how they abused her in every possible way. How she hated him, how being with me was her revenge against him.

And eventually, how crazy she was. How truly, chillingly insane.

She deceived me, and she's deceiving everyone around me, right now. That's not even her name, the one she's going by.

Her name is Jessica Forrest. My lover, my lunatic, my mistake.

I just can't live with the shame.

The cold circle is pressed against my flesh now, and I expect to hear the gunshot. I deserve that final, deafening roar signaling a bloody end to the harm I've caused so many. But the only thing that reaches my ears is the click of the trigger as my finger pulls it home. And my last thoughts shine like beacons in my brain, milliseconds before the bullet tears them into fragments, ending all thought forever.

I'm so sorry, Madeline.

Daddy loves you.

43

Friday, June 6, 12:25 p.m.

Brenda Westhall opens the door and stares at me. She reeks of alcohol and sweat, and she looks worse than the last time I saw her. "What do you want?" she sneers. "Going to try and have me arrested again?"

I look her in the eyes, and I say, "Jessica Forrest."

She blanches and shivers. "What about her?"

"My father knew her," I say. "And I need everything *you* know about her."

Brenda's shoulders slump, and she shuffles outside, closing the door behind her. "Don't worry, I'm not going to leave a ransom note on your car," she says with a smirk, and gestures to two folding chairs on the cement slab porch beneath the awning.

We both sit down. Brenda shakes her head and stares straight ahead, her hands folded between her knees. "What do I know about Jessica Forrest? Not much, unfortunately," she says with a heavy sigh. "I'll tell you, whoever she is, she's the real reason I was dismissed from the force. Sorry about blaming you for that, I guess."

I wave a hand. She can blame me for Hitler's rise to power if she wants to, as long as she tells me about this woman. I just know that somehow, the woman my father was paying off is connected to my daughter's abduction.

"Here's the thing," Brenda says. "Jessica Forrest is dead."

"What?" I say sharply. No, that can't be. She's the link to my daughter. There's no way she's dead.

"But that's not all!" she says with manic glee, like a game show host telling a studio audience about the fabulous prizes in store. She really is quite drunk. "You see, this damned dead woman left a fingerprint at my crime scene. Isn't that an amazing trick?"

"So she's not dead," I whisper as my guttering hope tries to flicker back.

Brenda laughs without humor. "You'd think that, wouldn't you?" she says. "I mean, dead people can't leave fingerprints. Oh, I was so *excited* when I found that print. I thought, this is it. We've nailed this bastard, this psychopath who's torturing innocent girls. But when the identification came back ..."

Suddenly she looks angry enough to rage herself sober.

"We knew the unsub was male. It had to be, because of the ... sexual trauma." She swallows once. "But this print came back female, 35, deceased. Jessica Goddamn Forrest," she spat. "Died in a house fire in Pennsylvania, a year before the murders started. She had a juvenile record for petty crimes, shoplifting and such, so her prints were in the system. That's how we matched it. And after the results came in, I was accused of mishandling evidence, because of course that fingerprint couldn't possibly exist. But I didn't mishandle anything." Her jaw clenched. "I did this one so by-the-book that you could practically read lines off me. I wanted to bring that sick son of a bitch down." Her fury faded, and she slumped forward slightly. "But you killed him, so at least he didn't live to be set free on a technicality."

I'm struggling to process all this, to voice the half-formed questions swimming in her head. "Is she the reason you had the theory about the accomplice?" I say. "Some of your notes said there might have been someone else working with Stewart Brooks."

"Nah, that was something else. A hunch, really," she says. "Nobody wanted to listen to my hunches, though. And after the fingerprint thing, I was persona non grata until they finally scratched up enough guts to kick me out."

I've got everything I need, and I have to speak to Detective Burgess. I stand to leave. "Thank you, Brenda," I say. "I think this might be the way to save my daughter."

"What, with a dead woman?" she says, rolling her eyes. "Good luck."

I go back to my car and get ready to drive to the police station. This is something I have to discuss with Tom in person.

44

Friday, June 6, 1:38 p.m.

Richard still isn't answering his phone, and neither is Ian. I try them both from the parking lot of the police station and there's no response. Now I'm getting angry, especially at Richard. How could he not scramble every time the phone rings or a text chimes in, at a time like this?

I try Renata's phone again, too. Nothing's changed. She's unavailable.

When I head inside, I discover the reason that Ian, at least, hasn't answered me. He's at the front desk, flanked by two uniformed officers, a furious look on his face as he scribbles something on a clipboard.

"Ian?" I say haltingly.

His head turns instantly, and his expression melts into deep sorrow. "Madeline, thank God you're all right," he says.

I frown at him. "Why would I not be all right?"

The officers look very interested in the answer to this question, too.

"I just ... I don't know. I'm worried about you," he says. "I hope *you* know that I didn't have anything to do with Renata's disappearance, don't you?"

"Yes, I do," I tell him. "I got your note."

A hopeful smile flickers on his face, but it fades quickly.

"Mr. Moody," one of the officers says. "You need to come with us."

"Wait, are you questioning him?" I say. "He didn't do anything. I already talked to Detective Burgess about it."

The other officer looks at me, stone-faced. "I guess you'll have to talk to him again," he says. "He's the one who told us to bring him in."

"That shit isn't mine!" Ian shouts, and then visibly forces himself to calm down. He meets my gaze with intensity. "I saw him, Madeline," he says. "I saw him, too."

My pulse starts to race. "You saw who?"

"Stewart Brooks."

"All right, Mr. Moody. Let's go. Now," the first officer says, shooting an eyeroll at his partner. "You can tell the duty sergeant all about the dead man you saw. Maybe *he* put those pictures in your bedroom."

I'm stunned and flustered, my mouth gaping open uselessly. I don't know what pictures they're talking about, but they must be bad ones. They can't be his. As the officers try to lead Ian away and he hesitates, gives me a desperate look, I say, "I believe you."

He shivers with gratitude and goes willingly.

I've got half a mind to go off on Tom Burgess, but I won't. Terrible as it is, I know he has to do his job, and I know they're going to find Ian innocent, because he is. The important thing is that he saw Stewart Brooks.

I'm not crazy. Somehow, it's *him* behind all this.

And just like Brenda Westhall's hunch that no one believed, I think he isn't working alone.

I find Detective Burgess in his office and walk right in without waiting for an invitation. He's on his computer, slowly typing something, and he startles when he notices me. "Let me guess," he says. "You're here to plead Ian Moody's case."

I almost smile. "Will it help?"

"No," he says.

"Then that's not why I'm here. I know your investigation will clear him, anyway," I say as I take the chair across from his desk.

"Well, that was the extent of my psychic abilities. I guess they're broken." He smirks and pushes back from the desk. "I do have a few updates for you, though. We're still holding Dallas Walsh —"

"Why?" I cut in. "He couldn't have murdered Frank Kilgore. He was in custody."

"Because we haven't proved that the person who murdered Kilgore is the same person who took your daughter," he says. "And we're still searching Walsh's property. We're also bringing Trevor Downes back in, because we found a hole in his alibi."

"Trevor didn't do it. Neither did Dallas," I mutter. "You're wasting your time. It was Stewart Brooks."

He stares at me. "I'm going to pretend you didn't say that."

I start to insist, but I know that's not going to get me anywhere. There's no way anyone else is going to believe that an alleged dead man is committing crimes. Except Ian. But I'm glad there's at least one person who saw him, and isn't me.

"Anyway, there's something else. This probably won't be easy to hear," the detective says, leaning forward with a concerned expression. "It's about Jan Shearman. I questioned and released her yesterday, but she came back in this morning with some ... additional information."

From the way he's talking, I think I probably don't want to hear it at all. But I have to. "All right, what is it?" I say.

He sighs through his nose, mouth pinched. "She *did* see you being abducted," he says. "But she never reported it, because she didn't want to admit that she was having an affair with your father. That's why she was in the area."

I wish I could be surprised about that, but I seem to have run out of shock at the things my father did. Apparently, I never knew him at all.

But the mention of my father lets me segue into the reason I came to talk to Tom.

"Speaking of him," I say. "I found out something from the original case, and I need you to look into it. Please."

The detective raises an eyebrow. "Your lack of reaction is a little disturbing," he says. "Isn't Jan Shearman your friend? I just told you that she slept with your father."

"Yes, well, apparently my father slept with a lot of people. I learned about that earlier today, too." Carson's wrenched face as she confessed what he'd done to her flashes through my mind, and my heart reaches across the years to her, wishing she could have told me then. "I'm only interested in one of them, though," I say. "Jessica Forrest."

Tom's eyes light up like a pinball machine. "I know that name," he says. "I've been looking at the case files from the SWK case. They found a fingerprint belonging to her at the crime scene." A frown slides over his mouth. "But they ruled it out as evidence, because she's listed as deceased."

"I don't think she is deceased," I say. "I think she's right here in Dayfield, and she's helping — the man who abducted my daughter." I catch myself before 'Stewart Brooks' slips out again. Can't have the nice detective thinking I'm crazy, not when he's finally listening to me.

"I'm not sure ... wait a minute," he says, turning to his computer and typing rapidly. "I do think this is worth looking into. It may not amount to much, but I'll grasp any damned straw I can right now." He types a bit more, and then looks at me. "I'm requesting copies of her juvenile records from the state department in Pennsylvania," he says. "At the least, we can find out more about her and see if there's some way she might ... not be dead." He shakes his head at that. "I can't believe I'm considering a dead woman as a suspect."

Why not, I think, when there's a dead man involved too? But I don't say that to him.

"All right. Thank you," I say. "How long will that take?"

He shrugs. "A few to several hours. Depends on how many requests they're getting through the records department today." He glances at me. "You're not planning to wait here for them, are you?"

"No, I've got something to do," I say. "You'll call me, though?"

"Of course."

I leave Tom to his report ordering and head for my car. Somehow I've got to get hold of my husband. He should know all of this, and I want to tell him that Ian's innocent. Maybe he can help clear his name.

Mostly, I want to tell Richard that we're getting close to our daughter. That soon, we're going to have her back.

This has to work.

45

Friday, June 6, 3:05 p.m.

It's strange being at the Rainforest Café alone. I've never come here without Richard. I'm not even sure why I did come here, unless it's out of a vague idea that this place and my husband go together, so maybe he would magically be here when I came.

He's not, of course.

I order a latte and take a seat by the window, looking out at the community center and fiddling absently with my phone as I wait for the drink to cool. My head is so full, it seems like at any moment, all my thoughts and worries will have to start leaking from my ears to make room for more. Everything in my life has changed so abruptly.

My friend isn't my friend anymore. I can't imagine remaining friends with Jan, knowing what I know.

My ex-friend is my friend again. I have Carson back. She has a son, and her son is my brother. I wonder if he knows that, if I'll ever get to tell him. If he *should* know. I'd like to meet him someday, if Carson doesn't mind.

My father was a rapist, pedophile, and philanderer, and my mother covered it up.

My ex-boyfriend, who despised me, still loves me. That diary still sticks in my mind, and I can't figure out where it came from or why. I'll have to ask Ian, if I ever get to speak to him.

My daughter is still missing.

And now, it seems, my husband is too.

Just then my phone chimes in my hands, making me jump. It's a text from Richard, as if my thoughts have summoned him. I only manage to read *Hey babe, so sorry I missed* before the partial text notification vanishes from the screen, so I tap through to my messages and open the conversation.

Hey, babe, so sorry I missed your call. Work records are more screwed than I thought. Sorry about Ian. I think you're right, he's not the one. Called Det. to say it's a mistake, they're prob. letting him go. Any news? Text me, calls not coming through here. Don't know why. Be home by 7. Love you.

My earlier irritation is edging on anger. At least I know he's alive, but ... work records? He'll be out until seven? I understand that his business is important and it's in trouble right now, but it almost feels like he's stopped caring about finding our daughter.

All right, that probably isn't fair. I'm the one who told him it was okay to go back to work. I just didn't think he'd throw himself into it like this. And I certainly can't tell him everything that's happened today in a text.

Suddenly I don't want a latte. I want to go home.

I leave the mug on the table and walk out of the café. My car is parked right out front, and for a moment I stand beside it, gazing at the community center across the street. Something about it's caught my eye, but I can't figure out what.

Then I see it, standing motionless near the back corner of the building, glaring across the distance at me.

I see *him*.

Instantly I'm sprinting across the street. My purse falls to the ground behind the car, but I don't give it a second thought. It's him, it's *him*, and I'm not letting him get away this time.

"Give me my daughter, you bastard!" I scream at the top of my lungs, my feet slapping the pavement, jumping the curb, dashing over grass. "You *can't have her!*"

I'm within fifty feet of him and he still hasn't moved. Just like the other times I saw him. Iron bands of panic tighten across my chest. Am I hallucinating? When I reach him, am I going to run right through him?

Just as I start to believe he's not really there, and I must be crazy after all, he pivots on a heel and dashes away from me. Toward the woods behind the community center.

"No!" I scream, already gasping for breath. There's a stitch in my side, rapidly spiraling toward agony, and then one foot comes down wrong and wrenches my ankle. I stumble a few steps and keep going, pushing faster, finding reserves of strength I didn't know I had.

I'm gaining on him.

I stop screaming and save my breath for running as the gap between us closes slowly. He doesn't slow down, doesn't look back. And then I spot something at the edge of the trees, a bulky, non-natural shape covered with camouflage paint.

It's a four-wheeler. He's headed straight for it.

I'll never be able to catch him on that.

"Please!" I cry, knowing that I can't possibly reason with this man, this killer of children. "Please, take me instead! You can kill me, finish what you started. I won't resist you. Just don't hurt my baby girl!"

He doesn't react to my begging. He reaches the bike, jumps on, and the engine roars to life.

"Stewart, *please!*" My scream splinters in my throat, drowned by the revving engine. He's still twenty feet away. I can't get to him, I'm not fast enough.

He's *right there*, and I can't stop him from hurting my daughter.

The four-wheeler blasts into the woods, kicking up vast clouds of dirt and mulch. I keep running senselessly, every step sending knives up my legs. I'll follow his trail, or the sound of the engine. Anything. He *can't* get away.

I stumble and fall to my knees at the edge of the woods, a long, agonized scream tearing itself from my throat. When my breath runs out, I collapse into wracking, shuddering sobs.

He's gone.

I've failed her.

Minutes, or maybe hours, pass as I kneel in the dirt, oblivious to everything but my pain. Through the white noise in my head, I hear someone running through the grass behind me, heading my way.

I lunge to my feet and whirl around, ignoring the pain. If it's him, if he's back, I'll kill him. Again.

But it's not him. It's Selma Ferguson.

"Madeline, what happened?" she pants, her breath heaving as she slows to a jog. "I was in my office, and I heard shouting, and then I saw you out here ..." She trails off with a look of horrified concern. "Did someone hurt you?"

I can't speak. I can't squeeze a single word from my grief-swollen throat.

I start to sob again, ugly snot-choked cries, and Selma's face falls. "Oh, child," she wails, wrapping me in her arms. "Come on, dear. Can you walk? We'll go inside, and I'll call someone. I think ... I think I should get you an ambulance."

Ambulance. Hospital. They'll keep me for hours.

It'll get dark.

"No," I rasp, trying to disentangle myself from her well-meaning embrace. "I'm okay. Just have to catch my breath."

Selma isn't convinced. "I really think you need —"

"I'm okay," I insist. The agony in my side is slowly fading, and my throbbing, trembling legs are starting to still. "Sorry, Selma. I just have to get home. My daughter ..."

Understanding floods her expression. "Of course," she says. "Do you need a ride?"

I shake my head. "My car's parked at the café across the street." I swallow and hack, swipe at my face, and a bolt of clarity hits me. She could be a witness. She could tell the police about Stewart, and they'll believe her. *She's* not crazy. Her office window looks out toward the woods. I can see it from here. It's the one with the blue curtains, the edges of them currently fluttering through the open window.

"Selma, did you see him?" I say breathlessly. "Did you see ... the man, on the four-wheeler? He rode off into the woods."

The look on her face drains me completely. I know what she's going to say before she says it.

"No, dear. You were the only one out here."

I beat back a swell of panic. How could I have possibly hallucinated a man running to a four-wheeler and driving away? I saw him, I *heard* him.

Selma must've heard him too.

"Your window," I blurt. "It's open. Didn't you hear the engine?"

Her look of concern deepens. "I heard you shouting, and then I ran right down and came outside," she says. "And then you screamed like that ... my heart was fit to burst. I thought you were dying. But there wasn't anyone else." She blinks several times. "Are you sure I can't call anyone for you, dear?"

I want to fall to the ground, pick up crying where I left off and stay that way. My mind is betraying me, sabotaging me. I'm having full-blown visions, complete with sound.

"No, thank you," I say, straining to pull myself together. "I just ... I want to go home."

Selma pats my arm. "Let me walk you to your car, at least," she says.

I nod in wordless agreement. I don't have the strength for more.

I plod back across the grassy lawn toward the street, with Selma slowing her pace to match mine. When we reach my car, my purse is still on the ground where it fell. The advantages of living in a town instead of a city.

It takes me a minute to find my keys. Selma hovers nervously at my side, glancing around like she's hoping someone will come and help. Maybe she thinks she needs saving from the crazy person who's hallucinating men and motorbikes.

At least she doesn't ask about calling an ambulance again.

"You drive safe now, Madeline," she says as I climb into the car. "Try to get some rest, if you can."

"Thank you," I croak.

Home seems a million miles from here, but at least I don't have to run them.

46

Friday, June 6, 4:20 p.m.

When I get home, I text Richard: *I am not okay.*

Seeing his earlier message as I reply reminds me that Ian has been released, so I text him too. *Call me.* I still want to know where he saw Stewart Brooks.

Because apparently, I *didn't* actually see him.

I shower until the hot water runs out and put on clean clothes. I'm starting to feel like a human being again, if a slightly insane one. And I've renewed my resolve to find my daughter.

It's almost time for my appointment with Dr. Bradshaw. I have to convince her to try hypnosis. I *need* to remember.

My broken memories are Renata's last chance.

I try calling her phone again before I leave for my session. Ring, ring, ring, the person you're calling is not available. I decide to text her, just in case she can see it.

I'm going to find you very soon. I love you so much.

The drive to Dr. Bradshaw's office is less harrowing than the one home from the community center. I'm regaining my focus. The week isn't over yet, and I will get my daughter back. Alive. I'll *make* my shattered mind cooperate, somehow.

When I enter the therapy room, Dr. Bradshaw rushes up to me and hugs me. "I won't ask how you're doing, because the answer is obvious," she says in a soft, kind tone. "You're directing this session. We'll talk about anything you want, with no prompting from me."

"Thank you," I say as I settle on the couch, trying to decide on the best way to approach my request. As I mull it over, I take the prescription bottle filled with the wrong pills from my purse and hand it to her. "This is the prescription I mentioned," I say.

Dr. Bradshaw takes the bottle, opens the cap, and shakes a pill onto her palm. She frowns at the fat yellow oval. "Yes, this definitely isn't pimozide," she says. "I don't understand how they could've gotten it so wrong."

I've ceased to care about the pills. I have more important things to worry about, and I've decided to just come out and say it. "Dr. Bradshaw ... I still want you to hypnotize me. Please, hear me out," I say as she opens her mouth to protest. "It's for my daughter."

She looks at me, and I can see her resolve cracking a bit. "How will this help your daughter?" she says.

I tell her as much as I can about what's happened, leaving out any mention of Stewart Brooks. His name is a red flag that paints me in crazy and makes people stop listening. "This person, whoever they are, is following in the footsteps of the Singing Woods Killer," I say as I wind down my pitch. "I just know he's taken Renata to Stewart Brooks' lair, the one the police could never find. I need to remember where it is." My throat clenches again, and my eyes burn hot. "Please. Help me remember."

After a long, tense moment, Dr. Bradshaw says gently, "All right. We'll try it."

Soon I'm lying on the couch, and Dr. Bradshaw has pulled a chair over by my head, angled toward me. She wheels a thin bracket table over, slotting the bottom under the couch so that the board-width surface hovers above my waist. She adjusts the table support to place the surface at eye level, and then sets something on it. A metronome, I think.

"I'm just going to dim the lights," she says as she heads toward the far wall. "Bear with me. I haven't done this in a long time, and it may take a few tries."

"That's fine," I say. If the goal of hypnosis is to put me to sleep, I'm already halfway there. I've slept so little in the past three days that just lying down is making me drowsy.

The light in the room fades to twilight levels, and Dr. Bradshaw returns to perch in the chair. She reaches forward and taps the little lever on the device, the metronome, and it starts swinging back and forth, slow and steady, with a sound like a heartbeat.

"Okay, Madeline," she says. "Close your eyes and take slow, deep breaths."

I do what she says. I can already feel myself slipping away.

"I want you to envision a peaceful, relaxing scene," Dr. Bradshaw says in a soothing, singsong voice. "Picture any place that makes you feel relaxed, and focus on it. Concentrate. Make it real in your mind's eye."

I see my own back yard. Lush green grass, fragrant flowers. A small child, three or four years old, extending a drooping bouquet of dandelions in her little hand. *'Look, Mommy, I pickeded you flowers!'* she giggles.

I see my baby, my Renata. Her beaming face relaxes me. The metronome is her heartbeat, lulling me into contentment.

"I'm going to count backwards from ten," Dr. Bradshaw drones musically. "When I reach one, you'll be in a deep, deep sleep. Your mind will be fully open. You will be able to remember anything, anything you want to."

I murmur something, thick sounds that may be intended as acknowledgement.

"Relax. Relax," she soothes. "Deep breaths. Focus on your relaxing place. I'll begin the countdown now." She pauses briefly. "Ten ... nine ... eight ..."

The last number I hear is four, and then blackness consumes me.

I see nothing. Feel nothing. Hear nothing.

I am nothing.

There's a flash of light in the darkness. A face hangs there, an afterimage, gone in an instant. It's a face I know.

I'm running through the woods, and death is chasing me. Death is coming to claim me.

Darkness falls again.

"Madeline!"

I swim toward the echoing voice, toward a growing light. It brightens and swells, beats against my eyes, blinding me. Another flash, brilliant as the sun.

A face. Laughing face, familiar face. Hated face.

Boards on the ground, covered by leaves.

The light fades away, and the only face I see is Dr. Bradshaw's concerned one. "I'm sorry. I had to bring you out of it," she whispers. "You were screaming ..."

I blink away the fog and sit up rapidly. She's already moved the table aside. "What?" I say. "What was I screaming?"

She shakes her head. "I couldn't understand you," she says. "It sounded something like ... habit whore."

Dull sorrow floods me. I'm never going to make sense out of that.

And I still don't remember anything.

I thank Dr. Bradshaw for trying and leave the office without using the rest of my session time. I need to think of something else, some other way to jog my stubborn memories. I'm not giving up.

As I reach the parking lot, headed for my car, my phone buzzes. I answer eagerly when I see it's Detective Burgess. "Find anything?" I say, skipping the greeting entirely.

Fortunately, he doesn't take offense. "I'm not sure, but maybe." There's a note of hope in his voice that hasn't been there before. "I've received some of the records on Jessica Forrest from the staties in P.A. It seems there was some sort of anomaly during the investigation of the fire that she allegedly died in."

"What kind of anomaly?" I say as I open my car door, praying for good news.

I can almost hear him smile as he says, "For a while, they didn't think the body was actually hers. Some things didn't add up. Eventually the case was marked as incomplete, but someone pulled it out and marked it closed years later, with no additional evidence."

"So she might still be alive, then," I say.

"Exactly. Can you come to the station right now?" he says. "I have a few files and an old photo I'd like you to look at. Maybe you'll recognize her."

I'm already starting the engine. "I'm on my way."

47

Friday, June 6, 5:57 p.m.

I use the hands-free to call Richard's phone on the way to the station. It goes straight to voicemail. I'm too fired up to worry about it right now, so I leave a hasty message telling him to call, and hang up.

My mind races as I'm driving, going over everything that's happened in the past few days. Still looking for any hints that will lead to my daughter. A parade of faces rush past, everyone I've seen, everyone I've talked to, everyone who had a reason to strike out at me. I wonder if one of them is really Jessica Forrest.

There's a sudden flash in my mind, like the one I had while I was hypnotized.

And I see something.

A door. A wooden door with an iron handle, and it's locked. I'm locked behind it. I'm pounding, screaming, begging and pleading. I want to go home.

The vision evaporates as quickly as it came, and my breath catches when I understand what it was.

I'm remembering. Oh, God, I'm remembering.

Please let me remember enough in time.

At the police station, I rush inside and head straight for Tom's office. His door is open. I go in to find him at the desk, a single folder on the surface in front of him.

He pushes it toward me. "Let's hope something looks familiar," he says. "There's a picture, but it was taken twenty-five years ago, so I don't know how helpful it'll be."

I don't bother taking a seat. I hold my breath as I flip the folder open, and an old, faded photograph stares up at me, printed on a sheet of plain white paper. The picture isn't the best quality. It's a slender girl, early twenties, outdoors and leaning against a low wooden fence with a lit cigarette in one hand. She's wearing cutoff shorts, a midriff shirt, and a sultry expression. Her hair is dark, and her eyes could be brown, or hazel. It's hard to tell.

At first my hope starts to fade. I don't think I recognize her. But the longer I stare at the photo, the more I believe she's familiar. If her face was aged, filled out a bit more, the sultry pout replaced with a warm, cheerful smile...

It all comes together with a shock so hard that my knees buckle, and I have to slam a hand on the desk to keep from falling. I *do* know her. I can see this girl in the face I'm familiar with. The face I was just looking at. The one pretending she was so concerned about me and only wanted to help.

The one who 'didn't see' what I saw.

Detective Burgess is staring, worried. I have to spit it out.

I swallow to ease my dry throat.

"That's Selma Ferguson."

He gapes at me. "Are you sure?" he says, spinning the folder so the picture's upright for him. He peers closely at it, and then practically lunges at his computer, typing madly. "Is her picture on the community center's website?"

"I have no idea." I'm mentally replaying every moment, every interaction with her. She's been here so long. She's a fixture of the community. She knows practically everyone, every family, and she's always so kind. Always has a warm smile ready.

I'm horrified at what that smile's been hiding.

"Got it," Tom says triumphantly. A printer on a filing cabinet next to the desk hums to life, the carriage racing back and forth as it slowly spits out a single sheet of paper. The detective stands, reaches over and snatches the printout, then places it on the desk, side-by-side with the photo from the Pennsylvania police.

The comparison leaves no doubt. Even looking at the photos upside down, I can tell.

Selma Ferguson is Jessica Forrest.

Minutes later, Tom and I are walking through the station. He's placed a quick phone call, and now he's barking orders into his CB, the unit crackling intermittently with responses. I see McKenzie rush by, headed for the parking lot.

Half of the officers he's sending out are going to the community center. The rest are heading to Selma's house at the north end of town, on Parkland Drive. All this time, and I never knew where she lived. Never considered it, because she seemed to always be at the community center.

She lives right at the edge of the Singing Woods.

We're approaching the exit, and Tom slows down slightly. "I think you should head home, Madeline," he says. "I've still got a detail at your house, and I'll send another squad car. You'll be safe there until this is over. Where's your husband?"

The question makes me flinch, and I feel guilty for not thinking about Richard in all of this. But Renata is the most important thing right now. "Honestly, I don't know," I say. "He went to work today, but his job site is always changing and I have no idea where it is right now. He texted me earlier and said calls weren't coming through." I press my lips together. "Ian. He'd know where he is. Did he mention where he was going when he left the station?"

The detective shakes his head. "When we released him, he rushed out of here like his hair was on fire and his ass was catching," he says. "Didn't say a word to anyone."

"Well ... Richard said he'd be home around seven." I realize that's it's almost seven now. "Maybe he'll be home when I get back. I'll text him again."

"All right. Just in case, I'm going to send a car out along the patrol routes to look for his truck," Tom says. "It's that big purple Tundra, isn't it?"

"Yes," I whisper as fresh panic ripples through me. "Oh my God, what if they have him? They could have my husband," I blurt. "Maybe that's why he hasn't answered the phone all day. Anyone could've sent a text."

"Take it easy, Madeline. I'm sure he's fine. It's just a precaution," Tom says, starting to frown. "Who is 'they'?"

"Selma and —" I stop myself abruptly. He's still not going to believe that Stewart Brooks is alive, but they're closing in on Selma. She'll be enough to recover my daughter. "I just assumed that a man abducted her," I say.

"Never make assumptions. That's a good rule for this job, and for pretty much everything in life." Tom smiles, and adds, "For what it's worth, I assumed that too."

I think about pressing my luck and mentioning my encounter with Stewart at the community center, but just then the detective holds a finger up and takes his cell phone from his belt. "Burgess here."

He's silent as whoever it is talks, but his eyes widen until they look ready to fall out of his head, and his jaw drops. "You've got to be kidding me," he says into the phone. "It's a full match? No doubt?" He pauses briefly. "My God. Okay, thank you, Templeton."

I stare at him as he replaces the phone, expecting an explanation.

"That was one of my lab techs," he says in an airless tone, as if he'd just taken a swift blow to the gut. "On a hunch, I decided to compare DNA from the Singing Woods case with your father's. We had it on file, because of the suicide. And ..." He gives me a look full of sympathetic horror. "There's an exact match between your father and Stewart Brooks."

I stagger back, a hand to my mouth. Stewart Brooks is — *was* — Jessica Forrest's son. And my father's. He was my half-brother, and he abducted me. Raped me.

I killed Selma Ferguson's child.

Now she was going to return the favor.

"You have to find her, right now," I say, clutching Tom's arm. "Please, hurry."

His expression is solemn. "We will."

I can only pray they'll do it in time.

48

Friday, June 6, 7:12 p.m.

I'm driving home, cutting across a quiet side street that leads to the main road in my neighborhood, when the wail of sirens swells behind me and flashing lights fracture my rear view mirror. I pull to the curb, expecting to see squad cars racing. Most of the Dayfield police department is converging on one of two locations right now.

But what rushes past me, throwing off warbling pulses and honking bleats, is the bright red of a fire truck. Then a second, and a smaller third one.

I shiver at the sight. The whole town seems to be crumbling apart, all at once.

My adrenaline is about to crash hard, and I stay pulled over for a few minutes trying to collect myself. My head is pounding. I reach up to massage a temple, and another flash of light rips through my mind.

I'm on a bed. Tied down. There's the wooden door, the locked one.

A man looms over me. He wears a mask, a ... balaclava, I think it's called. I can only see his eyes.

He's going to touch me.

I start to scream.

He puts a knee on the bed, and there's something behind him. Another balaclava.

A second man.

There are two of them.

The vision snaps away, leaving black-and-white images flashing behind my eyes like stuttering photographic negatives. There were two of them. I remember now, truly remember, at least that much.

There was *someone else* in the woods.

And it wasn't Selma. Both of the masked figures were male, but only one of them ever touched me.

I have no idea which one it was.

Tears streak down my face as I sit in the car, clutching the steering wheel. I'm so close. So close to remembering it all. It's maddening, a deep-seated itch that I can't reach. The vault in my mind has only cracked, allowing fractions of memories to seep out, but I need to break it wide open.

My ringing cell phone startles the breath from me. The pounding in my head increases as I answer an unfamiliar number on my screen with the fleeting hope that somehow it's my daughter. That she's escaped, found a payphone or someone with a cell phone.

But it's Sergeant McKenzie.

"Tom's driving right now," he says after he identifies himself. "We wanted to tell you..." He pauses, and there's a quick, muffled voice, as if he's covered the phone. "Sorry," McKenzie says when he comes back. "It's just ... Ian Moody's house is on fire."

"Oh my God." The tears that had dried up start rolling again. "Is he in there?"

"We don't know. The blaze is ... it's bad," he says. "And there's a car in the driveway. A blue Honda Civic."

That's his car. He rarely drives it, usually rides with my husband, but he wasn't with Richard when he left the police station.

He's there. And he could be dead.

"We'll let you know as soon as they get the fire out and have a look," McKenzie says. "I'm sorry, Mrs. Osborn."

"It's okay. Thank you."

I don't know what else to say.

I hang up and stare at the phone, daring it to ring with more bad news. When it doesn't, my finger hovers over the contact list. I know I've got to stop doing this, but I can't help it.

I call my daughter.

The phone rings, rings, rings.

My muscles tense as I wait for the recorded message.

And then, there's a small, weak voice in my ear, little more than a breath of sound.

"Mom ..."

"Renata?" My own voice barely crawls past my lips. Hearing her is so unexpected that I almost convince myself I'm having auditory hallucinations again. I almost hang up. But I banish those doubts as every inch of my body starts trembling. "Renata! Baby, where are you?" I'm nearly shouting, as if she won't be able to hear anything quieter. "Can you tell me where you are? Are you hurt? Is there anyone with you?"

"Mom." Her voice is a fraction louder, but it's enough to instantly silence me. I'm listening. "He says you have to come ..."

All of my joy implodes, and sick dread replaces it. She hasn't escaped. She's with *him*.

"Come where, baby?" I say roughly, wondering if I'll ever breathe again. "I'll be there. You tell him to let you go, and I'll be there."

"Come to the place ..." She's fading in and out. There's a muffled, wracking wet cough that makes my heart hurt. "The place where he left them. Drive as far as you can and wait."

The dumping grounds. The dirt road into the Singing Woods.

"All right, sweetheart. I'm on my way," I tell her. "Listen, baby, I love you—"

"You can't tell, Mom. You have to come alone." Her voice is flat, lifeless. "Or he'll kill me."

And then she's gone.

My shoulders shake with sobs as I toss the phone on the passenger seat and put the still-running car in gear. I will not fall apart. I will get to my daughter, and I'll save her. If I have to convince him to take me in her place, I'll do it.

With or without me, she's coming home tonight.

49

Friday, June 6, 8:15 p.m.

The woods are lovely, dark and deep.

The Singing Woods are not lovely. Lovely is for shafts of sunlight and singing birds, green leaves and deer drinking from streams. These woods are stark. Primeval. Densely packed rows of ancient sentinels a hundred feet tall, most of their branches bare and rattling all year round. Even in the daylight, this place is foreboding at best.

Now, in the dark, it's a living nightmare.

I creep along the path, intent on the glow of the headlights as I watch for shapes in the dark. Far above, a three-quarter moon shimmers in irregular facets, cascading silver-white diamonds filtered through the skeletal canopy of limbs. All around me, I can hear the ghostly, rattling foghorn of the wind whistling eerily through the trees, the distinctive sound that gives the Singing Woods its name.

My mind churns with questions. Will he bring Renata to me? Will he show up alone and simply kill me, and then go back to finish my daughter? Will Selma be out here somewhere?

Is it really Stewart Brooks? Or is it the other one?

Soon I can see the end of the path, where the side-by-side dirt tire tracks tumble into the underbrush and the trees press in closely. I ride the brakes to a stop just before the tracks end, put the car in park and turn the engine off. I leave the headlights on. Slipping the keys in one pocket and my phone in the other, I open the door and ignore the warning chime of the headlights as I get out.

I'm about to close the door when a female voice calls from the darkness, "Turn off the headlights."

Selma.

I shiver as I reach in and push the headlight knob. The velvet-black night swallows me as I close the door, and I stand still, listening for any sound. She's to my left somewhere. I'm not sure how far away she is, who or what she's brought to this place.

"Jessica," I say. "Is my daughter with you?"

"So you know my name. Bravo, Miss Maddie." The beam of a flashlight bursts from the trees, momentarily blinding me. "Get your hands up."

I do as she says. "My daughter," I whisper. "Please."

"We'll get to her. If you cooperate, do exactly what I tell you, I'll let you live long enough to see her." The light bobs and swells, and I hear footsteps crunching across the dry forest floor. She's walking toward me. "Empty your pockets," she says.

My hands shake as I drop my keys on the ground, and then my phone. I raise my arms again when I'm done.

"Look at you, being such a good girl without being told. Are you trying to score points with me, Miss Maddie?"

"I just want to see my daughter, please," I say. I need to stay calm, in control.

"Well, let's go see her, then." Selma is close enough now that I can see her face in the backwash of the flashlight. She's leering, no warmth left in her smile. The arm without the flashlight is stretched toward me, and there's a gun in her hand.

I guess now I know who murdered Frank Kilgore.

Selma lowers the flashlight and moves behind me. Seconds later, I feel the gun jammed between my shoulder blades. The beam of light wavers past me and steadies, forming an eerie, elongated circle of washed-out forest ringed with shifting shadows.

"Start walking," Selma says. "You'll know where to go."

I move straight ahead, away from the car. At first I think she means I know how to get to the lair, but I don't. I wonder what she'll do to me if I go the wrong way. Then she starts leading me, jabbing the muzzle of the gun toward my left or right shoulder when she wants me to change directions.

I want to ask her why she's doing this, but I already know. I killed her twisted, sick-minded love child. I decide to stick to the topic of my daughter. "Have you hurt Renata?" I say. "Is she okay?"

Selma laughs. "Not that it matters, but no. I haven't."

I swallow. "Has someone else hurt her?"

"Don't be like that, now. You'll spoil the surprise." She jabs me with the gun, straight on. That one was only meant to hurt. "I bet you've gotten it into that pretty little head of yours that I'm some kind of home-wrecker, right? The other woman? Well, child, the truth is that your father loved me. I was his long before *Judith*." My mother's name is a disgusted drawl. "Do you want to hear the story of how we met?"

No, I absolutely don't. I decide not to answer that question.

She tells me anyway.

"He chose me, you know," she says. "Over her, my rival. When it came down to it, to the choice between us, he strangled her to death so he could have me."

Apparently I hadn't run out of shock for my father's actions, after all. "Are you saying he *murdered* someone?"

"Oh, yes. Her name was Violet, and she was a sweet young thing. Pretty. I hated her." Selma's voice dips to a lower register. "I followed them into the woods, and I watched him kill her. Then we buried her together. It was *hot*. Turned me right on like nobody's business. That's when I knew that your daddy was the one for me."

I'm completely repulsed. The next time I think I'm crazy, if I live long enough for the next time, I'll remember Selma and realize how stone-cold sane I am next to her.

A touch of imposter syndrome is nothing compared to erotic homicide.

"The thing is, my stepdaddy was not a nice man." Selma seems determined to talk, as if I want to listen to any of this. Or maybe she's in love with the sound of her own voice. "I needed somebody else to be my daddy. I chose Wendell, and he chose me. We stayed in the woods together, at *his* daddy's hunting cabin. It was bliss." She sighs happily, like a new bride, and I want to vomit. "Then we had a baby of our own, and Wendell was a daddy."

I wonder how long this is going to go on. Her voice grates on me, stabs at me.

I wish she'd shut up.

"But he didn't know," Selma says in a puzzled whisper. "He left before I found out I was pregnant. He promised he'd come back, but he never did. He came here, and he had *you*." The gun shoves me again. "He was your daddy, not Stewart's. So I had to die and move here, become someone else, to get back at him. He deserved it, don't you see? He abandoned me." She sniffles softly. "I was supposed to be the only one for him. He told me so."

I can't take much more of this. Her deranged babbling makes me sick. "Stewart killed all those girls. He was going to kill me, too," I say, unable to keep the rage from my voice. "That's a lot of revenge for just one man."

"Oh, you dear, ignorant child," she says. "Those other girls were just a distraction, so no one would figure out the real target. That honor was supposed to be yours. But then you killed my angel." She snarls the last few words. "I had to do something special to get back at you," she continues in a normal tone. "You have no idea how long I planned, what I've done, what I've *sacrificed* to make sure every step of your life led to this moment."

The cold in me is bone-deep. "What moment is that?"

"The moment you watch your own child die, the way I had to watch mine."

That's not going to happen. Ever.

I tense and dart my eyes left and right, as far as the light reaches, searching for a weapon. Anything I can use. Ahead of me, at the furthest edge of the flashlight beam, there's a palm-sized stone on the ground, half-covered by twigs and debris.

Three more steps, and I drop and dive for it.

The gun goes off instantly, a thundering roar that echoes endlessly.

But she's missed, and my hand closes around the rock. I roll to the side, out of the light, and start running.

"Bitch!" Selma screams. There's another discharge from the gun, a quick strobe that throws all the trees into sharp relief for a few second. The flashlight beam finds me and I cut a hard right.

My toes slam against a tree root, pulsing agony through my foot. I grit my teeth and keep going.

"Do you really think you'll get away from me?" Selma bellows. "Out here in the dark, me with a flashlight and a gun against you and your desperation to save your precious daughter? I don't *have* to let you watch her die, you know. I could kill you right now and be just as satisfied.

My searching hand finds a tree trunk, and I rope and arm around it and swing behind, just as the flashlight beam passes me. She's coming this way.

"Madeline!" Selma snorts through her nose and picks up the pace, a charging bull. "Come out right now, or I'll make sure your daughter suffers for *months*, until I finally let her die."

I have to bite my tongue to keep a scream inside. She's almost close enough. Just a few more steps.

"I know you're right here somewhere!" she yells, stopping five feet from the tree I'm pressed against.

It'll have to work from here.

I rush toward her, raising the rock. She spots me instantly and gets the gun up, pulls the trigger, and the bullet grazes my side. It hurts like hell, but I won't let it stop me.

I swing the rock down on her skull with a sickening crack.

She warbles something nonsensical. Her eyes roll back as she sinks to her knees, crunching down on the forest floor. Moving quickly, I hit her with the rock again and throw it into the darkness, then snatch the gun and flashlight from her.

She's still on her knees, eyes open as a thick splutch of blood oozes down her forehead. I point the light and the gun at her, and she laughs.

It's the most chilling sound I've ever heard.

"You really think you're going to make it, don't you?" she says, her voice fading fast. "Maddie, child. Even if I lose here and now, I've already won. You'll never be safe. My son will make sure of that."

"I killed your son, remember?" I say. "Stewart Brooks is dead."

She gives another bubbling chuckle as she slumps completely to the ground. "Yes, he is," she whispers, her lips barely moving. "But I have ... two of them."

My finger tightens on the trigger without thought. The gun booms and kicks in my hand, jerking my arm back with the recoil.

And a black hole blossoms on Selma's forehead as the breath leaves her forever.

I cry out and fall to the ground, covering my face with my arms. I have the flashlight and the gun, but I'm lost. Lost in the woods, with no idea where my daughter is.

Except that she's with Selma's *other* son.

I have two of them.

Two Stewarts?

Twins. She had twins. That's why there were two of them.

That's why I kept seeing Stewart.

The sudden flash in my head is blinding, and I see ... trees, in the daylight. Tall, thick, lush green pines, three of them arranged in a triangle.

And in the ground, at the center of the trees, is something that looks like a section of stockade fence lying flat on the ground, half-covered in leaves and pine needles.

Habit whore.

Hobbit hole. That's what I was screaming when Dr. Bradshaw hypnotized me. The first time I saw that thing, that awful place where he kept me, I thought of it as a hobbit hole.

It was a door, and it led underground. To the lair.

That was the reason no one could find it.

And I remember where it is.

50

Friday, June 6. Night.

I'm not sure how long I stumble through the woods, headed doggedly toward the hobbit hole. Though I remember its location, the only time I saw it was during daylight, and there aren't many familiar landmarks in a dark woods. Every tree, every stone, every deadfall and cluster of bushes, look the same.

But I'm going the right way. I know it. And eventually I'm rewarded by the sight of three fat pine trees arranged in a triangle.

The trapdoor is in the center of them. I switch the flashlight off and give my eyes a few minutes to adjust to the near-total darkness, then creep forward as quietly as possible. The flashlight goes in my pocket, but the gun stays in my hand. I won't hesitate to shoot the other son the instant I see him.

Can they really be twins? That has to be it. The man I saw looks just like Stewart.

I reach the trapdoor and grip the edge. I remember that it lifts up, and that it creaks like a rusty spring in a screen door. There's a ladder against the edge of the opening to access the underground hideaway.

He'll hear me when I open it. I'll just have to hope that he thinks it's Selma coming back.

I decide to move quickly once I get started. I pull the trapdoor up, wincing as it squeals like a greased pig. There's a dull glow inside the hole, not coming from directly below, but I can make out the ladder. I swing onto it and start climbing down one-handed.

I will not let go of this gun until he's dead.

When I reach the bottom, there's an open doorway that leads to a simple living room with a dirt floor and dirt walls. A kerosene lamp burns low in the far corner. There's another open entrance kitty-corner from this one, and a closed wooden door on the back wall to the left.

My chest squeezes as I recognize it. That's the room they kept me in.

As I move carefully in to the living room, a youthful male voice calls from the open doorway, "Mom? Is that you?"

Thank God. He thinks I'm Selma.

Maybe if I get to him fast enough, I can kill him before he realizes I'm not.

I walk fast across the room, not bothering to hide the sound of my footsteps. I flatten against the wall beside the opening, say a silent prayer, and then swing around with the gun extended in both arms.

He's there, standing in the middle of the room. Stewart Brooks, exactly the way I remember him. Still twenty. He's holding my daughter's slumped, barely conscious form in front of him with one arm.

He has a gun pressed to her temple.

"Oh, it *is* you," he says in a cheerful tone. "Hi, Mom."

Mom?

Me?

"Stewart?" I whisper.

Even as I say it, I realize that's not really Stewart. It's a fake, an imposter who only looks like him. He's replaced Stewart, and now he wants to hurt me. Hurt my daughter.

The fake Stewart laughs. "My name's not Stewart," he says. "It's Wendell. After my grandfather."

Grandfather...

Oh. God. This is *my* child. Mine and Stewart's.

My other daughter.

"B-but you're a girl," I stammer. "I saw you, when you were born."

The cheery smile falls away. "Why don't you put the gun down,

Mom, before I have to hurt my sister? I don't want to," he — *she* — says. And then grins. "At least, not yet."

Shaking, I set the gun on the floor.

"Oh, and you should probably kick it over here."

I do it.

Renata moans and stirs, blinking blearily. She seems to look right at me for a few seconds, but then her eyes glaze over and her lids flutter closed.

"What have you done to her?" I whisper.

"Who, Renata? She's just stoned out of her mind right now," Wendell says. "Don't worry, she'll come around in a few hours. We've got plenty of time. Where's Aunt Selma?"

When I don't answer, Wendell shrugs. "You killed her, didn't you? Oh, well. That's okay, we can do this without her."

"Please," I rasp, weaving on my feet. "Please don't hurt my daughter."

"*I'm* your daughter," Wendell hisses, eyes narrowing. But then that terrible, cheerful grin resurfaces. "Well, I *was* your daughter. But now I can be your son. I look great, right?" Wendell waves the gun up and down at herself, and then socks it back against Renata's head. "You'd be amazed at what hormone therapy and plastic surgery can do these days. There were so many of them. So many surgeries." Her voice trails off, wavering into sorrow for an instant, but then it firms again. "It did help that there was already a strong family resemblance. And we had plenty of money for it, after Aunt Selma killed her stepdaddy. That bastard was loaded!"

Wendell's light, happy tone is a discordant note to the awful things that are so casually coming out of her mouth. It's nails on a chalkboard, amplified a hundred times and run through a distorter.

I change my mind about Selma. *Wendell's* the crazy one.

Selma would look normal next to her.

"Oh, there's just one thing, though," she says in a stage whisper, and points down. "I don't have any boy bits yet, so we'll just have to pretend they're there. Aunt Selma was going to get them done, but ... she hadn't gotten around to it yet."

Once again, that sorrow is back in her voice. Now I know what

Selma meant when she said she'd had to sacrifice so much to lead me to this moment. But she hasn't sacrificed anything, not really. She's forced this child, my child, to sacrifice everything instead.

And even though Wendell has a gun to my daughter's head, I feel absolutely awful for her. I'm so achingly sorry for what it must have been like, growing up with Selma and Stewart. I want to hold her and tell her that everything's going to be all right. But obviously, it's far too late for that.

I'd prayed for so long that her life would be better than what I could've given her. My prayers weren't answered.

I can only save one daughter now.

I swallow hard and try to look around the room unobtrusively. I have to get Renata away from her, get my daughter out of here. This is a rough sort of bedroom, dirt walls and floor like the living room, but there are patterns etched into the walls. Swirling, surreal designs that almost look like landscapes. There's a bed directly behind Wendell, against the back wall, and a table to her right with a kerosene lamp and a wind-up alarm clock. Against the left wall is a dresser, and on top of that is a heavy-looking, misshapen glazed clay bowl, a clumsy attempt at pottery.

Wendell must've made it. The child I've never known shares my interest in pottery.

God, how that hurts.

"Aren't you going to say anything, Mom?" There's a taunting edge to Wendell's cheery voice now. "I mean, you haven't seen me in twenty years. I thought we could chat and catch up, before I kill both of you. Her first, of course." She jerks Renata, and my daughter moans again.

"Wendell, you don't have to kill us," I say. "Selma's dead now. This was her plan."

"Wrong! Do not pass go, do not collect two hundred dollars," Wendell quips with manic glee. "The surgeries were her idea, so you'd be scared more, but I wanted to be the one to kill the two of you. Especially my sister," she spits as angry tears start to form in her eyes. "I *hate* her. She got you, and she got to stay a girl. And I had to be *this*." Wendell stares at me. "You didn't love me, so I had to be this."

"No, I did love you," I say shakily. "I wanted a better life for you —"

"A better life?" Wendell screams, spittle flying from her lips. "You think Aunt Selma was a *better life*?"

I shake my head. "She wasn't supposed to have you. There was a nice, well-off couple lined up."

"Yeah, there sure was. Selma's stepdaddy and his little tart. She was a real sweetheart, that one." Wendell pushes the gun harder against Renata. "I think it's time you said goodbye to your favorite daughter."

Renata jerks suddenly, her eyes flying wide open. "Mom!" she screams as her arm flashes out, knocking the gun away from her own head. "The bowl!"

I lunge for the dresser and grab the heavy, misshapen clay bowl. Wendell howls in sheer frustration as Renata squirms in her grip, flailing as hard as she can.

Then my daughter stomps a foot back hard, catching Wendell square in the shin. Her grip loosens, and as Renata drops to the floor, I smash the bowl across the side of Wendell's head.

There's a horrible crunching sound. Wendell drops like a stone, landing on Renata as she tries to squirm away.

"Oh, *God,* get *off!*" my daughter shrieks, shoving at the body.

I take Renata's hands and pull her forward, shoving Wendell's limp form aside with a foot. "Baby, I'm so sorry," I whisper. "It's over now. You're safe."

My daughter falls into my arms, sobbing, and I rub her back soothingly. And as I help her out of the room, across to the ladder, and up into the dark woods, my absolute relief is tempered by something Selma said to me, something I can't shake.

Even if I lose, here and now, I've already won.

She had. She'd taken something from me and twisted it horribly, until it was beyond all hope of salvation.

She'd taken my daughter.

51

Friday, June 6. Night.

Renata and I have been wandering the woods for quite some time as I attempt to retrace my steps back to the car. I still have the flashlight, so that makes things a little easier, but it's slow going. My daughter is weakened from what she's been through, and she does have some kind of drugs in her system. They just weren't affecting her as much as she'd pretended they were.

I believe I've mentioned that my daughter is a very intelligent young woman. I'm indescribably proud of her.

I'm more exhausted than I've ever been in my life, but I summon the will to keep going. We can't spend all night out here in the woods. We've talked little so far, both of us trying to conserve our energy, neither of us really knowing what to say about any of it.

Eventually, Renata sighs softly. "You know, Mom, I thought I was going a little crazy," she says with a little half-smile. "This boy kept telling me that he was my *sister.* I didn't know about all the ... surgeries and stuff, until he told you."

"I think maybe we're all a little crazy," I say as I put an arm around her shoulders. She doesn't even try to tug away. "And you know what? I think that's okay."

She laughs, and the sound goes a long way toward healing my

stricken heart. The knowledge that she can still laugh. "You might be a lot crazy, but it's the good kind," she says. "Did you really kill Selma Ferguson? The lady who runs the community center?"

I don't want to admit it out loud, and she already knows the answer. So I fudge the question, tilt the subject. "Her real name was Jessica Forrest," I say. "She was Stewart Brooks' mother."

"The guy who abducted you when you were my age?" Renata says, her eyes growing wide. "Wow. Our family is seriously fucked up!"

Renata Lee! is on the tip of my tongue, but I don't say it. Because she's right. She actually doesn't know how right she is, and I hope she never finds out.

I can almost see my mother's reasoning for not telling me about my father.

We fall silent again, and the wind whistles and hoots and rattles through the treetops as I shine the light ahead. Then I hear something in the distance. Shouting, what sounds like more than one voice, peppering the woods in various directions. And just ahead, dim pulses of light flickering through the trees.

"Do you hear that?" Renata breathes, suddenly going still. "It can't be ... it's not him, is it? Wendell?"

"I don't think so," I say as I take her hand and give a reassuring squeeze. "I think it's our rescue party."

She flashes a smile at me and we both break into a careful jog toward the voices and lights, moving as fast as the flashlight will allow us. As we get closer, I can make out words.

"Madeline!"

"Renata!"

"If you can hear me, come to the sound of my voice!"

At least one of those voices belongs to Detective Burgess.

"Over here!" I shout as loud as I can, waving the flashlight in wide arcs over my head as I slow my pace. "Renata, let's just stay here for a minute, let them come to us," I say. "It's easier."

She stops and retreats to my side. "Do you know who they are?"

"It's the police," I say. "They've been helping me find you."

Renata leans her head on my shoulder. "Well, they didn't find me," she says. "You did."

I have no words to say how grateful I am for that.

It's not long before the reach us, Burgess and McKenzie in the lead, with three uniformed officers right behind them. I realize one of them is Officer Jeremy.

Burgess heads straight for me and stops. His features pass through a gamut of emotions before he lands on an incredulous grin. "Didn't I tell you to go home, Mrs. Osborn?" he says.

"I am home," I say, hugging my daughter close. "Everything that means home is right here with me."

"Mo-om," Renata groans good-naturedly. "That's *so* mushy."

I don't mind the flash of teen drama, even a little.

"Well. There's an ambulance waiting for you ladies, right this way," Tom says as he gives a mock bow and gestures back the way they'd come from.

Everyone heads that way. "So, Tom," I say. "How did you find us?"

"Honestly?" he smirks. "After that little stunt you pulled with Brenda Westhall, I had a tracker put on your car. Just in case you tried anything else stupidly dangerous." He waves both arms in wide circles. "You know. Like *this*."

"I'm glad you did," I say with a smile. I'll explain everything to him later. Right now, I want to get myself and my daughter the hell out of these woods.

But there is one thing I have to tell him now.

"Detective," I say under my breath. "Did you find Selma Ferguson?"

He nods. "She's ... deceased."

I manage not to say *good*. "I'm sorry to tell you this, but there's another body." I point back in the direction Renata and I came from. "I can tell you where it is, but I don't think you'll be able to find the place until daylight."

"Do I even want to know whose body it is?" he says.

"It's an extremely long story. But her name is Wendell."

Tom blinks. "You mean like your father?"

"Yes." I don't have the strength to elaborate further. I'm thinking about Wendell, my poor doomed daughter, and the fixed, wooden expression on her face when she said I didn't love her. That she had to be this ... this thing Selma made her.

My daughter. Wendell was *my daughter.* But Selma said that she had two sons.

And Wendell couldn't have been working with Stewart when I was abducted. She hadn't even been born yet.

Selma wasn't talking about Wendell.

There was still someone else out there.

"Did you find Richard?" I say as my panic starts to rise, belatedly realizing that I still haven't talked to him all day. He doesn't even know that I've found Renata. "I mean, he should've been home by now. I just never made it back to the house before ..."

I trail off when I catch the look on Tom's face. "You didn't find him, did you?" I whisper. "He didn't come home."

The other son killed him. He killed him and buried his body in the woods, and you'll never find him. Never know what happened.

The detective is saying something, but I don't hear it, because suddenly the biggest flash of light yet bolts into my brain, and a flood of memories roar out like a waterfall.

My senses are so overwhelmed that I can't speak, and I sink to my knees, holding the sides of my head.

"Mom?" I hear Renata's voice from a distance, as if she's shouting through a tunnel. "Oh my God. Mom!"

I don't see her, or the woods.

I see the room. The door, the bed. *He's* in here with me.

I'm not tied down, at least. I *hate* him, hate the things he does to me, but I've managed to convince him that I like it. That I like him. It's the only way they won't tie me to the bed all day. Sometimes I'm afraid I'm a little too convincing, that I might have convinced *myself* that I like him, or it.

I don't, though. I feel dirty, disgusted, ashamed, violated. And *angry.* I'm angry all the time. I need to get out of here somehow.

But he's here, and he's going to do things to me. For some reason he's waited longer than usual today, just staring down at me, his eyes dulled marbles through the slit of his mask. I almost ask him if he wants something, but that's just *inviting* his repulsive touch.

Without a word, he reaches up and starts removing the balaclava.

"No!" I shout breathlessly, squeezing my eyes shut. I don't want to see his face. I haven't seen it, haven't seen either of them, and I know what happens when the bad guys let you look at them. That's when they kill you.

"Madeline." For the first time, I hear his voice unmuffled by the balaclava. "Look at me."

"No, I don't want to," I say in a small, trembling voice. "I don't want to die."

"I won't kill you." A hand squeezes my upper arm hard, until tears drizzle from my closed eyes. "*Look at me.*"

I have no choice. I look.

And I start screaming.

That's when I realize I'm actually screaming. Present Madeline in the woods, not past Madeline in the habit whore. Hobbit hole. I've seen his face. The someone else, the second kidnapper, the man who raped me. The father of Wendell.

The father of *both* my children.

Renata's trying to help me to my feet, while Burgess and McKenzie fire urgent questions at me. I wave them off and stagger a few steps as I attempt to remember how to breathe.

I didn't truly understand the vast machinations of Selma's scheme to ruin my life until this moment, this memory.

Richard.

Oh, Richard.

My husband is Selma Ferguson's other son.

52

Saturday, June 7, 12:27 a.m.

I haven't been able to tell Renata about her father yet. I can't bring myself to.

She's asleep in the other bed in our hospital room, the one by the window. She hasn't been seriously injured, thank God. Mostly bruises and scrapes. But she's dehydrated, and there are a handful of drugs in her system. Depressants, antipsychotics, and traces of marijuana. She'll need to stay here at least through tomorrow.

Once she'd dropped off, I had the long conversation with Tom. I had to tell him about Richard first. He was stunned, to say the least. I feel something beyond stunned, especially now that I remember that week in the woods, in the ground, with them. At least, I remember most of it. The only thing I don't know is how I escaped.

Stewart was the one who'd hurt me, the violent and angry one, but he'd never done anything sexual. And Richard had never hit me. He'd raped me repeatedly, gotten me pregnant, but he never struck me.

Then he took advantage of my blocked memory to worm his way into my life. I'd spent seventeen years married to this man, feeling *grateful* that he was so patient and loving, so understanding of my condition and the scars and the fallout from my horrific past. Oblivious to the fact that he'd been responsible for all of it in the first place.

He hadn't just violated my body. He'd violated my life, my existence.

I'd given Tom the diary, the one I'd supposedly written that Ian had ended up with. Now I knew that Richard must've been responsible for that, too, in some way. I still didn't know how he'd done it. But he'd fabricated the thing, gotten it to Ian so he'd leave me. And then he'd made Ian his partner so he could keep an eye on him, and make sure the man who'd actually loved me would never take me away from the monster I'd married.

I told the detective about the underground hideout, where it was in the woods, and whose body was in there. What Selma had done to Wendell, with the surgeries and conditioning. She'd probably had the child call her 'Aunt Selma' so Wendell would grow up knowing that she had no mother, that her mother had abandoned her and then had a different daughter, one she actually loved. Poisoning her mind with so much hate.

At least now, Tom could see that I wasn't crazy. I *had* seen 'Stewart' lurking around.

Detective Burgess has people scouring the town, looking for Richard. He's dangerous, of course, now more than ever since his secret's been exposed. But there's a chance he may not know that. He has no idea that my memories have returned, that I know what he's done to me. But for now, Renata and I are safe in the hospital.

I'm supposed to be resting and recovering, but I can't. There's someone else here I need to speak to.

I get up carefully from my bed and walk over to Renata's, gazing at my sleeping child for a moment. My strong, brave young woman. This experience will scar her, especially when she learns about Richard. She loves her father. But I believe she'll recover, that she has a good chance at escaping these shadows and living a life far better than mine.

Isn't that what every parent wants for their child?

I smooth her hair, kiss her forehead and slip from the room, leaving her to rest. He's just down the hall from us — Renata and me in 428, him in 416. His door is cracked open, and though it's late, I have a feeling he'll still be awake.

When I enter the room, his head turns toward me. He's the only one in here, in the bed by the window, and it's hard to see his injuries even in the low light. He has one broken leg, two broken ribs, three deep gashes that required stitches, and he's suffered smoke inhalation. His face is a patchwork of bruises. But his green eyes smile when he looks at me.

Ian survived the fire. Richard had beaten him unconscious and left him for dead when he set the blaze, but Ian managed to drag across his kitchen and throw himself down the basement steps. That was how he broke his leg. The rest was Richard's doing. They'd gotten the fire out before it reached the foundation, before it killed him, but the house is a total loss.

I sit in the visitor's chair beside his bed and take his hand, the one without the IV needle in it. "Hey."

"Hey," he says. One corner of his mouth lifts slightly. "You're alive."

"So are you." I pull a strained smile to cover the tears that want to come, knowing who's done this to him. Richard destroyed both of our lives, together and separately.

Ian shifts and winces slightly. "How's Renata?"

"She's doing great. Sleeping now." The shock of it all hasn't set in for her yet, and she'll go through a bad patch. But I'm going to be right here for her the whole time, helping her recover. Helping her understand that none of this is her fault.

All the things my own mother didn't do for me.

Ian nods and does that corner-smile thing again. "And how's Maddie?"

"Still breathing." I shake my head and smirk. "Do you feel up to talking for a few minutes? Now that you can finally tell me what you were going to say."

"Depends," he says.

"On ...?" I raise an eyebrow.

"Whether you feel up to listening." His stare is intense, the way he'd looked at me in the police station while he was being led away. "I don't want to upset you any more than you already are."

I manage a tired laugh. "Honestly, I don't think that's possible."

"Don't be too sure about that," he says. There's a small smile on his face, but soon it droops like a flag in a dying wind. "Maddie, I'm so sorry —"

"Hush. You've already apologized," I say, squeezing his hand gently. "I forgave you the minute I read all those ... horrible things. I'd have hated me, too."

"But you didn't write them. And I never should've believed that you did."

"It's hard not to believe what you see with your own eyes," I tell him, knowing the truth in that from personal experience. It's why Capgras Syndrome is so insidious. Your eyes see what's there, but your brain refuses to buy it. "How did you get that diary, anyway?"

He laughs weakly. "It was just in my mailbox one day, in a brown envelope," he says. "No address, no postage. I didn't even think about how suspicious that was. I just went with it." He fixes me with a stare. "But I shouldn't have."

"Well, it's over now. I gave it to the police, in case it's evidence of something," I say. "How'd you know that it wasn't mine?"

"That's what I wanted to talk to you about. It's kind of a long story, so bear with me." He closes his eyes, blanching under the bruises. "I'd been going over the company accounting. Richard always handled that, but I needed some numbers for the advertising budget and he was ... occupied. You know." He winces, and I understand he's talking about Renata's abduction. "So I checked the books myself. That's when I found out we were leaking a few thousand a month, that Richard was writing off as 'expenses' we didn't have. I wanted to know where the money was going."

This must've been what they were arguing about that morning. "He told me *you* were the one siphoning money," I say.

"Of course he did. Then he came up with that weak attempt to frame me for ... something, I don't know what, by putting pictures of Renata in my room."

A jolt of fear went through me. Richard had raped me. Had he done the same to our daughter? "What kind of pictures?" I whisper.

"Just normal ones. School and family stuff," he says, and I shudder with relief. "But he'd done things to them. Scribbled her eyes out in some, slashed up others, put red ink on a few of them trying to suggest blood. I guess he didn't have time to come up with anything better." He flashes a dark expression. "Anyway, I'm getting ahead of myself. After Richard tried to blame me for the missing money, I went looking through his stuff. That's when I found out the diary was fake."

"How?" I say.

"He had some of your old stuff. Essays and reports you'd written in high school. I don't know how he got them," he says. "But it was obvious he'd been practicing your handwriting, and I saw at least a few sentences that I'd read in the diary on the practice stuff. It must've taken him months to make that thing."

I remember all those months Richard came to the diner where I'd worked, every day. The little chats we'd have, about my apartment, my boyfriend, my everyday life. How we'd swapped high school stories.

He'd been pumping me for information all that time, so he could use it against Ian and remove him from my life. So *he* could take over.

"He always was very patient," I mutter, too hollowed out to cry any more. I wonder what he did with the money, but I imagine he'd been funneling it to Selma, maybe for Wendell. Supporting his 'family,' twisted as it was.

Ian's hand twitches in mine. "Have they found him yet?" he says. "You're not safe until they do."

"They're looking. They'll find him." If nothing else, I have faith in the dogged determination of Detective Burgess. "Meanwhile, I think I'd better let you get some sleep. And I should do the same."

Ian gives me a hopeful smile. "I hope we can be friends again someday."

I stand, lean over the bed and kiss his forehead, the least bruised part of it. "We're friends right now," I tell him. "And ... I still love you, too."

He shivers, and his eyes gleam. "Thank you."

I leave his room and go back to mine, where my daughter is waiting.

And I think, finally, I'll be able to sleep.

53

Saturday, June 7, 9:30 p.m.

Our home seems far less welcoming, now that I know the lies we've been living with all this time. But it's warm and familiar, and safe. There's been a constant police detail here since the beginning.

Before we'd left the hospital, I had to tell Renata about her father. That was the first time she'd really cried since I got her back. She sobbed in my arms for nearly an hour, and when she was done, she refused to talk about it anymore.

I know she'll open up one day, but it's going to take time. And time is something we have now.

We're both dragging as we walk inside the dark, quiet house. I turn the living room lights on and settle my daughter on the couch, handing her the remote from the coffee table. We've decided to make it a movie night, to just relax and be home for a few hours. We can worry about everything else in the morning.

"I'll go make some popcorn," I say. "You pick the movie. Anything you want."

Renata gives me an impish smile. "Even horror?"

I make a face, and she laughs. "Don't worry, Mom. I feel like I've just lived a horror movie, so I don't want to watch one. I'm thinking romantic comedy."

"That sounds perfect," I say, glad she's still able to make light of it. The shock of what she's been through will hit her at odd times, frequently at first. She'll have nightmares. Ordinary things will remind her of something else, something darker, and she'll burst into unexpected tears. But gradually the nightmares will fade, and the shadows will draw back, and the memories will sleep. Then she'll have peace again.

I know this, because I've lived it. And I'll go through it again with her now.

But we'll both see the other side.

Renata turns the television on and opens Netflix, and I head to the kitchen. The box of files from Brenda Westhall is still on the dining room table, the contents packed neatly inside, and I wonder what I'm going to do with it. Brenda may want it back, and I'll be happy to let her have it. If she doesn't, I'll probably burn it all.

There are enough memories in my head. I don't need to see them printed out in black and white, or on horrific glossy color photos.

I find the microwave popcorn and tear the plastic from two bags, and place the first one in the microwave. As it hums to life, I move to the cabinets for glasses. I think we have soda in the fridge somewhere, cola or root beer, and that'll go fine with the popcorn.

As I grab the handle to open the fridge, a sudden jolt of terror runs through me, freezing me in place. The file box.

I didn't put those files back in.

They were still spread all over the dining room table when I left for Dr. Bradshaw's yesterday evening, when Richard hadn't been back all day.

My heart stops beating as I stride through the dining room. I can see Renata through the entrance to the living room, seated on the couch. She's looking straight ahead, eyes wide, face white, the remote trembling in her hand.

He's there when I step through the doorway, standing in front of the television. His face is bathed with tears, but his expression is set, determined.

And he's holding a gun on our daughter.

"Richard," I say, my voice a sliver of sound. The rest of my words curdle and die in my throat.

He turns his head toward me. His movements are slow and jerky, and the light of insanity blazes from his reddened eyes. "I've been waiting so long for my girls to come home," he says. "Now that I've gotten Ian out of the way, we can talk."

I don't tell him that Ian survived. I'm sure that will unbalance him completely, if he's not there already.

"Richard, please," I say, trying to be the good me, the obedient me, the one who convinced him that I welcomed his assaults all those years ago. "If you really want to talk, would you please put the gun down?"

"I'm sorry. I can't," he says. "I have to end this. I'm the only one left."

I understand that he's talking about Selma's big plan for my life. He's part of it, probably the most important part. The one who kept me right here in Dayfield, under his falsely loving thumb, while she built her horrific trap from the broken pieces of my child.

"You don't have to. We're a family," I whisper. "You're not alone."

"She has to die!" he cries harshly, stabbing the gun in Renata's direction.

She bursts into tears.

"She's your *daughter*." I take a step further into the room. He makes a threatening motion with the gun, and I stop moving. "She loves you, just like me," I say, trying to impose a soothing tone on my shaky words. "We're not going to say anything to anyone. Are we, Renata?"

She hitches a breath and shakes her fiercely. "We won't, Daddy. Promise."

"You promise," he says as his eyes narrow on me. "The way *you* promised you'd never tell when I let you go?"

His words stun me, and my mind jolts to the past, where I discover one more memory waiting to be set free.

I'm in the locked room. It's been quiet for hours, after I heard them earlier arguing with each other. Shouting, screaming, breaking things. I can never make out the words, but I know they were fighting about me.

The other one, the one who hurts me, said that he was going to kill me tonight.

He's tied me down again. I'm dressed in a stained nightgown, shivering in the cold and dark as awareness beats at me like ocean waves pounding the shore.

I know I'm going to die.

It's an awful hollow sensation, the idea that I'll cease to exist, become nothing. And my memories will die with me. I'll never remember my friends or my family or that camping trip with Carson and Tricia the summer after freshman year, or my tenth birthday when Mom got me a guitar and I obsessed over it fiercely for two weeks and then put it in my closet and never touched it again, or how much I love pistachio ice cream and walking barefoot on warm sand.

I want those things back. I want more memories. I want to live.

But there's no chance of that now.

The ringing click of the lock drawing back makes me flinch, and I squeeze my eyes shut as the door creaks open. I wonder if he'll do it quickly, if I'll feel it at all. My heart is a bird trapped in my chest, fluttering desperately.

A warm, sour hand clamps over my mouth.

And I feel the leather strap around my wrist loosen.

It's *him*.

"Shhh," he breathes near my ear. "I'm taking you outside. You have to run. You can never tell anyone."

I nod beneath the heavy hand, my eyes opening to look into his. He's crying.

"Be very quiet," he admonishes as he moves his hand away, and then takes off the rest of the restraints.

I am. I'm very quiet. I don't dare to breathe.

I want to live.

He helps me off the bed, puts his arm around my waist as he leads me to the door. Turns toward me, a finger to his lips.

The other one is still down here.

We creep through the 'living room,' two silent mice. There's a light flickering in the other room, the one they take turns sleeping in, and I hear the faint rustle of pages. The monster is reading a book.

It's not something I'd ever have pictured him doing.

He brings me to the chamber and urges me up the ladder, toward the open trapdoor. I climb as fast as I can, with him right behind me. When I reach the top and spill out onto the ground, I breathe in a huge gulp of cool, fragrant twilight air and shiver at the silent forest all around me.

I look back down into the hole, into his upturned face. "Thank you," I whisper.

He nods once, his eyes flicking down. Then he stiffens.

The other one, the mean one, is moving around. I can hear his footsteps.

"Run!" he says.

I do what he tells me.

But I hear their argument break out behind me, and I know I'm not safe yet. The mean one is still going to kill me.

And now, twenty years later, the one who set me free is going to kill my daughter.

Richard sees the memory swim to my face, and he flashes a rueful smile. "She wanted you dead, like the others," he says. "But you were *special*, and the things she talked about doing to you ... horrible things. Gruesome things. All to get back at Stewart's father. I couldn't let her do that to you. I loved you." Fresh tears streak down his face. "I thought you loved me, too."

"I did love you. *Do* love you," I say, attempting to move toward him again. He doesn't seem to notice. For an instant I try to figure out why he'd said *Stewart's* father, and not *my* father, but I don't have time to dwell on that. "Your daughter loves you, too."

A thick, wrenching sob explodes from him. "She has to die," he whispers, his gaze swinging to Renata. She cringes away from him. "Don't you understand? She's tainted. She's got my blood in her."

"Daddy, *please*," Renata sobs in a high, breaking voice. "Don't hurt me."

He takes a single step forward. "It won't hurt, baby," he says. "I promise."

I can't wait any longer. I run at him.

He catches my eye for a split second, and I see the pain in his. The conflict. He doesn't want to do it.

When the thunder of the gun fills our living room, I scream. And scream, and scream, until my throat is ripped raw and there's nothing left in me to come out.

But it doesn't change anything.

My screams can't reverse a bullet.

54

six months later

I wake with a pounding head and the ache of sorrow nestled in my gut, the way I always seem to start my mornings these days. I can't stop dreaming of my child, and how it all went so wrong. But I won't take the sedatives Dr. Bradshaw keeps trying to prescribe me. I deserve this feeling, the guilt of knowing that I failed her.

For a moment I lay still as the last vestiges of the half-remembered dream slip away. Then I turn to the figure beside me in the bed, gently touching his arm.

He startles, and his eyes fly open. "Am I late?" he murmurs thickly.

"No, it's early," I whisper. "I just wanted to make sure you're still alive."

"Oh." His own smile is slow, sleepy, satisfied. "Yep, still alive," he says. "You?"

"Still alive."

"Good." He kisses me. "Five more minutes, then," he mutters as he turns away, pulling the blanket around him.

I watch him for a moment and then slip from the bed, letting him sleep. I never would've gotten through the horrible aftermath without Ian. He's helped me keep everything together when I was convinced it would all fall apart, just like he did when I was released from Brightside all those years ago. We're getting a second chance to start over.

I use the bathroom and then move from the bedroom into the hallway. My heart aches all over again as I look down the hushed, carpeted space to the closed door. How I used to love this place, this home. But now it's filled with tainted memories. We're putting it on the market soon, and we'll move to a different part of town, a new house for our fresh start.

One that's nowhere near the Singing Woods.

Before I head downstairs, I walk down the hall and stop in front of the closed door, where my eyes mist over with tears as they do most mornings. I reach for the knob and hesitate, my hand trembling slightly. I can't seem to stop this reaction. It's a bittersweet feeling, looking into this room, knowing how much worse things got for her in the end.

I wipe my dripping eyes so Renata doesn't see me crying before I open the door.

"Hey, sweetheart," I call softly. "It's about that time."

She shifts, groans, and shoves her head under her pillow, clamping it down tight, all without opening her eyes. "Can't you just homeschool me or something?" she says in a muffled voice. "It's cruel and unusual, how early they make you get up for school."

"Just wait until you start college," I say, and she groans again. "Come on, sleepyhead. Breakfast in ten."

Her arm shoots out, and she gives me a thumbs-up that somehow manages to be sarcastic.

I laugh as I close the door and head downstairs.

In the living room, I can't help pausing as I look at the place where he died. We've replaced the carpet and all the furniture, had the walls repaired and repainted, but I can still see Richard standing there, tears streaming down his face as he pulls his arm back at the last moment, shoves the muzzle beneath his chin, and pulls the trigger, splattering an unspeakable mess all over the television and the wall behind it.

With all my heart, I wish that my daughter had been spared that sight. It was the worst of everything that happened.

I find that I'm still capable of sympathy for Richard. He was a monster, and he'd done terrible things to me. He'd even driven me toward madness, forcing me to doubt my own sanity, during the week of Renata's abduction by tampering with my medication. I'd found my old prescription bottle, the one that was lost when I realized there was something wrong with the new pills, stuffed in the back of one of his dresser drawers. The real higher-dose tablets had been poured into the bottle, and testing showed that the yellow one's he'd replaced them with were just placebos. Sugar pills.

Being off my meds had gone a long way toward convincing me that Stewart Brooks was somehow alive.

But still, Richard had saved my life twice. He released me in the woods, and he killed himself instead of my daughter.

I couldn't have lived without her.

He'd also given me another gift, one that I'm sure wasn't intentional, when he'd said *Stewart's father.* I'd assumed, to my horror, that both of Jessica Forrest's sons were my father's as well, and that I'd conceived two children with my half-brother — though it didn't make me love Renata any less. But those words got me thinking, and eventually I'd asked Detective Burgess to find out what he could.

It turns out that while Stewart was my father's son, Richard was the child of Jessica Forrest and Clayton Osborn. Her stepfather. No one can figure out where the surname Brooks came from, but Tom's best guess is that Selma — Jessica — stole the identity of a dead person to give to Stewart, because she hadn't given birth to him in a hospital. He'd been born in the cabin in the woods where my father left Jessica, where she'd stayed until she was ready to begin her long journey to revenge. Richard was raised by Clayton and his wife, until Jessica killed both of them and took him back.

Horrific to consider, but it least it means that Richard wasn't blood-related to me.

Finally, I tear my gaze from the memory of death and go into the kitchen to start breakfast. Renata has school, and Ian's gone back to working for the town DPW for now, though he plans to start his own business soon. Not landscaping. He isn't sure what, exactly, but he doesn't want to carry on what Richard built.

I've gone into business for myself, too. I don't think I'll ever set foot in the Dayfield Community Center again, but I've opened a small pottery studio where I teach classes three times a week, and also make and sell my own pieces. I let any interested students offer their work through the studio on commission, and it's exciting for me to see them so happy when they sell.

Sometimes I think of the sad, misshapen bowl in Wendell's room, the evidence that my daughter and I had at least one thing in common, and I wonder what my life, our lives, would've been like if I hadn't given her up. If I'd figured out a way to keep her.

I couldn't have known what would happen to her, but that doesn't stop the guilt. She haunts my dreams. And not just because of my failures as her mother.

They never found her body.

The police were able to locate the underground lair in the woods with my direction, and they went there the morning after I brought Renata out of the woods. The trapdoor was open when they arrived. There was a lot of blood in the room where I'd struck Wendell with the bowl, and then a trail of it across the dirt floor of the living room, splashes of it on the ladder. But there was no sign of where she'd gone after that.

They'd decided that Richard must've gone there during the night and taken her body out, and buried her somewhere in the woods. He would've had time to do that and return to town before Renata and I came home from the hospital, though they can't explain how he managed to get back inside the house under the noses of the police detail.

I'm not so sure that's what happened.

I believe on the day Richard went to work, the day I couldn't reach him on the phone and he texted me, claiming that calls weren't getting through, that he was at the house then. His truck was found in the woods, where he must've driven it at some point. I think he parked it there, walked or gotten a ride from someone — maybe Selma — back through town, and then strolled right into the house while I was at my mother's, or Brenda's, or Dr. Bradshaw's, or the police station. At that time, no one would've looked twice at him. And he simply stayed there, hiding when he heard my car return from the hospital. He'd been there the whole time, waiting.

I believe this because of the file box. The one that was packed neatly on the dining room table, when I'd left everything scattered all over.

And I believe that Wendell may still be alive.

Maybe she's disappeared, moved far away to start another kind of life in a place that holds no memories of her, or for her. Maybe she'll come back someday to finally finish what Selma started, or maybe she'll stay away. Of course, it makes more sense that she's still in the woods somewhere. That Richard did bury her like the police believed, or that she simply crawled as far as she could before she died, and her body was destroyed by scavenging animals.

But whatever has happened, or will happen, I won't live my life afraid of the past anymore. I will embrace every day with my daughter, with Ian, and I won't constantly look over my shoulder at the shadows behind me. I'll spend time with Carson, meet her son, get to know my half-brother — the one who's *not* homicidal. I'll probably forgive my mother eventually.

And I'll stay right here in Dayfield, because this is my home. This is where my life unfolded, where it will continue until my daughter has children of her own, children she'll love as much as I love her. I won't fear the judgment of people who haven't walked in my shoes, who don't understand what it's like to battle through the fire and emerge on the other side.

I'm not crazy. I'm alive, and I'm free.

I've finally reached the summit and planted my flag.

And the view is fantastic from up here.

55

the darkest evening

This is the best part of my day.

She comes in every weekday morning for coffee, right around 8:30. I try to make sure I'm working the counter then, but I don't always make it. Sometimes Charlie Soames already has the register, and I have to grit my teeth and pretend I'm fine with that as I watch him exchange friendly banter and flirt with her, while I fill the orders. On those days I make it a point to go out and wipe down her table while she's still here, so I can talk to her.

So I can revel in her warmth, her friendliness, as she treats me like a normal person.

Like someone who isn't a threat.

Today I'm in my preferred position behind the register when she walks in, wearing dark slacks and a pretty sweater, with just a touch of makeup and her hair done up in a casual flyaway bun. She waits behind an old man who's counting out change with his palsied hands for his senior-discount coffee, and when she steps up for her turn, she smiles.

What a brilliant smile she has. So happy and well-adjusted.

So oblivious.

"Good morning," she says cheerfully.

I smile back. I've practiced the smile in the mirror until it looks natural. "Good morning. What can I get you today?"

"I think I'll have a mocha cappuccino with whipped cream. Oh, and a blueberry muffin," she says. "They look fantastic."

"They are. I baked them myself."

She laughs. "Well, you've done a wonderful job," she says. "So, just the coffee and the muffin, please."

"All right." I ring her up while Charlie starts assembling her order. "That'll be four-fifty," I tell her.

"What do you know? Just enough," she says as she hands me a five.

I place it in the drawer and return two quarters to her. "Charlie will have that right up for you," I say as I take a plastic tray from beneath the counter and set it to the right of the register.

"Thank you," she says, stepping aside to wait in front of the tray. There's no one else in line at the moment. "So, will I see you in class tonight?"

"Absolutely," I say. "I'm enjoying the coil method. It's more stable than pinch pots, and you can really get creative with the shapes."

She beams at me. "Your work is so impressive. So ... haunting," she says. "Have you given any more thought to selling some of your pieces?"

"I have. And I'm still thinking," I say with a little laugh. "Maybe I will someday."

"Well, it's certainly up to you. I think a lot of people would enjoy what you bring to the world."

That's an interesting thought. I wonder if *she* enjoys what I brought to *her* world.

The way I never enjoyed the world she brought me into.

Charlie sets the cappuccino next to her muffin, and she picks up the tray. "See you tonight, then," she says. "Have a good day, Katy."

"You too, Madeline."

It's so nice being a girl. They're friendly. Non-threatening. Easy to trust.

I did tell her that it's amazing what plastic surgery can do these days.

I watch her walk to a table, feeling my own kind of smile on the inside. The kind that scares her, the kind I'll wear one day when I put a knife to her daughter's throat and make her watch as I slit it wide open, into a red, red smile like mine.

Or maybe I won't. Maybe I'll take *her* life instead, and let her daughter suffer the loss of her mother. I lost *my* mother to her. It's only fair.

Then again, maybe I'll let them both live. She likes me now, and it's possible that her daughter may come to like me too. Love me, even. I could spend the rest of my life with my delicious secret, knowing that every time she looks at me, she fails to see the monster inside. The monster *she* let me become when she gave me away.

I can be very patient, just like my daddy.

I can wait forever.

And she'll never see me coming.

Thanks for reading!

If you enjoyed WHAT SHE FORGOT, please consider leaving a review on Amazon to share your thoughts. Reviews are a great way to help other readers find new books and new authors to enjoy.

ABOUT THE AUTHOR

S.W. Vaughn cut her reading teeth on Stephen King, Dean Koontz, and James Patterson, and has been hooked on thrillers and horror since. She lives in fabulous Central New York, where there are only two seasons (Winter and Road Construction) with her husband and son. An award-winning author, copywriter, and blogger, she's been writing professionally for the past 15 years.

Join the mailing list to receive email notifications whenever new books are released.

More books by S.W. Vaughn

TERMINAL CONSENT – a standalone crime thriller
How do you stop a killer whose victims are volunteering to die?

P.I. Jude Wyland books: crime thrillers
DEADLY MEASURES – a prequel novella
THE BLACK DIRECTIVE

House Phoenix series: crime thrillers (written under Sonya Bateman)
BREAKING ANGEL | Book 1
DEVIL RISING | Book 2
TEMPTING JENNER | Book 3
SHADOWS FALLING | Book 4
WICKED ORIGINS | Stories & Novellas

Made in the USA
San Bernardino, CA
29 May 2019